THORNS OF DECEIT

A CITY OF FOUNTAINS NOVEL

C.J. JOHNSON

PRESS

For all those who wear, or have worn, the badge.

CHAPTER
ONE

THE WINDS CUT across the parking lot, piercing the coats the girls were wearing, but the frigid air did nothing to dim their laughter. Hannah Reitzel and Tessa Kemp walked briskly towards their car.

"I can't believe you made me sit on Santa's lap," Hannah said.

"I can't believe you told him you wanted a man for Christmas," Tessa said. "You have to let me know if one is under your Christmas tree."

Giggling, Hannah said, "I suppose I better get one set up."

They loaded their packages into the back of Hannah's sports coupe then scanned the radio for holiday music while they waited for the windows to defrost. Satisfied with the condition of the windows and the selected station, they began the drive back to Hannah's house.

"Baby, it's cold outside…." Tessa sang.

Hannah laughed at her friend whose voice was off key and bordered on shrill. When the song ended, she said, "You know I always thought that song was rapey."

"Oh, lighten up," Tessa started. "I think it's sexy."

Hannah didn't argue, but to herself she thought, *"There's nothing sexy about a man not letting you leave when you want to go."*

Tessa continued to sing along with every song that came on the radio, and eventually Hannah began to sing with her.

They pulled into the driveway of the detached garage. Hannah started to put the car in park, but Tessa said, "It's starting to sleet, why don't we park inside so we don't get wet?"

Hannah pulled into the garage, pushed the button to close the overhead door, then stepped out of the car. She felt an explosion in her head. Hannah stumbled then fell to the ground and her world went dark. When she began to regain consciousness, Hannah noticed something was preventing her from moving her hands or legs and tape covered her mouth.

As though from a distance, Hannah heard Tessa. Then a man's voice. Or was it men? She lay immobile, feeling nothing until she felt pressure between her legs, beneath her dress. She tried to scream but the tape covering her mouth muffled the sounds. Gloved hands touched every part of her body, and although she could hear people talking, she could not understand their words. When the man, or men, were finished with her body, she felt a sharp pain as a shoe hit her back followed by another sharp pain in her head. The door to her car opened and Hannah heard the engine start and the garage filled with the sound of loud holiday music. The side door of the garage opened and shut, leaving her battered body on the floor.

Hannah could hear the creaking sound of the opening garage door as she lay on the cold, hard concrete floor. A sudden burst of wind blew across her body. She shivered as the air hit her bare skin. A stabbing pain, much like a sharp knife, bore through her skull leaving her powerless and unable to move.

The pain in her head was familiar but something about this was different. The pain extended beyond her head; it radiated through her face, side, and back. Suddenly Hannah realized the pain extended below her belly. She had been violated. Everything went black.

There was a flash of light, and Hannah could hear the voices of her neighbors, Kathryn and Julia. She could not understand what they were saying but the sound of their voices was frantic. Someone was hurt. Hannah wanted to help but was unable to move or speak. At that moment, she understood she was the hurt person they were talking about.

Flashes of memory invaded Hannah's thoughts. She had been attacked. She was hit from behind. She had been raped. Hannah knew the attack was not random and she knew who was behind it.

CHAPTER
TWO

THREE DAYS BEFORE THANKSGIVING, Detective Francesca "Frankie" Thomas stood looking out the window of her fourth-floor office. She watched the rain fall and silently hoped it did not turn to snow, or worse, ice. The streets of downtown Kansas City were deserted. The light from the streetlamps danced across the wet pavement giving the illusion of gold stars scattered on the ground; the windows across the street in the Richard Bolling Federal Building were dark. The only lights burning this late, other than at the police department, were in the county courthouse.

Frankie mumbled to herself, "Looks like Lady Justice is working late. Wonder who's there tonight?"

Looking out she marveled at the peaceful feelings the scene evoked. She had worked in the City of Fountains long enough to know a block or two in any direction the scene was anything but peaceful.

The detectives in her squad were in the field finishing up an area canvas for witnesses in one of their cases. It was the last night they would work together before the holiday weekend. Sergeant Baker had stayed behind to work on paperwork before taking them to dinner but was in his office with the door closed talking to a sergeant from the Assault Squad. Frankie knew nothing good could come from a closed-door meeting. She looked out the window and, almost as if it were an omen, the rain turned to sleet.

"I wonder if I should call home and let them know I'll be late?" She pondered aloud.

The ding of the elevator, followed by laughter through the open doors, broke her thoughts as her fellow detectives entered the squad room.

"You missed it, Frankie!" exclaimed Mia, laughing, as she and the other two detectives walked into the squad room, "I'm standing there talking to this crackhead and he's got his hand..."

Before she could finish Baker walked out of his office with Sergeant Millsap.

Baker interrupted, "Get ready for a long night."

CHAPTER
THREE

FRANKIE HAD WORKED for Baker long enough to know this was bad. She grabbed her notepad and pen.

"We have a new case and it's going to take all hands-on deck," Baker started.

This wasn't the first time this had happened - dinner canceled or cut short because of a case. It wasn't the first late night, or even the first all-nighter for any of the detectives, but something about the way Baker said those words caused all the laughter and horseplay to stop.

"This one's likely to generate a lot of media attention." He turned to Millsap, "Before I send the squad out, will you fill them in on the information you just gave me?"

"This isn't your typical case…"

Frankie mumbled under her breath, "None of our cases are typical."

"That's true, Frankie, especially when your name is attached," said Millsap, winking at her.

He had known Frankie since she graduated from the police academy seven years prior. They did not always see eye to eye, but he knew she had heart and could work circles around anyone in the room, himself included. Standing only 5-feet tall, what she lacked in stature she made up for in determination. She had the unflappability of someone who didn't join the police department until she was 30. This, combined with her relentless pursuit of truth, had earned her the reputation of being a bulldog. Working tirelessly the past seven years to earn the respect of her colleagues she had proven herself repeatedly with her never-give-up attitude, fierceness, and unrelenting work ethic.

"About two months ago my squad got called out to a scene in Waldo. The victim told us a white male wearing all black jumped out from behind her garage, put a gun to her head and threatened her. She said the man was taller than her with a thick Italian accent, but she didn't get a good look at his face. As quickly as he appeared he was gone. She didn't see a car but didn't think he could have walked far. He was wearing expensive loafers and didn't seem like the type to want to scuff them up.

"We investigated it, but she didn't have any injuries and there wasn't any real evidence to collect. We canvased the neighborhood but didn't find any surveillance cameras or witnesses, but we brought her downtown to get a statement and that's when it got weird. She told us she thought it was a mob hit; that this goon was sent to warn her because of a lawsuit she had filed a few months back. She said this guy she worked for was sexually harassing her and she finally had enough and got a lawyer. After she filed the suit, she learned the guys she was suing were connected to organized crime. We brought in detectives from the intelligence unit to assist when we heard that and - what do you know? One of the guys she is suing is being investigated for some… shall we say, questionable dealings."

"Who did she work for?" asked Frankie.

"Stevenson Automotive."

"Isn't that the Mercedes place on 104th?"

Millsap nodded, "Actually they sell all the high-end stuff. Mercedes, Range Rover, Jaguar, etcetera, cars worth more than my salary. Marzullo Automotive out of Detroit is the parent company. The Marzullo family has had strong ties in the northeast for over a hundred years. There are rumors Don Marzullo was an associate of Pendergast and Lazia back in the day."

Her eyes raised in surprise at the mention of those names. Like most Kansas Citians she recognized the name Pendergast.

"Tom Pendergast was a political powerhouse. He controlled all the government offices in Kansas City and Jackson County Missouri during the late '20s and most of the '30s. The police department was only one of many offices he controlled. Under his control salaries were kept low and, not surprisingly, the department was known for its corruption. Although he was not considered a mobster, Pendergast had close ties to the underworld. His right-hand man was Johnny Lazia, leader of the Northside Italians."

Not known for her patience, Frankie interrupted him. "Sarge, this is an interesting history lesson but what does this have to do with us?"

"Geez, Frankie, hold your horses, I'm getting there. Tonight, we got a call from your buddy Mac. He and his partner went out on a robbery in progress. They found a woman in her garage, tied up and unconscious with her skirt pulled up. There was evidence she may have been raped and the friend who was with her had also been assaulted. They were looking through one of their purses and found my business card. Turns out it was the same girl as before. The woman they found with her is the co-litigant in the lawsuit.   We think the two incidents might be connected. Since there was evidence of rape, I came up here."

Baker started issuing assignments, "Frankie, you go to the hospital and interview the women. Scott Fitzmeyer from the Intelligence Unit will meet you there but you're taking lead."

"Names?" She asked as she picked up the phone to call the Crime Scene Unit.

"Hannah Reitzell and Tessa Kemp," said Millsap. "Paramedics said they were taking them to county about 30 minutes ago. They should be there by now."

"Got it. Hey, Ash, it's Frankie. Have you been listening to the radio?"   She coordinated with the Crime Scene Unit while Baker continued giving orders. Upon hanging up, she grabbed her bag and said, "Sarge, Simpson and Yang will meet you guys at the scene."

"Got it, Frankie. We'll canvas the neighborhood while we're out there. Somebody had to see or hear something."

CHAPTER
FOUR

FRANKIE GOT into the unmarked police car and grabbed her phone to call home.

"Thomas residence. Tyler speaking." She smiled at the sound of her eight-year-old son's voice.

"Hey buddy."

"Hey mom! Guess what?! I got a hundred on my spelling test!"

"Way to go, Ty! Looks like all that practice paid off. I'm so proud of you."

"Yeah, I guess. I still don't like writing those words over and over and over," he groaned.

Frankie laughed to herself.

"Where's your sister?"

"Dani's in the shower. Are you going to be home in time to tuck me in, mom?"

"I'm sorry, Ty. I'm going to have to work a little late. I'm heading to the hospital. I'll come in and give you a kiss when I get home okay?"

"Sure." She could hear the disappointment in his voice as he said the word. "Be careful, mom. Keith said to be careful too."

She took a deep breath. "Always, bud. Tell Danielle I said to turn off the TV and go to bed after she gets out of the shower. Ok?"

"Ok, but she's not going to like it."

"I know." Frankie laughed, "Hey Ty, do you know how much I love you?"

"Yeah."

In unison, they both said, "More than all the sand and water in the sea."

By the time she said good-bye she could hear the smile in Tyler's voice.

Driving south on the deserted streets toward the hospital she thought about her children. To the air she said, "I'll never get used to this."

Frankie was good at what she did, and her work was important, but it didn't make her feel any less guilty about leaving her children at home to be put to bed by someone else. Tyler's father was killed when he was a toddler, leaving her to raise him and his sister Danielle alone. While her parents helped when they could they lived an hour away. During the week, she relied on her sister Sophie. Her neighbor Keith and his partner Bruce pitched in when Sophie wasn't available. They stayed at her house when she had to work the night shift every other month. It was a hard schedule but, somehow, they made it work.

"Shake it off," she said as she shook her head.

Frankie pulled into the hospital parking garage. On cold, wet nights like this she was thankful the entrance to the emergency department was underground, so she didn't have to endure the elements to get inside. As she walked through the doors of the ED, her focus returned to work.

"Hey, George," she called out to the security guard.

George was a tall, thick man with a deep voice that reminded her of James Earl Jones. She smiled and asked, "How's Miss Lainey feeling?"

His wife Lainey was an administrative clerk in the emergency department but had recently taken a leave of absence while she underwent chemotherapy treatment for breast cancer.

"Lainey's doing great, Frankie, thanks for asking. She only has one more treatment ahead of her then hopefully she'll be in remission. We'll see what happens from there. I'll tell her you asked after her. They're waiting for you in Exam Room 2 but before you go back a man's waiting in the lobby. He said he wanted to talk to you."

"Thank you, George!"

When she rounded the corner, she saw a man standing in front of the television. To herself she asked, "Scott Fitzmeyer?"

Sensing her presence, he turned his tall, broad-shouldered frame toward her. She noticed hints of gray in his wavy, sandy brown hair. She couldn't see a gun but knew by the way he carried himself that his KC Royals polo was covering his holstered weapon.

As she approached, he smiled. She was certain his smile had stopped the beat of many a heart. He took a step forward, extended his hand and said, "You must be Detective Thomas," His dark green eyes sparkled with laughter when he spoke.

Frankie returned his smile as they shook hands.

"You can call me Frankie. You must be Detective Fitzmeyer."

"The one and only. Most people call me Fitz. It's nice to meet you. Before we head back why don't you give me the skinny on what you know?"

She looked around the empty room to be sure no one had walked in behind her. When she was certain they were alone she told him what she had learned from Millsap. Once she finished, she asked, "Shall we head back?"

"Sure. I'll take a backseat on this one. I've met Hannah but I haven't met the other girl. Tessa, right?"

"That's right."

"Okay. When we're done, I'll fill you in on the history and background of these guys she's suing. Sound good?"

She nodded as they walked toward Exam Room 2.

WALKING toward the hospital room Frankie wondered what she would find. She had been on the job long enough that not much surprised her but something about this case had her unnerved.

Just outside the examination room was a uniformed officer standing guard.

"Hey, Frank-ee," he said in a rhythmic cadence.

"Hey Mac! Is this why I have five missed calls from you?" She exclaimed as she grabbed the officer's hand as though she were going to shake it, then pulled him in for a hug. She and Anthony "Mac" McClendon had been partners on patrol. The two had gotten into many close calls together in the field and had developed a bond closer than most siblings. Patting him on the back she asked, "How's my godson?"

"Growing like a weed."

Switching back to business she asked, "Give us a rundown before we head in."

"The call was dispatched about eight o'clock as a robbery in progress, a home invasion. Payne and I were riding two-deep and were just a couple of blocks away. You know me, I was hoping for some action, so we answered up. We were there in minutes.

"Hannah's neighbor was trying to wake her while administering first aid. The neighbor told Payne she found Hannah with duct tape wrapped around her feet and her arms were taped behind her back. She had removed the tape from her mouth before we got there.

"When we got there Hannah was still lying on the garage floor with her arms and feet still bound. She drifted in and out of consciousness until the ambulance arrived. The neighbor was the one that called 9-1-1.

"Hannah's friend, Tessa, had remnants of duct tape on one of her hands but was walking around crying. The ambulance was staging but we called them in right way. I rode to the hospital with Hannah while Tessa went in a separate ambulance. Payne stayed at the scene."

Frankie listened thoughtfully, "Do you know if the ambulances are still here?"

"I'm not sure Frankie, why?"

"Can you go find out for me? If they are, get the names of the paramedics and collect the sheets from the gurneys and recover them as evidence."

Training, experience, and common sense told her the bedding could contain evidence – loose hairs, skin particles, and fluids could have fallen from the victims' bodies. This evidence could lead them to the attackers if the paramedics had not disposed of it.

"Sure," he replied without hesitation. If anyone else had solicited this request, he may have grumbled but he knew if Frankie asked it was important. Not all detectives considered the small details, but she had a reputation for going the extra mile.

"Do you know what room they have her friend in?"

He pointed down the hall to the room two doors away from where they were standing. "She's in Exam Room 6."

"Thanks, Mac. I'll check in with you later."

Frankie took a deep breath and pushed the glass door open. She pulled the curtain back and saw a young woman lying on the bed, tears trickling down the cheeks of her tightly closed eyes. Her driver's license said she was 25 but the woman on the bed looked more like a teenager. The mint green hospital gown made her fair skin appear sallow. Her long, curly, auburn hair framed her heart-shaped face with a smattering of freckles across her nose.

When Hannah opened her eyes, Frankie looked into blue eyes so pale they were almost white. She had a small frame and couldn't have weighed more than 105 pounds. A purple bruise was already beginning to form on her right cheek making her appear even more fragile.

Seated in a chair next to the bed was a face Frankie recognized. "Hey, Beth."

Beth was a victim advocate with the local rape crisis center and frequently responded to the hospital and police station to support victims of sexual assault. She and Frankie's paths often crossed at work, in trainings and other community-based events. Eventually their paths began to cross in social settings and over time they developed a friendship common among workers serving those in crisis.

"Hey, Frankie, I was hoping you'd be the one to respond." She gently touched Hannah's shoulder and said, "Detective Thomas is here."

Frankie walked to the opposite side of the hospital bed and said, "Hi, Ms. Reitzell. Would you mind if I call you Hannah?"

Hannah nodded.

"Would you mind if I sit down?"

She looked at Frankie as though she was not quite sure what to say. After a brief pause, she softly said, "Yeah, sure."

Frankie sat down on the stool next to the bed, removed the notepad from her bag, and said, "Hannah, as Beth said my name is Frankie Thomas. With me is Scott Fitzmeyer. We are both detectives with the Kansas City Missouri Police Department. We have officers at your house and need to get a bit of information from you so they can process it for evidence. We will get a more detailed statement in a day or two but tonight I need to get a general idea of what happened."

"Okay."

"Do you mind if I record our conversation? It will help me when I write my reports later."

She leaned in listening to the words Hannah said, as well as the way in which she said them. She notated every observation for her reports.

"Okay."

Her voice was barely above a whisper, so Frankie laid the recorder on the bed next to her head.

"Before we begin, I would like to get your permission to process the scene for evidence."

She produced a form giving detectives permission to collect evidence from the garage and car. Absent a signed form, she would have to get a search warrant before officers could process the scene. After Frankie explained the form, Hannah read and signed the documents.

"Fitz, would you go call Sgt. Baker to tell him we have consent from Hannah? You can use my phone. Hannah, although I'm recording our conversation, I am also going to jot down a few notes while we talk. This way I won't have to interrupt you while you're talking. Take your time and please tell me what brought you here tonight."

Hannah took a deep breath, pushed her hair out of her eyes, and released a heavy sigh. Fresh tears began to roll down her cheeks. Beth reached over and patted her hand as the words started to flow.

CHAPTER
SIX

"I'M NOT sure where you want me to begin."

"That's okay. How about how you happened to be inside the garage?"

Frankie did not push. It was common for victims of crime to hesitate before telling what happened to them. They didn't know where to begin, what was important, and what was not. Victims didn't want to get it wrong by telling too much or not telling enough.

Hannah tried to raise her body up and nodded slightly.

"It's okay, you don't have to sit up."

Lying back on the bed she began to speak, "Tessa and I were coming back from dinner and shopping in Leawood. We were laughing and singing along to Christmas music on the radio on the drive back." She laughed lightly. "Tessa can't carry a tune to save herself. It had started to rain and sleet so when we got to my house, I pulled into the garage instead of parking on the street. We didn't want to get wet while we got our stuff out of the back. If only I had..."

Hannah covered her face with her hands as sobs caused her frail body to shake. Frankie waited while Beth spoke softly, comforting Hannah as she cried. Frankie was patient, allowing Hannah's sobs to lessen as she attempted to compose herself. Hannah eventually wiped her face, then continued.

"I pulled into my garage and closed the door with the opener before I got out. When I started to get out of the car, I felt something hit my head. At first, I thought I had hit the doorframe of my car. Have you ever done that?" Hannah looked to Frankie who nodded. "It really shook me. I couldn't get my balance, fell, and couldn't see anything at first and then things went blurry. I started to think maybe I had another aneurism."

Frankie raised her head up from her notepad with questioning look.

"About a year ago I had a brain aneurism rupture while I was at work. The pain was like that, but after a few seconds I could hear voices. One was Tessa's. The other was a man's voice. Or maybe two men. I'm not sure. I couldn't move my arms or legs and then I felt something between my legs…it hurt so much." Hannah's shoulders began to shake. Her voice was quivering as she asked to no one in particular, "Why me? I don't understand."

Frankie looked around the small room letting her eyes rest on Fitz. She had forgotten he was in the room. The laughter that had been in his eyes earlier was gone and the color had drained slightly from his tan face. With one look at him she realized how accustomed she was to hearing these kinds of stories. Until then she had never considered how difficult it must be for others to listen to them.

Hannah's voice broke her from her train of thought.

"I was lying on the ground, and I could feel someone's hands, but it didn't feel like skin touching me. Does that make sense? I could hear voices talking but couldn't understand what they were saying. At one point, I thought I heard thunder just as I felt another sharp pain in my head. I know that doesn't make sense, but it was a loud noise like the clapping of thunder. With the sharp pain and noise was a flash of light and then I heard my car engine running. That stood out to me because I was sure I had turned my car off. I don't know, maybe I didn't. The music coming from the radio was so loud, it was playing that song about mamma kissing Santa Claus. It was surreal. That was the last think I remember until my neighbor Katie was rubbing the middle of my chest real hard and saying my name repeatedly. I couldn't understand why she was in my garage or why she was so upset. I wanted to tell her I was okay, but the words wouldn't come out. I couldn't move. Then the police were there with an ambulance." She closed her eyes and dried the tears streaming down her cheeks. Suddenly her eyes flew open, and she asked, "Oh my gosh! Where's Tessa? Is she okay?"

"She's okay, Hannah. She's here at the hospital," Frankie calmly responded. Hannah let out a deep sigh as a nurse walked into the room. "Hi Jen. You ready to do the exam?"

Jennifer Jacobson was a short, stout nurse who had worked in the emergency department for over thirty years. She was a typical ER nurse with zero tolerance for nonsense: a force of nature with a big heart. She had been known to handle a belligerent drunk sternly one minute then move heaven and earth to help a victim of domestic or sexual violence the next. She built the forensic program from the ground up and had spent many a long night with victims trying to make an invasive, potentially humiliating experience as tolerable as possible. Frankie had learned about compassion, forensics, and people by watching and listening to Jen. Over time she had become both a mentor and friend.

Jennifer said hello to Frankie and Beth, then directed her attention to Hannah. "How are you doing, sweety? You ready to do this?"

Hannah looked to Jennifer, Frankie, Beth, and then to Fitz with a questioning look in her eyes. Frankie suddenly realized how it must look to her. "Detective Fitzmeyer and I are going to go talk to Tessa. We will stop back in before we leave - after the exam is finished. It's up to you if Beth stays. Okay?"

Hannah's shoulders immediately relaxed. She nodded her head and said quietly, "Thank you. Please tell Tessa..." She did not finish the sentence before the tears began to slide down her checks. "Beth, will you please stay?"

"Of course, I will. I'll be here as long as you want me here, Hannah."

CHAPTER
SEVEN

FRANKIE AND FITZ left the room as Jennifer began explaining the exam to Hannah. They walked the short hallway to Exam Room 6 to speak to Tessa. Before reaching the room Fitz stopped, leaned against the wall, and looked at Frankie. "I don't know how you do it."

She gave him a puzzled look, "What do you mean?"

"Listen to stuff like this. Deal with these kinds of cases every day."

"Some days are easier than others," Frankie admitted. "Most days I try not to think and just do. Ready for round two?"

They greeted the officer standing next to the door and walked into the room only to find an empty bed. Next to the bed sat a face Frankie recognized but she couldn't remember her name.

Thankfully, the young woman stood up and said, "Hi Detective Thomas. I'm sure you don't remember me, but we met and talked after the last advocate training. Olivia," she said as she extended her hand.

"Of course. Hi Olivia. Thank you for coming out tonight. This is my partner, Detective Fitzmeyer." She was preparing to ask where Tessa was when a woman stepped out of the bathroom and walked to the bed. She looked to the woman and said, "Hello, you must be Ms. Kemp. My name is Frankie Thomas and this is my partner, Scott Fitzmeyer. We are both detectives with the Kansas City Missouri Police Department. Do you mind if I call you Tessa?"

Tessa nodded quickly and got back onto the hospital bed. "Sure. How's Hannah? Is she okay?"

Tears began to pool in her eyes as she tried not to cry. When she reached for a tissue Frankie noticed a tattoo of a single red rose on the inside of her right forearm.

"The nurse is tending to Hannah. Can you tell me what happened?"

Tessa took a deep breath and looked toward Olivia. She exhaled, then began to talk.

CHAPTER
EIGHT

MUCH LIKE HANNAH, Tessa talked about the shopping, dinner, and singing Christmas songs but as she began to talk about going back to the house she stopped and closed her eyes, slowly describing the scene in detail. Pulling into the garage. The garage door closing. Opening the door to Hannah's car.

"I stepped out and saw a man. He was white, about 6-feet tall and was wearing a black hat. Actually, I think it was a black ski mask. He had on black gloves and was muscular. I couldn't see his hair color because of the hat but he had dark brown eyes. They were hard, cold, and mean. He was quick. He grabbed her before I could say anything. He was too fast. I couldn't warn Hannah."

She wept silently.

"A different guy grabbed me before I could get the car door shut. I tried to scream but he put his hand over my mouth. I felt my feet come out from under me and my body hit floor. He was on top of me, and his body was straddling mine. With his other hand, he held my arms behind my back. He put duct tape on my mouth and hit me on the head with something hard, I think it was steel. I heard Hannah screaming and then it went dark. I don't know how long I was out. Five minutes? An hour? I really don't know. But when I woke up, I felt the concrete against my face. I looked under the car and could see Hannah on the other side." She stopped and put her face in her hands and began to moan, "Hannah. Oh, Hannah."

Frankie looked over at Fitz as Tessa talked. She couldn't put her finger on it, but something didn't feel right. She was certain Hannah said she heard Tessa's voice during the attack, but Tessa said her mouth was covered, was duct taped right away, and lost consciousness. Frankie forced herself to stop speculating and refocus her attention on Tessa. She understood trauma affected people in different ways, so it was too early to make any judgments from this interview. But she also knew if there was something amiss, she would find it.

Tessa assessed her audience. She looked up at Frankie, then over at Fitz and Olivia, before continuing.

"The guy that grabbed Hannah was… he was doing…things to her. He had her skirt up. She was whimpering and looked so scared. I could hear the men talking; they were saying things like 'these bitches'll drop the lawsuit now,' 'I warned her.' The guy was kicking Hannah on her side and her legs. He had pulled the mask up and wasn't trying to hide his face so I thought he would kill me if he thought I was still alive. I've never been so scared in my life. When he came around the car, I closed my eyes and acted like I was dead. It didn't stop him. He still kicked me in the back. Hard."

"Can you describe the second guy?"

"He was tall and white. I'm not sure how tall but I think he was taller than my car. He had on expensive loafers. Both men left out the side door of the garage. They had turned the car on and left it running with the garage doors shut. I knew I should do something, but I was frozen in place. I don't know how long I laid there before I got up and went to the side door. I couldn't turn the knob because my hands were taped behind me. I looked around and saw a light on the wall, it was to the garage door opener. I pressed the side of my face against it and when the door opened the overhead light came on. I turned to look at Hannah and saw her lying on the floor and the first thing I noticed was blood. So much blood…a beer bottle with blood on it was lying next to her. I thought I was going to be sick, but I knew I had to get help, so I pulled myself together and ran across the street and knocked on the door.   Katie called the police and went over to the house to help Hannah."

Just as Tessa was finishing her sentence a nurse walked in and said she needed to take her for a CT scan. Frankie gave Tessa her business card and told her she was going to Hannah's house.

"Give me a call when you are being released from here. I don't want you going to pick up your car alone. I also don't think it's a good idea for you to go to your house tonight. There are some great shelters or a safe house…"

"I don't want to go to a shelter," Tessa said abruptly, interrupting her.

"They are actually nice but more importantly they are secure. It's your choice, of course, but until we identify who attacked you, I don't think it's safe for you to be in your home."

"But we know who did it! Or at least who's behind it! Why can't you just go arrest them?"

"We need to identify the actual attackers, Tessa, and that may take a few days."

"I'll think about it," she said reluctantly as she wiped the tears from her eyes.

"Okay Tessa. Think about what I said and don't forget to call me when you leave."

She nodded her head in agreement as the detectives left the room.

Frankie and Fitz returned to Hannah's room to check on her progress. Jennifer had just finished with the interview and initial photographic documentation and was preparing to begin the physical exam and evidence collection.

"Detective Fitzmeyer and I are going out to your house. Here's my business card. Give me a call when you are heading home. I don't want you to go back alone. I'd also like to do a more formal interview tomorrow. Would that be okay?"

Hannah took the card and nodded.

"I think it would be a good idea for you to go to a safe house or shelter until we can figure out who's behind the attack."

She looked at Frankie with wide, tear-filled eyes. Her voice cracked as she asked, "Can I go to my momma's? I just want to be with my momma and daddy."

"It's risky, Hannah, but in the end, it's up to you. I just don't think it's a good idea for you to stay at your house, at least not until we know who attacked you. I'm going to head out there now. Give me a call when you leave here, okay?"

She nodded.

CHAPTER
NINE

FRANKIE AND FITZ walked slowly to the emergency department exit in silence. The cold winter air hit their faces as the doors slid open to the parking garage.

"Where'd you park, Frankie?"

"Dammit I hate winter," was her response. She nodded to her car, "I'm just over there. Want a ride to yours?"

"No thanks. I'm not far. Meet you at the house?"

"Sounds good." She pulled her phone from her pocket. She was thinking of the calls she needed to make before getting to Hannah's house but before she could decide whose number to dial first it began to ring.

"Thomas."

"Whatcha wearin'?" asked the deep, sultry voice of Derek Kensington. The sound of his voice was as familiar to her as the sound of her own heartbeat.

A smile immediately brightened her face. "Nothing but a smile."

"Ugh…you're killin' me."

"What are you doing up so late? Don't you have an early docket in the morning?"

"I couldn't sleep and thought maybe you could sing me a lullaby…or better yet, come by and help me fall asleep some other way. You know I always sleep better when you're here with me."

"That sounds wonderful but looks like I'm not hitting the pillow anytime soon. I'm on my way to 73rd and Oak to a scene. Rain check?" She asked with hope.

"You know it, gorgeous. Be careful out there. I'll call you tomorrow."

"Always. Good night."

She disconnected. Forgetting the calls she needed to make she let her mind travel back in time as she drove. She met Derek while she was still in the police academy. He was a prosecuting attorney and had come to talk to her class about the judicial process. Seven years later she could still remember the day but, if asked, she could not remember a thing he said. While he talked, all she could think was, "He has to be one of the most brilliant and sexiest men I've ever heard."

During a break in his presentation, she made her way to the front of the room trying to think of an excuse to talk to him one on one. When she stood next to him it struck her, he was only about eight inches taller than her and, based on what he said during the presentation, she knew he was only a couple of years older. His hair was dark brown, cut military short, with just the right amount of gray at the temples. His suit was tailored and hugged his fit body in all the right places. He was charming and kind, looked her in the eye, and acted genuinely interested in what the naïve recruit had to say. While they talked, he gently touched her arm and when she looked into his hazel eyes, she immediately felt the breath escape her body. They shook hands as they said good-bye and with the touch of his hand, she felt a bolt of electricity that extended through her entire body.

Frankie saw Derek a couple more times before she graduated and when she did, he always asked questions that referenced their previous conversation. This told her he not only listened when she talked but also cared enough to remember what they talked about.

A few weeks before she graduated from the academy Frankie began to date Brad Thomas, an officer on the Tactical Response Team, and she forgot all about the handsome prosecutor. They had a whirlwind romance and were married within a year. Three years later, they had a son. Then two years after, just as they were preparing to celebrate their fifth anniversary, Brad was murdered while executing a search warrant. Frankie was devastated.

CHAPTER
TEN

A YEAR after burying her husband, Frankie had to procure a search warrant after hours. The prosecutors she normally worked with were at a conference and Derek was cover the prosecutor on duty. She drove to his house, and for reasons she didn't fully understand, felt butterflies in her stomach when he asked general questions. Before she left his house, he asked for her phone number under the guise of being able to call in the event he had follow-up questions. Without a second thought she gave him her personal cell phone number.

Derek called her before the week ended and asked her to lunch. Initially she hesitated but with a little prodding agreed to meet on her day off. They had been seeing each other casually since. At first, she tried to keep the relationship platonic - meeting him for lunch and the occasional dinner. She was a single mother, still grieving, and didn't have a lot of free time. When she did, she wanted to spend it with her kids. Derek understood and respected that her children always came first. He never pressured her to choose whom to spend time with nor did he expect to be included in their lives. Yet, on the rare occasions she could meet for dinner their meal would turn into hours of talking over cold bottles of beer or a shared bottle of wine.

During these long dinners, Derek told her about his childhood growing up in Northeast, a working-class, and somewhat impoverished, neighborhood in Kansas City. He was one of five children and had dreams of getting out and seeing the world beyond his neighborhood. His parents worked hard but did not make a lot of money. He knew the only way he would be able to see the world or go to college was on a scholarship, so he studied hard and excelled in sports. He played baseball for Northeast High School and by his junior year he had college scouts watching him and talking to his coaches. Then in his senior year a Marine Corps recruiter came to the school. That visit changed the trajectory of his life.

Instead of going to college to play baseball, Derek went to boot camp. After boot camp, he headed to the University of North Carolina on the ROTC program. He studied political science and graduated with honors at the onset of Desert Storm. His first assignment after the Basic School in Quantico was with 2d Marine Division aboard Camp Lejeune, NC. Within months of his arrival his unit deployed to Iraq. After two tours, two injuries, and one Purple Heart, he had fulfilled his contract but he was not ready to leave the Corps, so he transferred to the reserves and made plans to go to law school.

Before returning to UNC-Chapel Hill for law school he rented a cottage and spent a solitary summer on Ocracoke Island, NC. The slow pace of the island life was the balm he needed to begin healing the deep-rooted, psychological scars caused by war. Once he graduated from law school he returned to Kansas City, passed the bar, and got a job with the Jackson County Prosecutor's Office. He continued to serve as a Staff Judge Advocate in the Marine Corps Reserves and had been called up to active duty twice, going to both Afghanistan and Iraq.

Derek didn't like to talk about his deployments but on the rare occasion Frankie would stay at his house his memories would find their way to the surface. Occasionally he would wake her up screaming, his body thrashing about the bed in a fit of rage obviously caught in a horrible nightmare. It was on those nights they would lay awake, and he would share bits and pieces of his experience. He talked about the camaraderie, the brotherhood, and eventually the tragedy. They would laugh and cry together as he shared his memories. After his last deployment, the frequency and intensity of the nightmares increased. It was during that deployment where he lost his friend Kyle.

It was almost nine months after his last deployment before she heard the story. She was staying the night at his house and awoke to him screaming, his body drenched in a cold sweat. The pupils of his hazel eyes were dilated, making them appear almost black and his face was contorted in fear. She sat up and tried to talk to him, but his eyes bore through her as though he were somewhere else. She was frightened but she recognized he was having a flashback and her training quickly kicked in. She began to speak calmly to him, helped him get grounded, and slowly he worked his way out of the flashback. Once it ended, and he felt safe, Derek told her about Kyle.

Kyle had grown up in the northeast neighborhood with Derek and the pair enlisted in the Marine Corps together. They took different paths, but both went to college and law school. They rose up the ranks of the Corps together, each deploying twice – the final time with the same command. They were closer than most brothers.

As Frankie drove, she could see Derek rubbing a metal dog tag between his fingers and hear his voice saying, "During my deployment Kyle and I ended up together in Afghanistan. A call came in from one of the camps about a sexual assault. I was supposed to fly out to the camp to advise the commander but the night before I was scheduled to leave, I got food poisoning, so Kyle went in my place. He was gone for three days and although communications were not good, we were able to talk a couple of times and brainstorm about the case. The night before he was to return to camp, he called me, and we made plans to meet in the chow hall for dinner and strategize the case.

"On the day of Kyle's return I was walking across the camp to the showers when I saw a helicopter inbound. I stood helplessly as the helicopter exploded and erupted into a fireball. I watched as it fell from the sky just outside the perimeter of the camp. There were nine Marines aboard the helicopter; all nine died in the explosion. I didn't have to be told that Kyle was one of them, I felt it the moment the helo exploded. A part of me died that day with Kyle. All of me wished it had been me instead of him."

Years later Derek still carried one of Kyle's dog tags with him and on his left wrist he wore a metal band which bore the name of the helicopter and the date of the crash. It was a simple way for him to honor his friend and the other Marines who lost their lives, a way to carry them with him.

Frankie had strong feelings for Derek and was confident he felt the same way but neither had ever put their feelings into words. They enjoyed spending time together but also enjoyed their time apart. His job kept him busy and when he was in trial, she was lucky if she got a call, much less saw him. She kept him and the rest of her life separate. She understood when he got distracted and did not take it personally when he did not appear to have time for her. She was busy with her children, work, and volunteerism but enjoyed the fragments of time they got to spend together.

As Frankie drove the last few blocks, she pondered their relationship. She tried to imagine how he would fit into her world and she into his. They had never talked of the future but lately she had started to think about it. She was starting to want more but was not sure if she would ever have the courage to bring it up.

CHAPTER
ELEVEN

FRANKIE WAS grateful the rain-ice mixture had stopped. The unmarked police car she drove was no match for ice-covered roads. As she drove the final blocks, she listened to the patrol officers chatter on the radio. When there was a lull she keyed the mic, "1061."

"Go ahead 1061."

She smiled to herself, recognizing the voice of Laura Williams, a young woman she and Mac had mentored.

"Hold me out to 73rd and Oak."

"Copy. 1061 out to 73rd and Oak. 2315."

She thought to herself, "Is it really only eleven o'clock?" It seemed so much later. Her reverie was interrupted by the sound of her radio number being called.

"1060 to 1061 on private."

The private channel allowed officers to communicate one on one without interfering with regular radio traffic.

She picked up the mic, "Go ahead, Sarge."

"Safe route in is from the north on Oak. Park behind my car. And Frankie? There's media everywhere."

"Copy that, Sarge. Be there in less than five."

She exited Wornall Road at 72nd Street and drove east. Hannah's house was in a trendy area known as Waldo. It was a quiet, gentrified neighborhood with the "newest" house being over sixty years old. She loved the charm and character the houses that lined the streets. The trees in the yards were taller than most of the houses with branches broad enough for a large tree house or tire swing. In the autumn, when the leaves changed and fell, the streets and sidewalks were covered in a blanket of red, gold, and brown. They would scatter and swirl in the wind blowing through open garage doors causing them to stick and motion detected house alarms to sound.

When she worked patrol, part of her area included Waldo, so she knew the neighborhood well. Most of her time was spent in areas of distress and high crime, making alarm calls in Waldo a nice reprieve.

Approaching the scene, she thought to herself, "I love being a detective but some days I really miss working patrol. Driving with lights and sirens to answer a 9-1-1 call. Running after someone who had drugs, a gun, a felony warrant or a thousand other things that could come up in a shift. I miss the adrenaline rush of not knowing what's coming next."

As a detective, the rushes were fewer and farther between but when she got lost in a case or started doing an interrogation, she got a rush that almost matched. Almost.

She parked the car as Baker walked toward her.

"Hey Sarge, how bad is it?" she inquired as she stepped out of the car.

"The rest of the squad is inside the garage with the door closed. Crime Scene is just about finished collecting evidence. Media is everywhere so hold off on details until we get inside."

They walked the half block to the garage in silence. She felt an involuntary shiver from the cold but maintained a neutral facial expression as she looked around. She knew all the media crews would have their cameras running in the hope of catching a snippet of something. There was a good chance she would end up in a clip on the morning news and did not want her behavior to be seen as anything but professional.

They stopped in front of the detached garage located next to Hannah's house. Standing on the street, she pulled out her notepad and made a few notes about the placement of the structure in relation to the house and the vehicles that were parked on the street inside of the crime scene tape. She knew Coleman would draft a thorough crime scene report, but she wanted a sketch to help her later when she reviewed her notes. The overhead garage door was closed so they walked to the side entrance. On the side door, near the door handle, was a dirt stain that looked like a footprint.

"Hey Sarge, do you know if Coleman did anything with this door? Looks to me like someone may have forced their way in."

She made a mental note to make sure the door had been photographed and to ask Crime Scene if they could get a copy of the print for comparison purposes.

Mac's partner, Maria Payne, approached the pair before Baker could answer.

"Hey Frankie, I was just about to leave. Just when I think I've seen it all..."

Maria had been on the department for over ten years and was a former detective herself. She was a good officer who had heart and a reputation for rescuing stray dogs she found in the city, then finding good homes for them. She stood just over six feet tall with cornflower blue eyes and beautiful blond hair that fell to the middle of her back. She and her husband, a firefighter with KCFD, had twins that Frankie loved as if they were her own. They had been partners in the Sex Crimes Unit and friends for almost three years, spending a lot of time together on and off the job.

"Every time I say that it bites me in the ass," Frankie replied. "Who's taking the paper on this?"

"I'm up."

She was glad Maria was writing this one. Mac was a good report writer but had never been a detective. Maria was more experienced and would write a more thorough report, one with the end result in mind.

"It's okay. We had a four-car vehicular at Cleaver II and Oak down by the university right before we answered up for this. Mac is going to have a great time with the diagram. You know how weird that intersection is. We had stopped by the Quick Trip at 72nd and Wornall right after working that mess, which is how we got here so quick. I started the report, so it'll be in the system before I leave tonight."

Frankie laughed as she thought of Mac trying to draw the intersection that could best be described as a flattened star.

"Ha, better him than me! I hate writing accident reports - especially at that intersection."

Laughing Maria said, "Looks like my relief has arrived."

"Be safe and give the kids a hug for me."

"You got it. Stay safe."

As Frankie followed Baker into the garage she heard Maria tell the dispatcher she was en route to the hospital.

CHAPTER
TWELVE

"COLEMAN, tell me what we've got," she said, closing the door behind her.

"Rob just finished taking photos, but we were waiting on you before we started collecting evidence. Watch your step, there's blood on the floor by the driver's side door."

"Did you see the footprint on the door?"

"Yeah."

"I grabbed some photographs," Rob chimed in. "Yang will get an impression before we leave."

She put on gloves and looked around the room as she told the men what she had learned at the hospital. She was not quite sure what to make of what she saw. The garage was typical of those in the neighborhood. It was detached from the house and large enough for two cars - but only if the cars were small. Parked in the middle was a new red Hyundai Tiburon with both doors open and the headlights illuminated. In front of the vehicle were shelves that held colorful plastic containers. One of the containers was not sitting square on the other and had a lid slightly ajar.

"Hey Rob, did you take a picture of the shelves? One of these totes looks out of order. Yang, will you dust it for prints?"

She made a mental note to ask Hannah to verify if anything was missing from the tote or if she had been in it recently and not gotten it closed. Scattered about the floor near the driver's side door of were pieces of duct tape; the pieces appeared to have been cut and dropped quickly. Amid the scraps she observed red rose petals, the thorny stem of a rose and droplets of blood on the floor.

She let her eyes drift to the back of the garage toward the overhead door. The door was closed, and the corners of the garage contained piles of leaves. "Was the overhead door open when you got here, Rich?"

"No. Payne said they closed it when the media circus came to town."

She walked around the car as Rich talked. The garage was darker on the passenger side. She stumbled during her attempt to navigate around the yard tools and a bicycle propped against the wall. A second bicycle hung from a bicycle hook with an air pump attached. Rakes, a spade, and hedge trimmers hung from pegs on the wall next to the bicycle. Nothing appeared disturbed. To try and see what Tessa would have seen earlier in the night, she knelt to look under the vehicle.

"Hey Yang, did you take any pics underneath the car? It looks like there are some drops of blood and a beer bottle just under the door on the driver's side."

After Yang took the additional photographs, she retrieved the bottle to take a closer look. She looked at the empty beer bottle and saw what appeared to be hair, bodily fluids, and blood around its thick base.

"Damn. Just damn."

Baker bent down and looked at the bottle she was holding in her gloved hand. "Is that what I think it is?"

"Won't know for sure until it gets to the lab and gets processed but yeah, I think so."

She watched while Yang bagged the bottle then took a deep breath and continued looking around the garage. Coleman had already drafted a diagram of the scene and was making notes for the final report. She walked to the front of the garage and observed him writing a list of things they had seized and said, "Add a bottle to the list."

"Where'd you find a bottle?"

"It was lying just under the driver's side door on the floor. I wanted to see what Tessa described so I got down and looked under the car from the passenger side and noticed it. Looks like there might be some pubic hair, fluids, and possibly blood on the bottom of the bottle. There might be a good fingerprint on the neck of the bottle, too."

"What the fuck?" said Rich incredulously. "You don't think..."

She interrupted before he could say out loud what she was thinking, "Yeah, I do. I'll know more after I get their full statements, but I think Hannah was raped with the bottom of the beer bottle. He may have used the same bottle to knock her out. I'm not sure. Did you find anything else that may have been used as a weapon?"

He started to answer but the opening of the side door to the garage stopped him. Fitz walked into the garage and visually swept the room. Before she could tell them to shut the door, Mia and Brett walked in behind him.

"It's colder than hell out there," exclaimed Brett. "I freaking hate winter."

"I'm right there with you," Frankie said. "What'd you guys find out?"

"We knocked on doors two blocks in each direction. No one who answered saw or heard anything. A couple of people did say about six o'clock tonight they noticed a black Mercedes SUV parked a couple of houses down. One of the neighbors said she thought it sat there for a couple of hours. It stood out to her was because it was parked in front of the judge's house. This lady is your classic nosey neighbor, she not only told us the judge is out of town but said she doesn't have any friends or family who drive that type of vehicle. One of the other neighbors saw the SUV and thought it had a dealer tag but couldn't tell for sure. The nosy neighbor said she was going to call it in but when she went back to the window to try to get a license plate number it was gone. We left cards on the doors of those who didn't answer," Mia said.

"Were you able to find the person who called 9-1-1?"

"Yeah, it was the neighbor directly across the street," said Brett. "Her name is Kathryn Vergaro. She's a doctor at one of the local hospitals. She was pretty shaken up, so we just did a short interview. I told her you'd touch base with her in a couple of days to do a formal. Have you heard the call yet?"

"No. Is it bad?"

"Chilling is more like it. It's pretty powerful, Frankie. She found Hannah unconscious on the floor."

Just as Frankie started to tell the team she would listen to the call when she got back to the office her phone began to ring. "Thomas."

"HI DETECTIVE THOMAS," Hannah's voice was not much louder than a whisper. "You asked me to call when we left the hospital. My parents are bringing Tessa and me back to the house right now so she can get her car and I can get some clothes. Are you all still there?"

"Yes, we're still here. Crime Scene is finishing up with evidence collection now, but they should be done by the time you get here. Have you thought about where you're going to stay? I think we can get you into a safe house."

"I talked to my parents, and they think I should stay with them. I feel pretty safe there, they have a security system and a pretty big dog, so I think I'll be safe." She paused then added, "And my dad has a gun."

"Is Tessa in the car with you?" asked Frankie.

"Yeah."

"Can I please speak with her?"

Hannah answered affirmatively before handing her cellphone to Tessa.

"Hi Detective Thomas. Thank you for staying at the house until we could get there," Tessa said.

"Sure. Did you think any more about what we discussed at the hospital? Do you want me to get you into a safe house?"

"Do you think I need to? I mean, I live out in the country, and I have a couple of big dogs that I really can't leave alone overnight. If you're worried, maybe an officer could stay out at my house? I'm not sure what I should do. I don't have any family here," she rambled.

Frankie paused for a moment.

"I think it would be a good idea for both of you to go to a safe house until we can get to the bottom of this, but I can't force you to go. If you feel safe going home, I'll respect that. Please understand we cannot have someone stay out there with you. We don't have the manpower and your house is outside our jurisdiction."

She heard Tessa take a deep breath and exhale, "I understand but I think I want to go home. I don't feel like anyone will bother me there. The dogs I raise have been trained to work as police dogs and they are very loyal and won't let anyone get near me. I'm sure of it."

"Okay. We'll talk more about safety when you get here." Frankie disconnected the call then said, "These girls are refusing to go to a safe house. Fitz, just how bad are these guys?"

"As bad as they get, Frankie."

CHAPTER
FOURTEEN

"OUR UNIT HAS BEEN LOOKING at them for a couple of homicides, bombings, drugs, and weapons trafficking. We think they may also be trafficking women but so far, we haven't been able to make anything stick. These girls are suing a rough crew."

She looked toward Baker as he walked up behind Fitz, "Both girls are adamant they won't go to a safe house. Based on what Fitz just said can we get a dog out here to check for bombs before we let them leave?"

"That's a good idea, Frankie," Baker keyed up his radio mic. "1060?"

"Go ahead 1060," answered the dispatcher.

"Is K-9 working tonight?"

"764 is on the air. What do you need?" replied K-9 Officer Jordan Franklin.

"Stand-by," answered Baker. "1060 to 764 on private."

"Go ahead 1060."

"Is your dog a bomb detection dog?"

"Yep. Where do you need us?"

"We're out at 73rd and Oak. What's your ETA?"

"I can be there in ten. Do you need us to run hot?" Jordan inquired.

"No, normal speed is good. See you when you get here."

"Good deal. Thanks, Sarge. Hey Mia, can I talk to you a minute?" Frankie asked.

She motioned toward the newest detective on their squad. Mia was a talented detective with good instincts. Standing 5'6" she had short, spiky red hair, fair skin with freckles, and Irish blue eyes. Her hairstyle matched her personality - she was full of fire and spunk. Mia matched Frankie in her passion for the underdog, often championing those who couldn't stand up for themselves, but Frankie knew better than to let her sweet disposition and compassion fool her. Mia could hold a person to task, setting them straight without blinking an eye.

Frankie had been assigned to be Mia's training detective and in typical "Frankie fashion," she was baptized by fire. This meant working many late nights and challenging cases. As a result, the two bonded. They were not only work colleagues but best friends.

The Sex Crimes Unit did not have assigned partners but after the training period was over, they continued to work most shifts and cases together. The two frequently bounced ideas and theories off each other, even if they were not working the case together. Baker often threatened to separate them because it seemed trouble always found them but as much as he threatened, they both knew he was just teasing. They made a good, effective team putting together strong cases for prosecution. Frankie knew she could trust Mia with anything.

"What's up chica?" Mia asked as she bumped her shoulder into Frankie's causing them both to laugh as she lost her balance. "Man am I glad Sarge ran the media off. I think Killer's the only one still out there. Wish I knew what he said to them so we could use it next time."

"I know, right? Let's go to my car just in case Killer has his boom mic on trying to capture our conversation. I need to run something past you."

Frankie had known Gary Kinder, an on-air reporter for a local news station since she became a detective. He had earned his nickname because of his killer instincts on reporting news and his innate desire to report it accurately. Killer, or one of his staff, called the Sex Crimes Section asking about news stories several times a day.

The detectives walked to the car and once they were safely inside Frankie turned to Mia. "Something about this case just doesn't feel right. I can't put my finger on it but something's…I don't know? Off."

CHAPTER
FIFTEEN

"WHY WOULD these guys only rape one of the women instead of both? Why didn't they kill them? The men Fitz described don't strike me as the type to leave witnesses behind. And how'd they know the women would be together or when they would be coming back here? Were they watching them or did someone tip them off?"

Without hesitation Mia asked, "What does your gut tell you?"

She paused for a moment before replying, reflecting on what the women and the scene had told her.

"It tells me something's not right, but I don't have enough information to really make a judgment on what exactly that something is."

"A wise woman once told me to keep an open mind and always start by believing the victim, then let the facts drive the investigation." Mia winked at her.

Frankie chuckled as she wondered how many times she had said those same words. "Whoever told you that sure is brilliant."

She appreciated Mia making her eat her own words. When she conducted training workshops she said the same words to every officer, detective, nurse, victim advocate and prosecutor. She wore a bracelet that said, "I start by believing" and when she had any doubts in a case, she touched the bracelet and read the words. Those four words reminded her not to make judgments but instead to keep an open mind. She was the type of person who worked hard to practice what she preached.

"When are you getting their formal statements?"

"I told them to come in tomorrow. Given the way trauma effects memory, it's pointless to try to get a full statement tonight, it's just setting them both up for failure by allowing for possible inconsistencies in their statements."

Mia nodded and said, "True. I'm on tomorrow, want some help?"

"I was hoping you'd say that," replied Frankie. "Looks like K-9 just pulled up. I think the girls are pulling up, too."

They got out of the car and walked toward the police car with K-9 plastered on the side panel.

"Hey Jordan, I didn't know you were on," Mia exclaimed. Jordan Franklin stepped onto the street with her dog, Ero. Jordan had been Mia's field training officer when she was on patrol. The two continued to work the same district together until Jordan got the opportunity to go to the K-9 Unit and Mia went to investigations.

"Well, if it isn't the dynamic duo!" Jordan responded as Frankie greeted her. "What do we have here?"

"Two women were attacked in the garage behind us. Both women were bound with duct tape, physically assaulted, and one of the women was raped. Scott Fitzmeyer from the Intelligence Unit is here because we think there is a strong possibility this was a mob hit. The crew suspected is tied to a couple of bombings in town so we thought it would be a good idea if both of their vehicles were swept for explosives. The woman that was raped lives at this house and her car is in the garage. The white Range Rover on the street belongs to the other girl. Can you and Ero go around the vehicles before they leave?"

"No problem, Frankie. I'll start with the one on the street and give crime scene time to finish up inside." Jordan issued commands to Ero, and they walked to the Range Rover.

While Jordan and Ero walked around the vehicle, Frankie walked toward Hannah and Tessa.

"What are they doing?" asked Hannah.

Before Frankie could respond, Tessa answered, "The dog is looking for explosives."

"We asked them to come out just to be on the safe side. They will walk around your car, too, Hannah," added Frankie.

"I have an 8-bay kennel at my house where I breed and train German Shepherds for law enforcement and military units. That's why I don't think anyone would dare come there, my dogs would tear them apart. I always have two in the house." Tessa volunteered the information in rapid staccato as Hannah's parents exited their vehicle and walked toward the women.

"Do you really think that's something we should be worried about?" Hannah asked looking nervously from Frankie to Tessa and then to her parents.

Frankie tried to downplay her concerns, "It's just a precaution, Hannah, nothing to worry about."

CHAPTER
SIXTEEN

WITH AN EXTENDED HAND IN GREETING, Hannah's father introduced himself. "Detective Thomas, I'm Hannah's father Dave and this is my wife, Amber. Thank you for being so cautious regarding the girls' safety but we're going to take Hannah home with us."

"Nice to meet you both. I wish it was under different circumstances. If there is anything I can do to help ensure your daughter's safety, please let me know." She turned toward Hannah and Tessa and asked, "Would you be able to come to my office tomorrow? I need to get a formal, video-recorded statement and I'd like to do it as soon as possible."

Tessa quickly interjected her answer, "I'll come whenever you need me to."

Softly Hannah replied, "Me, too."

"My shift starts tomorrow at 3:00, but I can adjust my time if you would like to come in earlier."

"Three works for me," said Tessa. Hannah nodded in agreement.

"Great." Frankie handed each woman a business card. "This card contains some important information. First is the address where you need to come tomorrow afternoon. You can park in the lot on the side of the station. Second are my office and cellphone numbers. Normally I don't give my cellphone number out but since both of you will be staying outside of our jurisdiction, I want you to have it. If there is an emergency, call 9-1-1. When police arrive, if they do not take you seriously, give them my number and I'll explain what's going on. Lastly is the number for the local rape crisis center. If you need to talk to someone about what happened, they are there for you, 24 hours a day, 7 days a week."

She paused to give the women an opportunity to digest the information and ask questions. When neither said anything, she asked, "Would you like to have an advocate with you for the interview tomorrow?"

Hannah nodded her head and quietly said yes.

"Do you think they will send Beth?"

"I'll ask. They always do their best to accommodate when they can. Beth is a full-time employee so it should be easy to get her to come. What about you Tessa?"

Tessa took a moment before responding but then said, "Sure. If you can, ask for the girl who was with me at the hospital. She was great."

Just as Tessa finished speaking Jordan approached and asked to speak with Frankie privately.

"What's up Jordan?"

"Ero hit on something on the car in the garage. It doesn't look like a bomb to me, but I called the bomb squad just to be sure. They'll be here in thirty."

"Okay, I'm going to send these women on their way. Hopefully we can do it without freaking them out." She walked back to the group. "Hannah, would you mind leaving your car here tonight?"

"Sure. Is everything okay?" Her voice trembled.

"Yep. We just wanted to finish processing the scene and didn't want to hold you up any."

Hannah nodded affirmatively.

"I can ride with my parents and pick up my car tomorrow."

"Do you have any questions before you leave?"

Both women shook their heads as they looked to each of the officers. Frankie reminded both women to call if they needed anything. As the women got into their cars to leave, they thanked the detectives and told Frankie they would see her the following day.

Baker walked up behind Frankie and asked, "Did Jordan tell you?"
She nodded. "Show me what Ero hit on."

CHAPTER
SEVENTEEN

BAKER AND FRANKIE walked into the garage with somber expressions. Frankie had a nervous feeling in her stomach and wondered as they entered if it really was safe to do so. In the back of her mind, she knew no one would be in the garage if they thought it was unsafe but adrenaline still coursed through her veins.

Jordan and Ero stood at the rear of the car. "Everyone needs to make sure their phones and radios are turned off. The bomb squad is en route. Frankie, there are some wires and what looks like a piece of C4 under the bumper of this car. From here it does not look like the wires are attached. It's almost as though the intent was to frighten, not actually cause an explosion."

"I wondered why you let us in."

Frankie laid on the floor and looked under the bumper. A small gray square wrapped in plastic was stuck to the underside of the bumper. A black cell phone was attached to the gray square with red, green, and blue wires hanging from it. Just as Jordan said, the wires were not attached to the gray square. She could not help but think it looked staged, which caused her to ask the question, "Why?"

BAKER ORDERED the team to evacuate the garage. Ero had been put back inside the police car while everyone else waited for detectives from the bomb squad to arrive. Frankie looked around the neighborhood and let out a sigh of relief when she realized Killer had left and there would be no news covering the latest development.

When detectives Haggerty and Paridis arrived, Jordan provided a description of the device and location where Ero hit. The two detectives donned their protective gear and slowly walked inside the garage. Only a few minutes passed before they returned with a bag in hand.

"We recovered the device and will send it to the lab," said Haggerty.

"What can you tell us about it?" inquired Baker. "Why didn't it go off?"

"This thing wasn't set to detonate. My guess? It was placed there to scare the shit out of whoever owns that car. It was definitely not put there by a pro either. Hell, based on initial examination it looks like someone got directions off the internet. Or worse, some damn television show."

"Thanks for coming out, guys. I appreciate you recovering the bomb...or whatever it is. I'll put a lab request in tomorrow. Maybe we'll get lucky and get a print or DNA off the plastic," said Frankie.

CHAPTER
NINETEEN

IT WAS after midnight when Frankie left the scene. The air was crisp and smelled of cold; winter was coming quickly in the City of Fountains. She caught a glimpse of the moon and stars as they tried to peak out from behind the clouds. Her mind was going a million miles an hour as she drove, one thought cascading over another. She tried to piece together in her mind what happened in that garage, all the while knowing she did not have all the pieces and it was too early for the images to be clear.

She parked her police car outside of the headquarters building and debated on going inside to start her reports. She knew the office would be quiet and with no distractions she could knock the reports out quickly, but she was too restless to work. Instead, she grabbed her bag, climbed into the red Jeep Wrangler, and began driving north on Interstate 35. As she crossed the Paseo Bridge, she picked up her cell phone and dialed the number she had memorized a year prior.

After one ring, she heard someone clear his throat, followed by a husky, "Hello?"

"Whatcha wearin'?" she inquired in a sultry voice.

"Nothin' but a smile. How you doin' babe?" inquired Derek.

"My mind is going about a million miles an hour. This case is going to be a doozy."

"Want to come by and knock the cobwebs out?"

Sophie was with her boyfriend, so Keith was at her house. Bruce was working the night shift and wouldn't be expecting Keith, so he'd be asleep on the couch. The kids were in bed, so she didn't need to hurry home.

"I was hoping you'd ask. I'll be there in ten."

She hung up the phone, drove a little faster, turned the music up, and sang along loudly as the sounds of Daughtry filled her vehicle.

Derek lived in a small house on ten acres at the north edge of the city limits. The further north Frankie drove the fewer streetlights and the clearer the skies. By the time she reached the road to his house the clouds were gone, and the full moon shone bright enough that she could see for miles.

He had grown up in the heart of the city where a car couldn't fit between the house. Derek loved the feeling of freedom he had knowing his closest neighbor was half a mile up the road. The back deck of the house faced a pond and on Sunday mornings he could often be found sitting on the deck, drinking a cup of coffee, and reading the Kansas City Star or just watching the wildlife and fog as it rose from the water. When it was too cold to sit outside, Derek would sit in a chair by one of the windows that faced the same scene.

Frankie knew she would leave before him, so she parked directly behind his garage door. As she got out of the car there was a low, deep bark.

"Hey Bear. What are you doing outside?"

The twelve-year old black lab licked her hand. She rubbed the dog's head as she walked the moonlit path to the back door.

"Come on, let's go inside where it's warm."

Frankie let herself into the house through the unlocked door. She dropped her coat on the chair by the door and placed her keys and duty weapon on the kitchen table. She slipped her shoes off and walked down the hall. It did not enter her mind to turn a light on to navigate the house she knew so well. Frankie's feet padded softly down the carpeted hallway which housed a gallery of photographs of Derek's family. A sliver of blue light escaped the semi-closed door. She opened the door slowly. The television lit the room, showing replays from the Monday night football game. Derek was propped up on the bed with his only cover a light sheet, despite the frigid outdoor temperatures. The glow from the television reflected in his dark eyes. A smile spread across his face as he watched her walk into the room. Frankie felt something catch in her throat. The look in her eyes said everything that needed to be said.

Derek didn't say a word as he gestured for her to come to the side of the bed. She stood at the edge and put her cold hands on his bare chest. A shiver ran down his spine as he put his arms around her back and pulled her toward him. He placed his lips lightly against hers, reminding her of their first kiss.

The kisses started soft and sweet but quickly turned deep and fervent making her quiver, wanting more. Without removing his lips from hers, he quickly removed her clothes and pulled her onto the bed and under the sheet. His hands caressed her shoulders and breasts as his lips worked their way down her neck. She moaned as his lips brushed her nipples on his way further down her body. She ran her fingers through his hair and let them wander down his taut, muscular body; a body she never tired of exploring. His lips made his way back to her mouth while she caressed his hard body and guided him inside her. They made love until they were both spent and collapsed in a heap together.

"Do you want to talk about your night?" Waiting for an answer, he caressed her arm and ran his fingers through her hair causing an involuntary shiver down her spine.

"Not tonight," she replied. "I just want to enjoy this moment."

He knew he didn't need to say anything more as she lay in his arms, and he drifted off to sleep.

When his alarm sounded a couple of hours later, he leaned over to tell Frankie the time and noticed she was gone. On the pillow where she had been lying was a red paper heart.

"Call you before I go in. XO Frankie" with a heart over the i.

He smiled and walked into the bathroom to shower, thinking how lucky he was to have her in his life.

FRANKIE AWOKE to the sound of cartoons coming from her television and Tyler laughing. He was dressed for school and sitting on the end of her bed. She left Derek's house as soon as he dozed off and had fallen asleep the minute her head hit the pillow on her bed.

"Hey buddy."

"Hey mom! You're awake. Are you going to take me to school today?" Tyler spoke quickly, bouncing up and down on the bed without taking his eyes off the cartoons playing on the television screen.

"Yep. Do you have your backpack together? Have you brushed your teeth? Combed your hair?"

"I'm going to go do it now. I had to wait on Dani. She takes forever," he answered, drawing out the syllables of forever. He jumped off the bed and walked to the bathroom he shared with his sister.

Frankie slowly stretched out in her bed, extending her legs and toes as far as they would go. Her mind began to drift. She looked at the time on the alarm clock sitting on the table next to her bed. 7:05. Derek was probably in the shower preparing for a day at the courthouse. Thinking of the soap covering his naked body and streams of water running down his taut back, she smiled. A wave of guilt swept across her as she thought of Brad.

"Mom!" yelled Dani, jarring Frankie from her thoughts.

She slowly crawled out of bed. It was time to start the day.

"Mornin' Angel-girl. What's wrong?"

"Where is my purple scarf? I can't find it and it is spirit week. I have to wear it today. I can't find mine; can I just wear yours? Please mom?" Dani begged with just a hint of whining like only a girl can.

"Yours is in the hall. In your basket. I put it there when I got home last night. You know if you put things away when you came home…"

"I know, mom. You tell me that every day."

Before she could respond her cellphone started to ring. She winked at Dani. "Saved by the bell. Thomas."

"Hey Frankie," said an unfamiliar voice. "It's Scott Fitzmeyer. Do you have a minute?"

"Sure Fitz, I'm just getting my shoes on so I can take the kids to school. What's up?" She mumbled, "Dammit, where are my keys?"

"When are the girls coming in to give their statements?" He inquired adding, "Try looking where you last had them."

"No shit, Sherlock," she said, laughing. "They are supposed to be at my office at 3:00. I'm heading in about 1:30 to prep."

Fitz heard papers rustling and things being moved about. A distracted Frankie continued to look for her keys while they talked.

"I think we should talk first. Mind if I meet you there?"

"Sure. Come on guys, we're going to be late!" She yelled.

"Okay, I'll see you then. By the way, my guys are going to hit the mall where the girls had dinner and look at any surveillance footage they have. Hopefully it'll give us…I don't know, something."

"Call me if they come up with anything solid. I can't figure out how these guys knew when the girls would be coming home. Just doesn't make sense to me, but man, those injuries – you can't deny they were attacked."

"Mom, come on!" yelled Dani. "I can't be late to first period."

"Hey Fitz, can I call you back? Chaos is abundant in the Thomas household this morning. Found 'em!" Frankie exclaimed. She grabbed her keys off the floor by the entryway table. They must have fallen when she tossed them toward the table the night before.

"No problem, Frankie," he replied. "I'll meet you at HQ at 1:30. If my guys find a smoking gun, I'll call you."

"Thanks, Fitz." She hung up the phone and grabbed her gym bag yelling, "Come on guys, let's go!"

Frankie dropped her kids off at their respective schools and each went about their normal routine. She was exhausted but instead of going back to bed she headed to the gym. She preferred to run outside with her golden retriever, Isabelle, but when the air was cold, she left the dog at home and hit the treadmill at the community center. To her running was better than therapy. It was a place for her to think and clear her thoughts; a place to try to answer the questions that raced through her mind. She blasted music through her earbuds and got lost in the sounds. The beat of the music, rhythm of her breath, and the pounding of her shoes as they hit the belt were cathartic.

After spending 45 minutes on the treadmill, Frankie grabbed her towel and cellphone and went into the dry sauna. She had just laid down on the wooden bench when her phone began to vibrate. She looked at the caller ID and couldn't help but smile at the site of Derek's face. "Hey babe."

"Are you all hot and sweaty?" He asked, knowing her routine as well as she did.

"Just a bit. I was a little tired this morning so I wouldn't have won any races but at least I showed up."

He laughed and asked, "Is that a complaint I'm hearing?"

"Not at all," she answered. "Definitely worth the fatigue."

"Did you solve all the world's problems on your run?"

"Hardly," she laughed, wiping the sweat from her face.

"Are you taking the girls' statements tonight?"

"Yeah, they are coming in at 3:00. I'm going to head in about 1:30 so I can look over my notes and talk to Fitz first. How's trial prep coming?"

He had a murder trial starting the Monday after the holiday. The case involved a shootout between rival gangs; the result was the death of a four-year-old child. He was relentless in all the cases he tried but when the case involved an innocent child the fire in his soul was lit even higher. Because of this he would probably work late hours and into the weekend preparing.

"I've got a witness on their way in now for an interview. Once I'm finished with them, I will start working on my opening statement. This one's going to be tough. Some of the witnesses are having second thoughts about testifying. I think the 51st Street F.O.G. is making threats against the family but I can't prove it." Frankie heard knocking on his office door. "Hey babe, looks like they're here. Call me tonight?"

"Definitely," she answered as she grabbed her towel and wiped her face. It was time for her to head home to get some lunch, take a shower and get ready for work.While Frankie prepared for work, she and Baker texted back and forth about the case. She had only worked for him for about a year, but he had proven himself to be an irreplaceable leader. She learned quickly if you were wrong, he would take you to task but if you were right, he would back you endlessly. They were close in age and had formed a strong professional bond. It was not uncommon for them to brainstorm ideas and occasionally vent to one another about cases and department issues.

She updated him on her plan to meet Fitz at 1:30 and invited him to join them so he could update them together on the background of Stevenson Automotive and those who worked there. He said he was working his off-duty job but would be in the office after he got relieved. Like most police officers, he worked approved security jobs to help supplement his income.

Frankie grabbed her dinner and her workbag and walked out the door. She looked back at Isabelle and asked, "I wonder what surprises await me today?"

CHAPTER
TWENTY-ONE

BEFORE FRANKIE COULD TAKE her coat off and put down her bag, she was bombarded with questions from the detectives on her sister squad. She told them what she knew while she put her things away.

"Hey Frankie," said Fitz as he walked through the door of the squad room. "Looks like a full house today."

"No rest for the weary," answered Dustin Kramer, sergeant of 1050 Squad. "How've you been Fitz?"

Kramer and Fitz attended the police academy together but, with a department of 1500 sworn officers, their paths had not crossed much over the twelve years since they graduated.

"Doing good. How's the family?"

While Fitz and Kramer made small talk, Frankie grabbed her pen, notepad, crime scene photographs, and case notes from the night before and went to the conference room adjacent to the squad room.

Fitz called out, "I'll be right in, Frankie."

She laid the pictures on the table side-by-side. She couldn't put her finger on it, but something wasn't right. The photographs depicted two attractive young women lying on hospital beds with red, watery eyes but that's where the similarity ended. Hannah had purple and black bruises on her cheek, arms, ribs, and upper thigh. The bruises were consistent with someone who had been grabbed, knocked down, held, bound, and kicked or stepped on. The bruise on her thigh had the distinct outline and shape of a man's dress shoe. Additional photographs showed long scratches on her inner thighs from her groin to her knees - scratches that didn't have an obvious explanation.

The doctor had placed six staples on the top of her skull and multiple sutures on the right side of her cheek and forehead from where she hit the ground. In contrast, Tessa had one bruise on her arm, slight redness on her wrists and bruising on the exterior of her upper thigh. To Frankie, the bruising looked old. She also had a knot on the top of her scalp but, unlike Hannah, she did have to get any sutures or staples.

Pushing those photographs to the side, she pulled out the photos from the crime scene. She looked over the photographs and tried to recreate in her mind's eye what happened in the garage. She was lost deep in thought, analyzing each photograph. The sound of the door opening and Fitz walking in startled her, causing her to jump slightly in her seat.

"A little jumpy?" he teased.

Chuckling she answered, "No, just lost in thought."

Standing, she turned toward him. The light bounced off the bald head of the man following him into the room. She glanced at the pocket of the navy polo and read to herself, "Federal Bureau of Investigations."

"Damn," Fitz said as he looked at the photographs scattered about the table. "Don't you have this locked up yet?" He winked at her as she smirked. He gestured behind him and said, "Jim Craven meet Detective Francesca Thomas. Jim's a special agent with the FBI's Career Criminal Unit. He's got a lot of experience with the men these women are suing and offered to work with us on the investigation."

She shook Jim's hand before returning to her chair.

"It's nice to meet you. Thanks for offering to help," she said, hesitating slightly. "Please call me Frankie.

She had heard bad things from other detectives about the FBI's offer to "help." They had a reputation of making the locals do all the work and then taking all the credit for closing the case. Frankie was a little uneasy and reluctant to accept help from this new addition, but Fitz was one of theirs. If he trusted Jim, then she would give him a chance.

With a slow, southern drawl, Jim replied, "No problem. I've been workin' these guys for a while and would really like to get somethin' that will stick so we can bring down their organization. I don't want to get in your way, but I've got loads of resources that will be at your disposal if you need them. You need anything, just say the word."

He was not surprised by her less than warm reception. He had been a police officer in Chicago for eight years, with three spent as a detective before joining the FBI. He knew he would have to earn her trust and it might take some time. She would have to believe he was there to help her, not take over her case or take credit for her work.

She nodded then asked, "Fitz, did your team find any surveillance footage, witnesses, or anything of value when they went out to Mayfaire?"

"Jared King and Corey Fields went out there this morning and viewed the footage at a few of the stores. The security teams were busy getting ready for Black Friday, so they don't have anything downloaded yet, but they promised to have discs burned by the end of the week. King scanned the video but didn't think there was anything unusual. Since we don't have the girls' full statements it's hard to tell if they missed something. Once we get the full story, we can watch the videos ourselves and see if there is anything of value. Fields said he would pick them up for you this weekend."

"That would be great, thanks! Either way it will be good to have them on hand. At the very minimum it will help set a timeline." Switching gears she asked, "So what do you know about these guys they are suing?"

CHAPTER
TWENTY-TWO

FITZ WALKED to the dry erase board and began to draw a diagram as he talked.

"It goes without saying but none of what we are about to tell you is public knowledge and should not be repeated. I'll try to make this as easy to follow as I can, but the connections can get a little twisted.

"You already know the girls worked for Stevenson Automotive, which is owned by Marzullo Automotive Group out of Detroit. I knew there was a connection between Marzullo, Stevenson and, I suspected, a third organization but it wasn't until today that Jim was able to confirm my suspicions. Marzullo Automotive Group is associated with the Dante Group out of Chicago. The head of that organization, Anthony Michael Dante, is a well-known crime boss in Chicago with affiliations in Detroit, St. Louis, and Kansas City. They have their connections hidden well but the FBI has been tracking Dante's activity for a while because of some of their other suspected dealings. I am pretty sure there are some familial relationships underlying the business connection. Does the name Charles Carrollo sound familiar?"

Frankie shook her head. "Should it?"

"Carrollo was Johnny Lazia's oldest friend and bodyguard. We think Dante is part of the Carrollo family."

"Which means his organized crime roots are deep in KC," she said.

He nodded and let the information resonate with those at the table.

"As for Dante and his crew, some of their activities we're looking into include racketeering and trafficking of drugs, women, and weapons. These guys are no joke, Frankie. We need to take it slow and methodical connecting the dots in this case. We do not want them to know we're looking at them until we are ready to make an arrest. Moving too quickly can jeopardize both of our cases and put the women in even more danger."

He looked to Jim who was pulling a manila folder from his bag. "Jim, why don't you show Frankie what you have."

"The photographs I am about to show you are graphic. I could probably get in trouble for sharing these, but I think you deserve to know what you're up against."

He laid the file on the table and pulled out 8x10 photographs. She picked up each photograph, looking at them carefully. The first photograph depicted three bodies piled and stuffed into the trunk of a full-size black sedan. Duct tape bound each person's hands and covered their mouths. The woman's skirt was pushed up around her waist and her panties were torn.

The next series of photographs showed each person lying on the slab in the morgue. The report said cause of death for each was a single gunshot wound to the back of the head - execution style. All three had injuries from being beaten but the injuries the woman sustained were significantly more severe. Their faces were swollen making them unrecognizable. All three were ultimately identified by their fingerprints. The medical examiner's report said a forensic examination of the woman revealed evidence of being raped. Frankie was memorizing the details of the photographs while Jim talked. As he started to put the photos away something in the photograph of the woman caught her eye.

"Can I see that photo again?"

"What is it, Frankie?" asked Fitz.

Jim handed her the photograph of the woman from the morgue.

"I want to get a better look at the tattoo on her wrist."

She examined the photograph carefully. On the inside of the woman's wrist was a tattoo of a single rose. She handed the photograph back to

Jim, "I've seen that tattoo before. I think one of the women from last night had the same tattoo on her wrist."

Fitz and Jim looked from Frankie to one another. Fitz broke the silence and said, "Coincidence?"

She shrugged her shoulders with a look on her face that told the men she did not believe in coincidences.

"Those three were found in the west bottoms, over by the stockyards. The car was abandoned behind one of the steakhouses, so no one realized it was out of place for several days. Fortunately, it was cold, so the bodies had not decayed too badly. The woman was identified as Katarina Schlovik, a dancer from a strip club on 12th Street. She was last seen leaving the club with the guys she shared the trunk with. Guess who underwrites the club?"

Fitz and Frankie sat silently.

"Marzullo. The two dead men were believed to be soldiers for the Finnegan family who are direct competitors of the Marzullo family. Speculation was Katarina was either being recruited by the Finnegan's to dance at one of their clubs or she was romantically involved with one of the men or both. It doesn't really matter what her relationship with the soldiers was, the Marzullo family saw her association as a form of betrayal."

"A betrayal that cost her life," said Frankie softly. "I remember hearing about the triple last summer, but I don't remember hearing if anyone was ever charged."

"There haven't been any charges filed. Yet. I worked with your homicide guys a bit but there wasn't much physical evidence. They collected some swabs from the forensic exam of Katarina, but the DNA results haven't come back yet. I'm not expecting them to identify anyone. These guys are no amateurs," explained Jim.

She sat quietly, absorbing what he had said. Were these the same people that attacked Hannah and Tessa? They were certainly capable, but it seemed unlikely they would leave anyone alive that could identify them. The attacks had some similarities, but Schlovik and the two men were beaten unrecognizable. Hannah had some bruising on her face, but Tessa barely had a scratch on hers. There appeared to be a connection between this case and the triple homicide, but Frankie was slow to force it. She knew things were often not what they initially appeared.

Before she could comment Mia opened the door and said, "Hey Frankie, Beth just called and said she and Olivia are downstairs with the girls from last night."

"Thanks, Mi. Would you mind going down to get them? Fitz is going to sit in with me, but I'd like you and Jim to watch on the monitor if you have time. Maybe take notes on anything you think is important."

"I was hoping you'd ask! I have to go see a girl from one of my cases later but otherwise I'm free until 6. If you're done with your interviews, I may need a little help with mine."

"You got it."

She turned to Jim and said, "The monitors are in the squad room. I'll start the video recording before Fitz and I go into the interview room. There's water and sodas in the fridge, help yourself to anything you want."

She showed him where to sit, started the recording, grabbed her notepad, pen, and photographs before closing the squad room door and heading down the hallway toward the interview room.

CHAPTER
TWENTY-THREE

THE INTERVIEW ROOM was a small square room about twenty feet from the squad room. It was used to interview victims, suspects, and witnesses so it was sparsely furnished with no art on the walls. A closed-circuit camera hung above the door, pointing toward the back wall. Frankie had just shown Fitz where she wanted him to sit to allow the camera to be focused on Hannah when she heard the ding of the elevator doors opening. After grabbing a chair for herself and bottles of water for everyone she went to greet the women.

Frankie met them in the hallway and said, "Hello ladies. Thank you for coming down. Hannah, if you don't mind, I'd like to talk to you first and then we'll talk to Tessa."

She directed Hannah and Beth to the interview room while Mia escorted Tessa and Olivia to the waiting room. The room, a clear contrast to the interview room, had three walls painted the color of a sandy beach and the fourth a deep navy blue. Artificial ferns, lamps, and artwork adorned the walls. Magazines, coloring books and miscellaneous brochures were strategically placed on the tables inside the room. She had turned on the table lamps in lieu of the fluorescent overhead light to make the room seem less sterile and put people at ease.

Frankie walked into the small interview room and closed the door behind her. "Hannah, there is a camera in the corner of the room that will be recording our conversation, but I will be taking notes, so I don't have to interrupt you while you talk. If at any time you need to take a break just let me know. We are not in a hurry so take as much time as you need. Think of it like we are running a marathon, not sprinting a race. Okay?"

Hannah nodded her head and cast her eyes downward toward the table.

Frankie began to ask demographic questions, verifying Hannah's address, date of birth, place of employment, phone numbers, and next of kin information. She made small talk with Hannah in between questions and watched her shoulders slowly begin to lower. With each exchange, she relaxed and started looking up when she answered the questions. After about fifteen minutes Frankie laid her pen down and took a deep breath, she knew the rest of the interview would be more difficult for Hannah.

Gently she said, "Hannah, I want to talk to you about last night, but I think it's important for me to understand what led up to it. Do you feel comfortable talking about the lawsuit?"

Hannah nodded, took a drink of water from a bottle she produced from her bag and then answered, "Sure. How far back do you want me to go?"

"As far back as you feel you need."

Taking another long drink, she began, "I started working at Stevenson Automotive about two years ago. I had just graduated college with a degree in finance. Since I didn't have any experience selling cars or working in finance, they started me out as a receptionist. It wasn't what I wanted but I figured I had to pay my dues so didn't complain. I worked hard and paid attention to what everyone else was doing.

"Soon after I started working at the dealership Tessa took me under her wing and showed me the ropes. She became my mentor and quickly my best friend. Within just a few months I was on the sales floor. I really don't think I would have gotten there so fast without her help. It became normal for us to do stuff together on the weekends and we always went to work functions together. By early spring car sales were up for both of us and we were making a ton of money. Life was great. Then we got a new general manager.

"Anthony Maggio arrived in late May and immediately started

paying an overt amount of attention to us. He began asking us to work late, took us out to expensive lunches and routinely invited us to happy hour at one of the nearby bars. We offered to pay our own way, but he always insisted on picking up the tab.

"After a few months, he talked us into modeling for print ads for the business. It seemed like a great idea and a way for us to increase our personal sales, so we did a few layouts for a couple of the local magazines and even discussed shooting a television commercial. Maggio seemed genuinely interested in any ideas Tessa and I proposed. He told us we were going to revolutionize the car sales industry and make loads of money. Looking back now I can see that Maggio was just playing us. He was always super flirty but at first it was not a problem. He's attractive for his age and intelligent so, to be honest, it was kind of flattering but he's at least my dad's age, so I wasn't interested in messing around with him. I thought I made that very clear and even though he would sometimes say offensive stuff initially he didn't take things too far.

"On the 4th of July we were all invited to a party in Brookside. Stevenson's marketing rep, Alexandre Kristof, was the host. We had worked with Alexandre a lot on the marketing campaigns, and he often invited us to join him and his friends at his house. But his parties...his parties were legendary. He didn't specifically mention to us that he had invited Maggio but since Alexandre's firm represented the business, we weren't surprised when he walked in. There were so many people at the party we didn't initially have much interaction with either of them.

"Like I said, Alexandre is known for his parties. He has this unbeliev-able house in Brookside, complete with an in-ground pool, hot tub, sand volleyball pit, and a stage for live music. He always has a couple of bars strategically placed at his parties and the drinks are always top shelf. And free.

"That night an '80's cover band was playing on the stage. Tessa and I were having a blast dancing and laughing at the crowd. There were a lot of little umbrella drinks and bottles of wine floating around. We were enjoying the free drinks and the mixed crowd of people at the party. Alexandre had plenty of friends from all walks of life with one thing in common - a lot of money. Tessa was particularly intent on mingling with as many of Alexandre's friends as she could, giving out her card to everyone she met.

"After a few drinks our paths crossed with Maggio's and as always, our conversation turned to business. We talked about using Alexandre's house for a commercial or photo shoot. It seemed like the perfect place, super sexy with just the right amount of class. He really liked the idea and suggested we pitch the idea to Alexandre. Tessa and I were so excited and began brainstorming what it would look like. A few more drinks later we found Alexandre sitting in the hot tub alone so we asked if we could join him.

"We had just gotten in when Maggio walked up and asked if he could join us. Neither of us thought it was a big deal. In fact, we thought his timing was perfect since we planned to pitch our idea to Alexandre, but that wasn't his intention. After sitting in the hot tub for a few minutes Maggio stood up and moved over and squeeze in between Tessa and me. He didn't even ask; he just wiggled his way in between and threw one arm around each of our shoulders and asked Alexandre what he thought of his girls. Weren't we gorgeous and sexy? Didn't we look awesome next to him? Alexandre said we were 'picture perfect.' I started to feel uncomfortable, but I thought his BS was just part of his sales pitch. Then Maggio asked Tessa if she and I were lovers."

"Are you?" interrupted Frankie.

"No. I'm straight but it is well known around the dealership that Tessa's gay. By this time Maggio had a history of making rude comments to both of us. Unfortunately, this wasn't the first time he had asked something like this. Occasionally, during happy hour, after a few drinks, he would ask Tessa and I if we ever messed around. We always told him no but that didn't shut him down. Instead, he would say to call him if we did so he could watch. Normally we just let it go but one night he asked us to kiss for him. We had all been drinking and Tessa told him to back off. She told him he was out of line which made him angry. I had never really seen that side of him. He started telling us we didn't know who we were dealing with. He said he was 'connected' and knew people that could make problems 'go away.' He told us he had been burned by females in the past and if it ever happened again, they would wash up in the Missouri River and he knew where we both lived."

CHAPTER
TWENTY-FOUR

HANNAH TOOK A DRINK OF WATER, then continued, "Then, like a light had switched on, he started laughing; like he was trying to play it off as a joke. I didn't know what to think. A part of me was afraid he would show up at my house uninvited and make a move on me but another part of me figured he was just drunk and harmless."

Fitz asked, "Did he ever elaborate about the people he knew?"

"No. Like I said, I was not even sure it was a real threat at first. It wasn't until I was attacked the first time that I put all the little comments together."

"Hannah, can we go back to the party at Alexandre's. Did anything else happen in the hot tub besides him making rude comments?"

"I'm sorry I didn't mean to go down that rabbit hole. Like I said earlier, Maggio sat between us with his hands on our shoulders. He began caressing us as he talked to Alexandre. Tessa stood up and told Maggio to fuck off and got out of the hot tub but all I could do was just sit there in a drunken stupor. I had been in a situation like that before and it didn't end well so I froze. His threats started coming to mind and I was not sure what to say or do. I think I sat there for about five minutes until Alexandre got up and sat on the edge of the hot tub. That's when I got my towel and got out. As I walked away Maggio laughed and asked

Alexandre what he thought of my tight ass. I could hear Maggio tell Alexandre he had 'hit that.'

"I was furious. Maggio and I never had sex. Never. We never kissed, held hands or anything remotely close to that. I never put out any signals that I wanted to have sex with him. It makes me sick to think of it. I found Tessa and we ordered an Uber and left. As we rode back to my house, we talked about what happened and what Maggio said after she left the hot tub. I was ready to report him to human resources then, but Tessa convinced me that Maggio was just drunk, and I should let it go. Besides things were going so well at work we didn't want to mess it up. Tessa said if we reported it things would change. I figured Tessa was probably right so I decided I wouldn't tell anyone. I was mostly angry Maggio told Alexandre he had sex with me. It was important to me for Tessa to know it was not true. I worked hard to get where I was and didn't want her or anyone else thinking I got ahead by sleeping with the GM. She seemed to believe me.

"The weekend flew by, and we did not mention the incident again. I went to work on Monday with a good attitude, ready to make some sales and forget all about the party. Everything was fine until Maggio came over to talk to me. He asked me if Tessa and I had a slumber party over the weekend and without thinking I answered him honestly and told him Tessa had stayed at my house after the party. Maggio gave me a sly look and asked if we had a pillow fight in our panties. I must have given him a weird look because he leaned down and quietly whispered in my ear. He wanted to know if we made any good 'home movies' during our sleepover and if we did could he watch them? I feel stupid now but at the time I wasn't sure what he was talking about. It didn't register, so I didn't say anything. At lunch, I told Tessa what Maggio had said and when she explained he was asking if we had made sex tapes I started crying.

"The next day Maggio invited Tessa and I to meet him at the Intercontinental on the Plaza for happy hour and dinner so we could discuss the next round of print ads and a possible commercial for the dealership. I told Tessa I was very uncomfortable with Maggio and didn't want to go but she convinced me it was good for our careers. He suggested he was going to invite Alexandre, so I thought it was legit and said I'd go. Looking back, I don't really think he invited Alexandre.

"Tessa and I rode together, and on the way, we discussed the situation and made a game plan. We decided we would sit across from him and keep the conversation focused on business. When we got there, we did everything like we planned and, at first, it was fine, but after a couple of drinks Maggio started in on his antics.

"At first it was almost innocent but gradually got worse. He started by telling us how beautiful we were and how Alexandre was really excited about working on more print ads with us. He told us we were sexy and assured us 'sex sells' so we would sell the hell out of some cars. As he talked to us, he kept inching closer and closer to me and then started touching my leg under the table. I was wearing a skirt, so he was touching my bare skin. I didn't want to make a scene in the restaurant so I told Tessa I wasn't feeling well and asked if we could leave. I seriously thought I was going to be sick.

"On the way back to my house I told Tessa what Maggio had done. After we talked it over, we decided I needed to make a report to human resources. The next day Tessa and I went and tried to file a report. It was a joke. The HR director, Bob DeSalvo, basically gave us the verbal equivalent of a pat on the head. Mr. DeSalvo told us he would investigate it and called Maggio into his office. We could hear them laughing from out in the hallway. It was demoralizing.

"A few days later the head of Marzullo Automotive group, Joe Marzullo, flew in from Detroit and asked to meet with Tessa and me. He told us he had brought his checkbook and wanted to know how many zeros it would take to make this all go away. We told Mr. Marzullo we didn't want his money. We explained we loved working for the company but wanted to feel safe and wanted to make sure Maggio did not harass anyone else. He told us he would talk to Maggio but was not sure there was anything more he could do.

"We went back to work, and I tried to go about business as usual, but I was so angry. Over the course of the next month, we both noticed some changes. We were not getting as many customer referrals. Co-workers who used to be friendly started avoiding us. Several employees at the dealership started being swapped with employees at the dealership

Marzullo owned over in Merriam. We were being ostracized, co-workers stopped asking us to go to happy hour and other work functions. They were talking about us behind our backs - especially me. The things they said really hurt. People were being nice to my face but then Tessa would tell me the cruel things they were saying behind my back.

"After a couple of weeks, I got called into Maggio's office to talk about my low sales numbers. I was nervous at what he might do but he was very professional. He told me if my sales didn't increase, I would have to find another job. He hinted there might be a way to make it all okay but before he could elaborate, I asked him if I was still on track for becoming a finance manager. Maggio told me he no longer thought I was a good candidate for that position. I was devastated.

"A couple more weeks went by and what used to be friendly banter with coworkers turned nasty and dirty. About four weeks after Mr. Marzullo's visit Maggio took things to a new level. He started talking to co-workers about Tessa and I. He described sex acts as though he had witnessed us engaging in them, graphically depicting our body parts – or more accurately how he imagined them. He didn't say anything to us directly but made things uncomfortable for both of us. It became a normal occurrence for me to lock myself in the bathroom so no one would see me crying. Tessa went and talked to Mr. DeSalvo a second time and this time they transferred Maggio to the dealership across the state line. We thought with him gone things would change but instead they got worse."

Hannah grabbed a tissue off the table and wiped her nose and eyes as Frankie wrote on her notepad.

"Our coworkers didn't like the new GM and the new GM didn't like us. They all seemed angry that Maggio had been moved. This ostracized us even more. It got to the point I wasn't getting any sales referrals at all, and Tessa only got a couple a week. Eventually I got fed up and decided to talk to an attorney who initially asked Tessa to come in as a witness but after going over all the incidents Tessa and I decided to file a joint lawsuit against Maggio, Stevenson Automotive and the parent company, Marzullo Automotive. The basis of our civil suit is sexual harassment, gender discrimination, hostile work environment, and retaliation."

CHAPTER
TWENTY-FIVE

FRANKIE WAS SHOCKED at what Hannah had told her. It was surreal to her that Maggio had gotten away with as much as he had without so much as a slap on the wrist. Laying her pen down she said, "Wow! I am sorry you had to go through all of that. I appreciate you sharing. It helps me understand a lot more."

Fitz had been sitting quietly, listening, and taking in all the information. After Frankie finished, he asked, "Obviously, this is a motive but is there anything else that makes you believe your attack is connected to the lawsuit?"

"We started depositions for our civil suit earlier this month. They had already deposed Maggio and some of the other people at work and my attorneys were threatening to subpoena Mr. Marzullo. It made him angry. Marzullo's people had already threatened me once, so I think this time they were following through with their threats."

"Okay Hannah, I need you to tell Detective Fitzmeyer and I what happened yesterday. Tell us what you remember, however you remember it."

Hannah took a deep breath and looked down toward her clasped hands resting on the table.

"Where do I start?" she asked without expecting an answer. She didn't say anything for a few moments, then lifted her hands and took the strings from her hooded sweatshirt and let them slide through her thin fingers.

"I've been kind of depressed the last few weeks because of all the depositions and the way their attorneys were acting. It's been a real stressful month having to go over everything repeatedly, but Tessa's been a rock. Yesterday morning she called and asked if I wanted to go do something to take my mind off the lawsuit. She thought I needed to get out of the house.

"It started out one of those rare November days. The sun was out, and it was warm. Tessa said bad weather was moving in so we should enjoy it while we could." Hannah paused briefly then said under her breath, "Why didn't I just stay in bed?

"Since it was such a nice day we decided to go to the park and walk the trail. Tessa said she would come to my house and pick me up. We talked while we walked and eventually our conversation turned to the lawsuit and how we thought it was going. Some days it feels like we are wasting our time but other days it feels like we might be making progress, like we might win. About a week ago they really seemed to be running scared and offered each of us a settlement of $250,000. We had talked to our attorneys and were supposed to give them our responses by close of business today. We weren't sure what we should do so while we walked, we discussed the pros and cons of settling. Our cut of the money would be good, but this guy was going to continue working and harassing other women, so it didn't seem right to me to just let him get away with it. Plus, he had the power to blackball both of us from getting jobs at any other high-end dealerships, so settling might not be a good financial move. Basically, we were trying to decide if we should just take the money or gamble on going to trial.

"After walking around the park for about an hour we still had not made a decision, so we decided to go to dinner and maybe do a little Christmas shopping to get our mind off things."

Hannah stopped for a moment to take a drink of water. Frankie sat and waited. Every victim tells his or her story in their own way and the best thing she could do was give Hannah time.

"We went back to my house so I could change clothes. While we were there, we grabbed a light snack and a beer, then left for the mall. Tessa had driven to my house and to the park, so I told her I would drive us to the mall. We grabbed our coats and purses and headed to the garage. It was already starting to get cold. When I got ready to get in, I realized I still had my beer bottle in my hand. A few months ago, I got a ticket for an open container, so I didn't want to take it with me. I sat it by the door and figured I would throw it in the barrel when I took the trash out at the end of the week."

CHAPTER
TWENTY-SIX

"WE LEFT my house around 4:30 and talked the whole way there – finally about something other than the lawsuit. We listed off stores we wanted to go to, gifts we needed to buy and where we were going for Thanksgiving dinner. Tessa and her girlfriend had recently broken up and her family lives in southern Missouri so I invited her to my parent's house so she wouldn't have to spend it alone.

"It was just starting to get dark when we arrived at Mayfaire. We went into a few shops and looked around. I bought some lingerie at Victoria's Secret and found some leather gloves for my dad's birthday. After we finished shopping, we went to a sushi bar near the shopping center for dinner. I'm not sure what time it was when we finished but by the time we got outside it had gotten really cold and was starting to drizzle. The drizzle had formed a thin layer of ice on my windows, and I couldn't find my ice scraper, so we sat for a while to let the ice melt and the car warm up.

"Once my car warmed up, we drove back to my house. One of the radio stations was playing Christmas music and we were both feeling the holiday spirit, so we turned it up and sang along. We were laughing and having so much fun," her voice broke as she said "fun" and tears filled her eyes.

"I started to park on the street by Tessa's car, but it was still drizzling so Tessa asked me to pull inside so we wouldn't get wet while we unloaded the car. I pulled in the garage and grabbed my purse and opened the car door," she paused and took a deep breath. She looked down at the table and continued to play with the jacket strings. She appeared to be lost in thought as she alternated the strings between her fingers.

"I stepped out of the car and before I could get the door closed, I felt a sharp pain in my head. It felt like a heavy object hit the back of my head. My ears started ringing and my vision got blurry. At first, I thought I had gotten out of my car too fast and hit my head on the top of the doorframe or maybe I had another brain aneurism like before. But then I realized someone had hit me on the back of my head. As I stumbled I grabbed onto my car but before I could catch my balance I felt something hard hit me again. This time I fell to the floor and may have hit my head again on the concrete because that's when things get murky."

Her voice had softened almost to a whisper and when she finished tears streamed down her face.

Frankie let her collect herself while she reviewed her notes. After a few moments, she looked up and asked, "Can I ask you a few questions?"

Hannah nodded her head in agreement.

"What door (or doors) did you use to go in and out of the mall?"

She sniffled and then answered, "The door right by Victoria Secret. We went in and out the same door. The sushi place is about a block away from Mayfaire. When we got there, we thought we could walk to the restaurant but by the time we left the air was wet and cold, so we drove."

"Okay. I need to ask you more detailed questions about what you've already told us. It will help create a better picture of what you experienced. The questions may be difficult, so if you need to take a break, just let me know. Okay?"

She waited for Hannah to nod her head in affirmation.

"Let's go back to the mall. Do you remember seeing anyone or anything unusual? Anything that may not have stood out at the time, but now makes you wonder?"

Hannah looked at her hands and continued to play with the string. Suddenly she stopped, sat up straight and said, "There was a guy."

CHAPTER
TWENTY-SEVEN

HANNAH HESITATED as she second-guessed herself, "It's probably nothing."

"Go ahead," encouraged Frankie.

"There was this guy at the mall. He was about forty and wore a real nice suit and expensive shoes. When we walked to the door of the mall, he was ahead of us. He held the door open when we walked in. I wouldn't have thought anything of it except I saw him again at Nu, the sushi place. He was sitting in a car near the restaurant. I noticed him when we were walking in because the car was backed into the parking space, and we had to walk right past it. I said something to Tessa, and she made a joke about him following us. It kind of pissed me off that she was making jokes like that after what happened to me a few weeks ago. She knows I'm real anxious and on edge. We sat at the sushi bar, and I don't remember seeing him come in after us."

"What do you remember about the man?"

"He had short, black hair with a bit of gray. He wasn't skinny but he wasn't fat either. He had some facial hair, but I couldn't tell if it was because he hadn't shaved, or he was trying to look scruffy. His shoes were expensive, and his suit looked tailored, just like the guy from before."

"Was there anything else that stood out about him? Or his car?"

She thought for a moment then said, "His smell. Is that weird?" Not waiting for a response, she exclaimed, "I remember his smell."

"No that's not weird at all. Our memories are tied to our senses, especially smell. What did he smell like?"

Hannah closed her eyes in thought.

"Cologne. I'm not sure exactly what brand, but I think it was Calvin Klein. Truth maybe? It smelled a lot like the cologne an old boyfriend of mine wore."

"What about the car? What do you remember about the car?"

"It was dark. Black or navy blue. It was the new S-Class Mercedes sedan. Very high end."

Frankie did not know much about high-end cars, but she knew Hannah did.

"Did you see the license plate?"

"I don't remember seeing one on the car, but I wasn't really looking at the bumper. We walked in front of the car to the restaurant. There may have been something on the back but I'm not sure."

Frankie made notes. Based on what Hannah said the car was either registered in the state of Kansas or had a temporary or dealer's tag on it. Vehicles registered in Missouri were required to have license plates on the front and back of the vehicle. Kansas only required a tag on the back of the vehicle. Temporary and dealer tags were always on the back, either on the window or license plate holder. It wasn't much but it was a start.

"Hannah, a couple of times you've an incident that happened to you a few weeks ago. This is probably as good a time as any to talk about it. Can you describe what happened?"

She looked at Frankie then back to her hands. She closed her eyes and Frankie watched as another tear squeeze through her eyelids. After a few moments of silence Frankie was about to inquire again when Hannah began to speak.

"It was the end of October. It had to be about 6:30 in the evening. I know the time because I was on my way to a Pilate's class that started at 7. It was a cold night, and the wind was blowing hard. I was wearing my boots, gloves, and a long coat over my workout clothes. I had my yoga mat in one hand and was holding my coat closed with the other. I was almost to the garage when this goon jumped over the fence behind my garage and grabbed me so quick I dropped my mat and almost fell to the ground. He twisted me around so I could not see his face and held his hand over my mouth. I attempted to scream but his hand muffled any sound I tried to make. He growled in my ear, 'drop the fuckin' lawsuit or I'll fuckin' kill you.' He pushed me towards the garage door and ordered me inside the garage. I was so scared. I didn't know what to do. I thought he was going to rape me. He was stronger than me so it wasn't like I could fight back. The minute he got me through the door he let go of me. He was gone before I could turn around. I called the police after I stopped shaking and could dial the phone. I think I called Tessa, too."

"Tell me what you remember about the man, Hannah."

"I never saw his face," she said.

"It's okay," Frankie assured her. "Tell me what you do remember."

"He was taller than me. Maybe 5'8"-5'9". Or taller. I couldn't see his face, so I don't know old he was or what color hair or eyes he had. He wasn't skinny but he wasn't fat either. He had big hands and a deep voice with an accent. It sounded like he might have been from New York or New Jersey." Hannah lowered her voice and said, "Drop the fuckin' lawsuit or I'll fuckin' kill ya."

"What else can you tell us?" prompted Frankie.

"He was wearing expensive shoes and seemed clean. I mean it wasn't like he was homeless or anything. In fact, he smelled pretty good. Like citrus and leather mixed with a good cigar."

Frankie thought for a moment then asked, "Did you recognize his voice?"

"No, but I think I would it if I heard it again. It was very distinct. Can we take a break? I need to use the bathroom."

"Sure, Hannah. Beth, can you show her where it is?"

Beth nodded.

Frankie turned to Fitz and said, "Let's go into the squad room for a minute."

CHAPTER
TWENTY-EIGHT

WHEN FRANKIE and Fitz walked into the squad room Baker, Mia, and Jim were clustered around the monitor. Frankie stretched and twisted her back as the door closed behind her.

"Damn."

"What's next?" asked Jim.

"I'm going to let her have a minute then we'll go back in and delve into the details of the assault. Mia, can you call Nu and see if they have surveillance video and if so…"

Mia interrupted her and said, "Hold onto it. Yeah, I know the drill. I'll call when you go back in and see if they can pull it tonight. Do you think the guy she described is involved?"

"Thanks Mia. I'm not sure but it's worth checking out. It may be our first real lead. Sarge, can you ask Millsap to send up the case file from the assault? See if they have the 9-1-1 call, too."

"Already ahead of you, Frankie. Millsap is sending it up and communications is going to email me the 9-1-1 call," he answered. "Mia, run her in the database and see if there are any other reports with her name. She said she thought the guy was going to rape her and referenced something like it had happened before. We need to know when 'before' was. Before we bring up that trauma with her let's see if we can find some information out on our own."

"I'm on it, Sarge," Mia replied.

"Thanks. Fitz, what do you think?" asked Baker.

"I think it could be the same guys but…"

Before Fitz could finish Frankie said, "Something is off."

"There's no doubt something happened to her, but I have a lot of questions," Fitz said. "If it was the same guys, I'm surprised they left either of them alive."

Hannah and Beth entered the interview room, their presence on the monitor stopping the conversation.

"Time for us to get back in there."

Frankie and Fitz walked back to the interview room and sat down on the hard, unforgiving chairs.

"Hannah, can we talk some more about last night?"

She nodded.

"I want you to let your mind go back to leaving the sushi place. Walk to your car. Do you see the Mercedes?"

She closed her eyes. Frankie watched her eyes move back and forth beneath her eyelids as her fingers tapped the table. After a few moments, she said, "No. I don't think it was there. It had gotten colder while we were inside. I'd left my coat in the car, so I was hurrying across the parking lot. It could have been there, but I don't remember seeing it."

"Did you see anything unusual? Any other cars or people stand out?"

She shook her head and said, "I didn't notice anything, but I wasn't really looking either. I was more focused on watching the ground so I wouldn't slip and fall."

"Fair enough," said Frankie with a smile. "What streets did you take after you got off the highway?"

"We got off the highway at Wornall Road. I turned onto 75th Street and then onto my street." She was starting to understand why Frankie was asking these questions and added, "There wasn't hardly anyone on the road. I definitely didn't see the Mercedes. It would have stood out."

"Good. Are you familiar with the cars and people who are normally in your neighborhood?"

"Sure. I've lived there about a year, and I think I've met just about everyone on my block. I know what my closest neighbors drive. Even with the holidays there haven't been that many different vehicles in the neighborhood."

"When you got back to your neighborhood do you remember seeing anything unusual? Any cars or people?"

"No. I saw Tessa's SUV parked on the street, but I wasn't really paying attention to anything else. I was focused on pulling into my garage."

"Okay. What do you remember seeing when you got out of the car?" Frankie asked softly. Recall was about to get a bit more difficult for Hannah.

Hannah sat quietly for a few seconds and then closed her eyes. Her hands began to tremble, then she began to lightly tap the table in no discernible pattern.

"Tessa and I were singing along with the radio. I remember one of the songs was the one where the girl was trying to leave and told Tessa it was 'rapey.' She told me to lighten up and turned up the radio. When the next song came on, I started singing with her. The rest of the way home we sang really loud and laughed at each other. When we pulled into the garage, I grabbed my purse and keys and opened my car door. I stepped out," she paused for a moment as though she were trying to picture it in her mind. "I started to close the door with my hip. That's when I felt something hit the back of my head. I stumbled so I'm not sure the door ever closed. I felt the keys and bags fall from my hands. Then I felt something hit me again."

"What did the object that hit you feel like?" asked Frankie. "Can you describe the size, shape, or texture?"

"I think I was hit with two different objects but I'm not sure. The first object was smooth, hard, and didn't have any edges. I'm not sure that makes any sense. The second object was a lot harder than the first. It was…like…metal. Not really metal, more like steel. It had edges on it. They weren't sharp edges but edges just the same."

"Did you notice any odors when you got out of the car?"

"Just my car." Hannah took a drink of water from her water bottle and looked toward Beth who had been sitting quietly by her side. Frankie started to ask her another question, but Hannah broke in and said, "Cigar. I think I smelled a cigar. Not like someone smoking but that tobacco smell that stays on a smoker's clothes. It was faint but it was there. It wasn't cheap tobacco either. It smelled almost like going into a cigar shop."

Hannah stopped.

It had been almost twenty-four hours. Based on the way trauma impacts memory, Frankie knew it was possible Hannah could recall more information than she had the night before. She paused before saying, "Hannah, last night you said you didn't remember anything else after getting out of the car, but I need you to try."

CHAPTER
TWENTY-NINE

TEARS BEGAN to creep out of Hannah's eyes as she recalled the details. Frankie watched her hands tremble slightly. Beth handed Hannah a tissue and they all sat in silence for several minutes.

"On the ground…I remember pain in…pain in my vagina. I. Remember. Being. Raped." She tried to choke out the words through her sobs. She sobbed loudly for several minutes. Beth spoke quietly and attempted to comfort her.

Once she had composed herself Frankie asked, "What do you remember about the rape?"

Her voice trembled, "I remember bits and pieces, like flashes. I thought it was just a nightmare, but I know it really happened. There was something thin and sharp inside me scratching me inside my vagina and down my inner thigh. There was something else, too. It was an object – not a body part. Oh. My. Gosh! I think he used my beer bottle. The bottle I left inside the door. I think I heard the other guy tell him to."

Hannah cupped her face and cried openly.

After a few moments Frankie asked, "Is there anything else you can remember? Anything else that was said?"

She closed her eyes and appeared lost in thought for several minutes.

"I thought I heard Tessa's voice, but I must have imagined it. She said she was duct taped, too, so she couldn't have been talking. I think I passed out because the next thing I remember is my neighbor Katie rubbing my chest. Hard. She was crying but I couldn't understand why. Then I heard sirens and was trying to process why they were getting louder and why Katie kept telling me it was going to be okay." Hannah's voice cracked, "I feel so bad for her. I'm so sorry, Detective Thomas. I really don't remember anything else."

"It's okay, Hannah. You've done great today. And if you do remember more, you can give me a call," Frankie said reassuringly. "Is there anything else you want to add to this statement?"

She shook her head.

"If you don't have anything additional, I think we are finished for today."

"Can I wait in the waiting room for Tessa? We rode here together."

Frankie nodded to her as she escorted her from the room.

WHILE HANNAH WAS BEING INTERVIEWED Tessa and Olivia sat in the waiting room waiting. Tessa flipped the pages in a magazine without reading the words as Olivia clicked the channels on the television and tried to make small talk. The two had little in common and the attempt at forced conversation made the time pass even more slowly. They both looked up in relief when Hannah walked into the room.

Hannah's face was red and tear stained. She held a tissue in one hand and her purse in the other. She looked at Tessa and feigned a smile.

"Are you okay?" asked Tessa. She reached out to hug her.

Hannah's body stiffened, "Yes. I think Detective Thomas wants to talk to you next."

Frankie walked through the waiting room toward the squad room and stopped to say, "Tessa, give me just a minute to grab something then we can get started, okay?"

She nodded and then asked, "Can I get another bottle of water?"

Frankie nodded as she entered the squad room. She looked at her over her shoulder and said, "I'll be back in a sec."

Frankie closed the squad room door and stopped at her desk to check her cellphone. One missed call. "Hmm I wonder what Brooklyn wants?" She thought to herself.

The number belonged to one of the teenage girls she mentored. She had started a mentoring program called "VISION-Visualize and Integrate Successful Individual Opportunities Now" about two years before she became a detective. The group of ten youth were between twelve and eighteen years old and lived in the urban core of Kansas City. They met at least once a month to discuss opportunities for their futures to include college, jobs, military and personal growth. Several times per year they also did volunteer work and the day before Thanksgiving they were going to prepare a meal for the Ronald McDonald House adjacent to the children's hospital. She provided the food, but each teen was expected to assist in preparing and serving the meal. If the family could afford it, they were asked to donate something to the house from their wish list. She assumed Brooklyn was calling to ask for a ride to the event, so she sent her a text telling her she would call when she finished her interview.

"Ready Fitz?"

Frankie grabbed a couple bottles of water and headed to the door.

"Tessa, will you and Olivia come into the other room with us?"

She led the group down the hall, held the door for the women, and gestured to them where to sit.

THIRTY-ONE

FRANKIE STARTED the interview with Tessa the same way she had with Hannah, asking basic demographic questions. Tessa's answers were quick and to the point. After she got the basic information she needed she asked, "Tell us what you remember about yesterday."

"Where do you want me to start?"

"Wherever you feel is important."

Tessa began to repeat the same basic story Hannah had given. She talked about picking up her friend and going to the park.

"I thought she could use some retail therapy, so I suggested we head over to Mayfaire. Hannah has been real down since our attorneys started taking depositions. The opposing attorneys have really given her a hard time since that goon attacked her. She has been a complete wreck."

Frankie made notes to follow up on the depositions.

"Hannah was wearing yoga pants so we had to go back to her house so she could change. While she was getting ready, we had some cheese and crackers with a beer. I offered to drive but she said since I had driven over from my house, she would drive to the shopping center.

"We did some shopping, then went to Nu for sushi after. By the time we left it had gotten cold and started sleeting, but the roads didn't seem too bad. We were listening to Christmas music, singing as loud as we could, laughing and having a good time. When we got to Hannah's house, she pulled into the garage so we wouldn't get wet when we got out."

"Did you ask Hannah to pull into the garage?" Fitz interjected.

"Hmm? What? No, I think she just did it out of habit." She appeared surprised at the question. "We were laughing at the radio as we gathered our stuff to get out of the car. She got out before I did and..." Tears filled her eyes, and she began to choke up. "I wish I had gotten out first. Maybe I could have protected her."

Olivia handed her a tissue and patted her hand as she tried to calm herself.

"When I got out of the car, I felt something hit me on the head and I fell to my knees. He hit me again and I fell to the floor. A man wrapped duct tape around my arms and face. I may have gone unconscious. I'm not sure. While I laid there I looked under the car and could see Hannah just...she was just lying there. She was all tied up and this guy...this guy," her voice broke, and tears fell from her eyes. Tessa held her face in her hands. Her shoulders shook and her hands trembled as the sobs wracked her body.

Frankie saw Tessa glance up, then quickly avert her eyes back to the table. She gave her time to collect herself before softly asking, "What do you remember next?"

"I was looking under the car and saw two sets of shoes. One of the guys was holding Hannah's legs down. I couldn't see his face because he was wearing a mask and gloves. The other guy, he was doing...things... to Hannah. He had put a hand around her throat, and she was gasping and coughing. Finally, he released her throat and put tape over her mouth. Through the tape I could hear her, 'uhm, uhm, uhm' like she was in pain and was trying to get him to stop. Her skirt was pushed up and her tights were torn. He had a single rose in his hand. He moved one hand to her shoulder and his other...she started wiggling around and moaning in pain, then he took the bottle... he put the bottle..."

Tessa described Hannah's rape in broken sentences. Tears were streaming down her face as she described what she saw.

"When he finished, he told the guy that hit me they should check on me. I was afraid they were going to rape me, too, so I played dead. He came around and kicked me. I bit my lip to keep from screaming. When I didn't move, he told the other guy I was out, and they could leave. They turned the car on and left the driver's side door open with the music blaring. The men left through the side door of the garage. I waited - I don't know how long. Three minutes. Five. I don't know. When I was sure they were gone, I rolled over on my side and sat up. I was terrified but knew I had to do something to help Hannah. My hands were bound behind my back so I couldn't open the side door. I looked around and then realized I could hit the garage door opener with the side of my head. When the door opened, I ran outside and went over to Katie's to get help."

AFTER SHE FINISHED FRANKIE SAID, "Okay. I need to ask a few follow-up questions. When you went to the mall, do you remember seeing anyone or anything that seemed unusual or out of place?"

Tessa thought for a moment before responding.

"I didn't see anything that seemed unusual. Hannah told me she saw a guy at Nu who had also been at the mall. To me that wasn't all that odd since Nu is close to the mall and popular. That said, I didn't notice him, so I don't know if it was the same guy or not. Honestly, Hannah has been acting paranoid lately, so I didn't really pay attention."

"Did you notice any unusual cars or other activity when you got back to Hannah's house?"

"No, but I don't really know what cars would be normal in her neighborhood."

"Think back when you pulled in the garage did you notice anything?"

Tessa closed her eyes for a moment. Her voice quivered as she answered, "No, there were shadows and stuff, but it was dark, and the only light was from the small garage door light so I couldn't really see anything. When I got out, he hit me hard and fast."

"Did you notice any smells when you got out of the car?"

She closed her eyes and raised her head up as though she were looking at the ceiling through her eyelids. After a few moments, she lowered her head, opened her eyes, and said, "Tobacco. But not the cheap cigarette kind. More like the expensive cigar kind. And leather. I smelled leather."

"Great. That's great. What did the object that hit you feel like?"

"Hard. Like a steel rod but square not round. Kind of like a tire iron."

Frankie thought for a few moments and reviewed her notes before asking, "What else did you feel?"

She used her hands to make gestures as she answered, "Gloves. I didn't feel bare skin. He was definitely wearing gloves, but they weren't latex. I don't think they were leather either. They felt like riding gloves - the kind cyclists wear. You know, the kind with small, raised dots for good gripping. The jacket was soft leather but since it was dark, I couldn't tell what color it was. I think he was wearing jeans and expensive loafers."

"Tell us what you heard after you got out of the car, Tessa."

"There were two men talking," she paused for effect. "They sounded like they were from the northeast. Maybe New York.

"The one that hit me sounded like Al Pacino. He was giving a play by play to the other guy, telling him what he was doing to me. After he got me tied up, he went around the car and started helping the other guy. Like I said, I could see them under the car. The guy that hit me held Hannah down while he put duct tape on her legs. She was wiggling, twisting her legs back and forth. I could hear her moaning, 'mhm mhm' through the tape that was across her mouth. The other guy was barking orders at the guy that hit me. He told him, 'Hold her down. Help me get these tights off. Grab that bottle.' One of them ripped her tights and the other laughed. The guy barking orders was the one that used the bottle on her. When they finished the guy that hit me made some crack like, 'bet them bitches drop the lawsuit now.' The other guy mumbled something, but I couldn't make out what he was saying. The music was still blaring from the radio. I'm not sure why I just now remember that. Then I heard the side door to the garage open. It creaked loud before it slammed shut."

"Did you hear either of them call the other by name?"

"I don't think so."

"Did you happen to hear any car sounds, engine, another door, etcetera, after they left?" asked Fitz.

She shook her head, looked from Frankie to Fitz, and said, "The music was too loud, and the car was running."

Fitz looked at the notes Frankie was taking and then asked, "When you ran out of the garage what did you see?"

Tessa wiped the tears from her cheeks and took a long drink of water.

"Streetlights. The light on Katie's back porch shed a cone of light down the sidewalk that met the driveway. I could see lights on inside, that's why I ran there. It was still drizzling but I don't remember the road being slick as I ran across. I was moving my arms around trying to get the tape loose. The tape on my mouth came loose so I screamed for help. I had to use my head to pound on her door. Cars were just going by on the street in front of Katie's house like nothing had happened."

She put her face in the palm of her hands and cried.

Frankie reviewed her notes then told Tessa they were going to take a break. She and Fitz left the interview room and went to the hallway to talk quietly.

THIRTY-THREE

AFTER A FEW MOMENTS, they returned to the room to ask another follow-up question.

"You're doing great, Tessa. We only have one more thing to follow up on. Okay?"

"Sure, Detective Thomas, but I'm not sure what else I can help with. I told you everything I remember."

She was twisting in her chair and fidgeting with obvious impatience.

Fitz directed the follow-up question to her, "You mentioned Hannah has been paranoid and referred to someone laughing at her. Can you elaborate on that for us?"

She perked up slightly and became animated. Her shoulders relaxed.

"Those bastards we are suing. Did Hannah tell you about the lawsuit?"

Frankie and Fitz nodded.

"Well, a couple of weeks ago Hannah was walking to her car and some goon jumped her and told her to drop the lawsuit or he would kill her. After he left, she called the police, but I don't think they ever got anywhere with the investigation. The following week we started the second round of depositions on our civil suit. Our attorneys knew about her getting jumped and during the depositions they mentioned it to Maggio's attorneys. The jerks being deposed started making stupid comments and accused Hannah of lying. As if she would make something like that up. It got so bad Hannah left the room crying. I went after her and tried to calm her down. She kept saying she wanted to drop the lawsuit. She said it was just too hard and it was unfair. Hannah was upset they were being so mean, and the attorneys didn't stop them. In fact, their attorneys joined in. Well, I convinced her giving up was not the way to go. We must see this thing through, or they win. It's not right that they should get away with treating us like that."

"Was a settlement ever offered?" inquired Frankie.

Tessa sat up straight and with contempt in her voice said, "They offered us a measly $250,000. Maggio would get to keep his job and we would get blackballed at every high-end dealership in the area. Hannah and I decided we weren't going to accept. We were supposed to give them an official answer today but with all of this going on I think our attorneys told them they would have to wait until next week for an answer."

Frankie took notes and nodded as Tessa talked. She suspected this would be one of many interviews and follow-ups to come.

"Let me go get Hannah and then we'll finish up."

She walked out to the waiting room and before returning with Hannah and Beth she turned to Hannah and asked, "By the way, did you and Tessa ever decide what to do about the settlement?"

"No, we were going to meet with our attorneys again today and decide after talking to them. Why?"

"No reason, I just realized I had forgotten to ask." Frankie escorted them to the interview room where Tessa and Olivia were waiting. "Thank you for coming in today. I am sure it was not the easiest thing for either of you to do but it gives us a good starting point. As we work the investigation Detective Fitzmeyer and I will have follow-up questions, so please do not be surprised if I call you or ask if we can meet up again. I want to make sure I do the best job possible for you. On the flip side, if either of you have any questions you can call us. You both still have my cell number, right?"

Both women nodded.

"Good. I'm supposed to be off tomorrow night, but I'll have my cell phone on should you need anything. Do you have any questions for either of us?"

Hannah looked at Tessa and then looked back at Frankie. Her lips parted as though she were about to ask a question when Tessa cut her off and said, "I don't think we have any."

"Hannah, you looked like you have a question," Frankie said.

Hannah shook her head in dissent.

"Okay, if you think of any just let me know."

Frankie escorted all four women to the door of the building and told them she would be in touch. Before she could get back to the squad room Fitz and Jim stopped her in the hall.

Jim said, "I took one of your cards and left my numbers on your desk. I need to run and check on a wire but call me and let me know what I can do to help you."

"Thanks, Jim. I'm on until eleven, so if you think of anything give me a call." She wrote her cell phone number on the business card he was holding.

Fitz said, "Frankie, I'll holler at you tomorrow. The security teams from the mall called my guys and said the videos are ready. I'm going to go pick them up now. I'll let you know if there's anything good on 'em."

"Thanks Fitz. Be safe guys."

THIRTY-FOUR

WHEN FRANKIE GOT to her desk and checked her cellphone, she noticed she had three missed calls from Brooklyn and a text that said, "Call me. ASAP. It's urgent!!"

Before she could dial the number, Mia bellowed, "Hey Frankie, do you have time to go with me to talk to this girl tonight? Should be an interesting interview."

"Yeah, can you give me five? I need to make a quick phone call."

"Yeah. I'm working on a lineup now, so I'll be a few minutes anyway."

She grabbed her cell and went to the empty interview room so she could call Brooklyn. She looked at the time on the clock and noticed it was ten minutes to six.

"I should be able to catch her before they sit down for dinner."

Brooklyn lived with her grandmother who was a woman of routine. They sat down to dinner every night at six o'clock like clockwork and she was not allowed to have her cellphone at the table during dinner.

The phone rang twice before a soft voice said, "Hey, Miss Frankie. I'm sorry I kept calling but I didn't know what else to do."

"It's okay, Brook. Were you calling about a ride for tomorrow? If so, I can pick you up."

"No. I mean, yes ma'am I'd like a ride but that's not why I was calling. I'm calling for my momma." Her voice cracked as she choked back tears. "My momma's been hurt, Miss Frankie, and I don't know what to do."

She sat up straight in the chair, poised for action. "Where are you Brooklyn? Are you safe?"

"I'm okay. I'm at Grandma Laurice's. Momma called me and said she'd been attacked. She was up on Prospect and took a ride from some guy and he hurt her, Miss Frankie."

Brooklyn began to cry openly on the phone.

"I tried to get her to call the police, but she kept saying it was her own fault and the police wouldn't help her. I told her I was calling you. What should she do Frankie?"

"I'm sorry Brooklyn. I know you must be scared. Did your Momma tell you how she was attacked?"

"I think she was raped and beat up. She said he hit her in the face and took it from her. I think she might have been high but I'm not sure. I thought she was clean. At least that's what she told me. I believed her but now I don't know." She was rambling and her sentences were coming out staccato.

"Can you give me her number?"

Brooklyn grunted a negative response.

Frankie spoke slowly and in measured tones as she explained, "Okay, tell her to go to the county hospital. If she was raped, she can get an anonymous forensic exam for free. She does not have to call the police to make a report. She can get medical treatment without it and if she wants to file a report later, we will have physical evidence to work with. More importantly she needs to get a medical exam to make sure she does not have any other injuries. If she wants to make a report, tell her I can meet with her later but to go get the forensic exam today. Do you understand, Brooklyn?"

"Yes ma'am. I'll try to call her now," Brooklyn said quietly.

"You can give her my number if you want. Text me if she wants to talk to the police and I'll meet her, okay? I'll take the report instead of a uniform."

Brooklyn's voice cracked, "Okay, I'll text you later. Thank you, Miss Frankie."

"Anytime. And Brook?"

"Yeah?"

"You can only do what you can do. Remember that okay?"

Brooklyn mumbled then disconnected the call. Frankie sat in the interview room for a few moments and closed her eyes picturing the tiny girl with caramel skin and soft, doe-colored eyes.

She met Brooklyn at the high school she worked at on one of her many trips to the office. She was a junior in high school with a penchant for getting in trouble. Brooklyn did not warm up to Frankie quickly but once she earned her trust she opened up about her life. Her mother, Asia, was addicted to crack cocaine and had a long history of doing whatever she had to do to support her addiction. Because her mother did not have a stable life, Brooklyn lived with her grandmother, but her mother still called occasionally, usually begging for help.

Over time Brooklyn shared stories of using her babysitting money, allowance, and even her birthday money to pay her mother's debts. She was always trying to protect her from being beaten or raped by her dealer. She had experienced more in her sixteen short years than most adults would experience in their lifetime. Knowing her background, Frankie couldn't help but wonder if the ride Asia accepted started off as an effort to get money for crack. She hoped, for Brooklyn's case, that was not the case.

Frankie had compassion for women used in the sex industry; women whose addictions were exploited primarily by men. In most cases these women were vulnerable and helpless and that is exactly what perpetrators looked for. It was a challenge to get these cases filed in court because of the perceived credibility of the victim. She not only understood the challenges, but embraced them, these women were the underdog and she believed in standing up for the weak.

Frankie's thoughts were interrupted by the sound of Mia asking, "Hey you ready?"

Frankie looked up from her cellphone and answered, "Yep, let me grab my coat and I'll meet you at the car."

CHAPTER
THIRTY-FIVE

MIA WAS in the driver's seat when Frankie got outside. The air was crisp and smelled like snow even though there wasn't a cloud in sight.

"Where are we headed, Mia?"

"Twenty-third and Bellefontaine. I need to show a lineup to this girl from the other night. She was at a party and this guy put his hands down her pants. I have another case with her, too, and since it's taken me awhile to find her, I'd like to get a statement from her on both. Neither one should take too long."

As Mia drove, she and Frankie talked about Tyler and Danielle. Tyler was precocious and prone to saying anything that came to mind, which usually led to entertaining stories. Dani was the bossy big sister and that caused the two to butt heads pretty frequently. Mia laughed as Frankie filled her in on the latest Tyler-isms and other antics of the Thomas household. Mia wanted a house full of children someday, but she and her husband had just gotten married, worked opposite shifts, and weren't ready to start their family.

As they approached the house Frankie asked, "What's this girl's name?"

"Allie Wheaton. She's twenty-three and from what I can tell, pretty transient."

They approached the house at an angle, rapping on the doorframe firmly. After a couple of knocks, the door opened slightly. The young girl standing in the doorway was tiny but not frail. It was obvious she was wearing a wig, but it was not immediately obvious why. Her skin was smooth and the color of espresso, her eyes the color of melted caramel. Mia introduced herself and Frankie as Allie invited them to sit at the kitchen table.

Mia began asking Allie questions about the case. Frankie had to fight back a smile at her choice of language and colloquialisms. Listening to Allie speak, Frankie could tell she was not from the Midwest, her accent was a combination of southern bell and California valley girl.

During the interview, she revealed she had grown up in North Carolina and moved to southern California while in the Navy. Frankie and Mia looked to one another with a bit of surprise and admiration.

"Why did you leave the Navy?" asked Frankie.

"I was, like, at a party and ended up leaving through a plate glass window. Like, they didn't want me anymore after that."

Frankie did not ask any additional questions but wondered what made Allie leave through a plate glass window. Had someone hurt her?

Mia questioned Allie about the assault from her report, then brought out a photographic lineup for her to look at. Without hesitation, she identified her attacker. Mia returned the file to her bag and pulled out another file folder.

"Allie, there was another report I wanted to talk to you about. It was from about six weeks ago. Can you tell me about it?"

"You mean that dude that raped me in his car?"

"Yes. Can you tell us what happened?"

She didn't miss a beat.

"I was, like, walking to the house I was staying at, and this dude pulls up to talk to me. I wasn't wearing my glasses, so I had a hard time seeing. The dude and car looked familiar, so I walked over to the window to talk to him. He asked me if I wanted a ride and the house I was staying at was, like, a long walk so I got into the car. Dude seemed nice at first. Then when he started driving - it was like he changed. Like he was two different people.

"I told him where to drive but when I, like, told him to turn to go to where I was staying but dude drove past the street and refused to stop. I yelled at him to fucking stop. He slapped me in my face like I was a dude. He turned down an alleyway and when he parked, I tried to get out of the car but he, like, pushed me into the back seat. I tried to get out, but the doors wouldn't open. The doors were locked from the inside and, like, wouldn't open – like a cop car.

"He climbed into the back seat on top of me and started to pull at my clothes. I fought him. I pushed him. Wiggled. Grabbed at him. His shirt was off, so I grabbed at his underarm hair and yanked. I got some of his hair, too. I gave it to that cop that came."

Frankie and Mia exchanged a look. Frankie wondered if the hair was collected as evidence. She could tell by the look Mia gave her that she was wondering the same thing.

Allie continued, "I was trying to get him to stop so I told him, 'Dude, like, I have AIDS.' I don't really have AIDS, but I thought if I told him that he would stop. I didn't want to get raped again. I was desperate. I was able to get to my purse so I grabbed my Butane can and lighter out of my purse. By this time, he had pulled my pants down and was trying to stick me. He wasn't looking at my face, so I sucked the Butane into my mouth, and like, when he looked down, I blew in his face. Then I tried to light my lighter. I was trying to burn his face, but the lighter totally didn't work. He got mad and grabbed my purse and threw it all out the window. Then he backhanded the shit out of me.

"He started sticking it in me hard. I, like totally tried to talk to him. I thought I could psych him out. I told him, 'Like I can't feel it' and stuff like that. But he wouldn't stop. He just got angrier. The more I fought the crazier he got. He slapped me a few times but when he punched me in the face I just gave up and let him do whatever he wanted. I didn't want him to punch me again. I thought he would kill me if I kept fighting."

Her voice got quieter. She twisted the ringlets on the wig and described the rape in more detail.

"When he was finished, he dragged me out of the car and threw my clothes and shoes out the opposite side window. It was dark so all I could find was my jeans and sweatshirt, I couldn't find anything else. I was scared if I stuck around and kept looking, he would hurt me worse. He told me he had a gun, so I wasn't taking any chances. So, like, I grabbed my clothes and ran to the first house I saw. I pounded on the door, but no one answered. I went to three or four houses before someone finally answered."

She began to fidget in her seat, twisting her hands and pulling at her wig.

Mia asked, "Tell us what you remember about the guy that picked you up and the car he was driving."

Allie took a long drink out of her forty-ounce Colt 45.

"He was a black guy with glasses. He had a fade and pits on his face. He seemed pretty tall, like, he kept hitting the roof of the car while he was raping me. He was old - like probably forty or fifty. His car was nice. It was white or gray and had four doors. It smelled new." She took another drink and paused before saying, "I saw a license plate, too."

Suddenly Frankie perked up and asked, "Do you happen to remember the plate number and maybe what state it was from?"

"Uh, yeah," Allie guffawed. "78H Y8B. It was Missouri."

"Do you think you would recognize him or the car if you saw them again?" Frankie inquired as she tried to conceal her excitement at this tidbit of information.

"Yeah. Dude was totally memorable. He wasn't ugly or anything, but I'd remember him."

"Did he tell you his name?" Mia thought it was a long shot, but one worth taking.

"Allen?" Allie said questioningly. "I kind of remember laughing because my name is Allie and he said his was Allen. He probably lied to me though."

"Do you remember anything else about him or his car or is there anything else you'd like to add?"

She chewed on the fingers of her right hand as she tapped the top of her beer can with the left.

"He scared me. This wasn't, like, the first time I've been raped. This is like, the eighth time. But, this guy, he totally scared me. He's going to kill somebody. This," pointing at the wig, "is because of him. I was so freaked, I started pulling out my hair. I pulled out so much, I have to wear a wig now."

Mia told her she'd be in touch and left her business card in case she remembered something else. As she and Frankie walked to the car Mia let out a large exhale and said, "Let's head back."

CHAPTER
THIRTY-SIX

THE SOUND of Frankie's phone ringing broke the silence in the car as the detectives tried to piece together what they had heard.

"Thomas."

She took notes while Mia listened to the one-sided conversation. Mia did not say anything, knowing Frankie would update her when she hung up the phone.

"That was Fitz. He went out to Mayfaire to get the surveillance. He and Jim will be by the office in about an hour to review it. He talked to a few people over there but no smoking guns yet. He also said they had some more information on the lawsuit."

"Jim is hot," said Mia. "Like, Vin Diesel or The Rock hot. Fitz is pretty nice to look at, too, and I've heard he's a damn good detective. Been in the Intelligence Unit a long time. If I wasn't married…"

Frankie laughed in agreement.

"I'm curious at what this video shows."

"Me too. Hey, did you ever hear from Brooklyn?"

Frankie shook her head. She grabbed her cell phone to look and see if she had missed any text messages or phone calls.

"Dammit. Her mom called her but wouldn't agree to meet with me."

"There's only so much you can do, Frankie. Maybe she'll change her mind later."

"That's exactly what I told Brook. Maybe I should take my own advice. Do me a favor, let's take the long way back. Head up to the Avenue and see if she's out. Maybe I can talk to her a little and at least get her to go to the hospital."

Frankie was not one to give up easily and when it involved someone she cared about, she was even more zealous. She was quiet on the drive. She pulled up a booking photo of Asia on their in-car computer so Mia would know who they were looking for. She had only met Asia once but had heard plenty of stories. She did not think Asia was a good mother, but she knew Brooklyn loved her and worried about her mom more than any teenager should. She wanted to be angry with her but found herself having compassion. She understood Asia had an addiction, which caused her to make poor choices and be in places that made her vulnerable to victimization. As for Brooklyn, Frankie would do whatever she could to help her.

Mia drove north on Prospect from 23rd Street. She slowed down when she saw women congregating on the corner or standing near an abandoned storefront. On either side of the street were abandoned businesses and homes, once inhabited, now boarded up. Young men congregated on the corner wearing sagging jeans, hooded sweatshirts, and stocking caps. Most walked away when they saw the unmarked car approaching. Young girls approached passing cars when they slowed down but quickly waved the car away when Mia squawked the sirens.

As they approached Independence Avenue Mia asked, "Which way?"

"Let's head towards Van Brunt. Brooklyn said she normally hangs out around Independence and Indiana. If she's not there we'll head back."

Independence Avenue used to be a hub of social activity in the early 1900s but the buildings which once held successful businesses, churches, schools, and storefronts were now lifeless and abandoned. Mia drove slowly so she and Frankie could scan the sidewalks. The large row of buildings which lined the street had more vacant storefronts than occupied ones. The nail salon, liquor store, and check cashing store all had bars on their windows. The abandoned storefronts had plywood boards covering the windows and doorways. A chain store pharmacy served as a makeshift grocery carrying milk and bread, but the prices were considerably higher than a traditional grocer, extorting those who lived nearby and couldn't go to a grocery store. The once vibrant neighborhood was now full of blight.

Frankie scanned the area for Asia as they drove past an abandoned church and sidewalks covered with litter. When they approached the convenience store at Benton Boulevard she said, "Slow down. It's dark and I don't want to miss her."

Mia drove about two more blocks before Frankie said, "There she is. She just walked into the laundromat."

Before Mia could put the car in park Frankie had the door open and was walking toward the laundromat. She took a deep breath and opened the business door. Asia was sitting alone at a folding table with her face cradled in her hands, an ice pack pressed to her face. She looked both frightened and defeated with her tiny body slumped in the chair. Her skin, normally the color of rich espresso beans, was ashen gray. Frankie saw a towel with ice against her swollen face. She looked into Asia's almost gold, almond shaped eyes and saw the look of a wild cat.

Asia raised her head when Frankie said her name.

Softly Frankie asked, "Do you remember me? I'm a friend of Brooklyn's."

"Yes," was the hushed response. "How'd you know where to find me? I told Brooklyn I didn't want to talk to no damn police."

"Don't be mad at her, Miss Asia. She's just worried about you. I'm not here to make you file a report, I just wanted to make sure you're okay."

She grunted and looked at Frankie, letting her eyes go from her shoes to her face and back. Frankie knew Asia was sizing her up, wondering if Frankie was judging her and if she could trust her.

"Do I look like I'm okay? I'm hurtin' and don't want any damn cops in my business. Tell that girl I'm fine."

"Okay I'll tell her but Miss Asia, I'm really worried about your injuries. Do you want to go to the hospital?"

"I said I don't want a bunch of people in my business. I'll be fine."

"Did you know you can get a forensic medical exam at the county for free? Just to make sure you're okay. They can also collect evidence without you having to file a police report. My partner and I can give you a ride if you want."

Asia studied her face before asking, "Why would you help me?"

She didn't answer quickly, instead she took a breath and chose her words carefully. She knew her answer could make the difference between Asia getting help or going into hiding.

"Because you are a mother, a daughter, and most importantly, a human being. You didn't do anything to deserve to be assaulted or hurt in any way. You deserve to be treated with dignity and respect. You deserve to go to the hospital to make sure you're okay."

Tears pooled in Asia's eyes, but she turned away and coughed before any trickled down her cheeks. Asia spoke quickly and with gruffness, "Well if it'll make Brooklyn to stop worrying about me then I guess I'll go. You sure they ain't gonna make me talk to the damn police?"

"Yes ma'am. I'm sure. Just tell them you want an anonymous kit done and they won't call the police. I won't even go in with you unless you want me to."

Asia stared at her with a hard look before saying, "Okay, let's go." She grabbed her bag off the table and stood up.

Frankie led her to the car, opened the door and allowed her to sit in the front seat. They drove to the hospital in silence and when they arrived Frankie asked if she wanted her to go inside with her. Asia shook her head and started to walk away.

"Here's my card. When you're ready, you can call me. Anytime. Okay?"

"Yeah."

Asia began to walk toward the door then stopped. She turned back to Frankie and said, "Thank you. You'll look after my girl, right?"

"Absolutely."

"I'M TELLING YOU FRANKIE, it was a dude," Mia shrieked as the elevators opened to the fourth floor. "He had an Adam's apple!"

"Seriously?! Did you see those legs? Those didn't look like a man's legs," argued Frankie. The banter between the two detectives could be heard down the hallway to the squad room.

"What are you two arguing about?" asked Baker.

Frankie and Mia answered at the same time, "Nothing Sarge."

Mia followed up with, "There was this man at the county hospital wearing a dress and bright red, six-inch, spiked heels. Frankie is convinced it was a woman but I'm certain it was a man. I could see an Adam's apple and I'm not so sure I didn't see his…"

Baker cut in and said, "I get the picture Mia. Frankie, Fitzmeyer and Craven are in the conference room waiting for you. They have surveillance from the shopping center pulled up on one of the monitors."

Mia gave Frankie a knowing wink at the mention of Craven's name. Frankie rolled her eyes and followed Baker into the conference room. Mia trailed behind.

"Whatcha got, Fitz?"

Frankie could not help but notice that Jim stood when she walked into the room. His dark brown eyes bored into hers as he extended his hand to shake. The smell of his cologne, a blend of patchouli, red cedar, and sandalwood invoked a deep-seated memory from her youth. His voice was deep, with just a hint of a southern accent.

"Hey Frankie. Sarge. Mia. We picked up some surveillance footage and talked to a few people. I have one video here and there may be something on one of the other videos, but I won't know until tomorrow. One of my techs is trying to clean it up so we can get a tag number off a car."

Frankie said, "Great. What else did you find?"

"You really are impatient, aren't you?" Fitz asked.

Frankie stuck her tongue out as Fitz winked at her.

"You've got her pegged," said Baker. "Did you find anyone that saw these girls being followed?"

"No one even really remembered the girls at the mall, but we did get surveillance of them going in and out the main doors. The guy Hannah said held the door for her is there but he kept his head down, so we didn't get a clear shot. We showed their photos to the host at Nu, and he recognized both of 'em. He said he remembered them because he thought Hannah was hot and wanted to find a way to slip her his phone number. His girlfriend came in right before they left so he missed his shot," said Fitz, laughing.

"Classy," Frankie and Mia said in unison.

"Ah, give the kid a break ladies, he was barely eighteen. He said he watched them leave the restaurant but didn't notice anyone following them. When they were walking out he said Tessa was messing with her phone and almost ran into him. He wasn't sure if she was texting or doing something else."

Frankie doodled on her notepad as she listened to Fitz talk. "Where did the video Jim mentioned come from?"

"There is a small drive-thru coffee shop in the parking lot. It has exterior cameras, but they don't extend very far. The camera caught a car matching the description Hannah gave but it was too grainy to see a plate or even get a good description of the driver," answered Jim. "They should have it ready tomorrow. They know it's a priority."

"Thanks, Jim," said Frankie averting her eyes from his as they bore into hers. The surge of electricity between them was palpable.

BY THE END of her shift, Frankie's shoulders ached, and her eyes burned. Only a couple hours of sleep and a long night of work made here double thankful she was off the next day and the kids were out of school.

"I'm going to sleep until noon tomorrow," she said as she walked to the lot with Mia and Baker.

"Whatever, Frankie. You say that now, but Tyler is going to be jumping on your bed begging for breakfast and Isabelle is going to bring you her leash for a run and you're going to do it." Mia laughed and shoved her friend on the shoulder while they walked.

Frankie laughed in agreement. They said good-bye when they reached their cars. "Call if anything comes up tomorrow, Mee. Have a good holiday, Sarge."

"I'll be in town if anything comes up this weekend, Frankie," replied Baker. "Text me if you get anything good."

"You got it, Sarge. See you Thursday, Mia." Frankie nodded at Mia and waived at Baker as she climbed in the Jeep. She put the key in the ignition just as her phone beeped notifying her of an incoming text.

"Dinner tomorrow night? Or at least dessert? ;)"

She smiled at the text message from Derek.

Wish I could but doing volunteer stuff. See you after work Thursday?"

"Okay, I'll see you then. Sweet dreams, sexy."

She put her phone back in her bag and drove the ten minutes home in silence. Isabelle barked the moment she put her keys into the door. She pushed the door open and immediately felt a surge of love course through her heart as she observed Tyler asleep on his beanbag while Sophie sat watching a movie with Dani.

"Hey guys."

Dani barely looked up from the movie, "Hey mom. How was work?"

"Busy, angel-girl. What are you still doing up?

"No school, remember? So, no bedtime." Frankie ruffled Dani's golden-brown hair before kissing the top of her head.

"Any problems tonight, Soph?" Frankie knew her life would be much more complicated without her sister there to help her.

"No. Quiet night. We left you some chicken and rice if you're hungry. We're going to finish this movie then I'll head upstairs. Want to join us?"

"Thanks Sophie. Let me grab a beer and get into my pajamas."

She opened a bottle of Bud Light and walked toward her bedroom with Isabelle at her heels. After getting her pajamas on she plopped down on the couch with Dani who laid her head onto Frankie's lap. Isabelle laid at her feet.

She stroked Dani's hair while they watched a movie they had all seen a dozen times. Sophie and Frankie made small talk while Tyler snored softly in the beanbag. After discussing Thanksgiving weekend plans and her next on call schedule Sophie asked, "What time is your VISION meeting tomorrow?"

"I have to pick up a couple of the kids and I want to have dinner ready by 6. We'll probably leave here by 4. Are you coming to help?"

"I'm planning on it unless mom says she needs help. Keith said he would help too."

Keith and Bruce enjoyed joining VISION in their volunteering efforts, so she had invited them when the event was scheduled.

"Bruce has to work. He's pulling a double and working Thanksgiving so one of the other guys can go out of town."

Keith was a paramedic and Bruce a firefighter for the Kansas City Missouri Fire Department. Like a lot of people who work in the emergency response field, Keith and Bruce met on the job. Frankie watched their friendship as it grew into a romance. About a year after they started dating, she helped Bruce move into Keith's house next door. Five years later they were still as in love as they were the day they met.

"That's sweet of him. Want to ride with us or will you meet us down there?"

"I'll meet you. I have to work and may not be ready to go by the time you leave. Besides, you won't have room in your car after you pick up the kids," Sophie replied.

"Yeah, I guess that's true."

They finished the movie in silence and once it ended, Frankie jostled Tyler and told him it was time to go to bed. Sophie grabbed the blanket and stretched out the length of the sofa.

"Night sis," Sophie said. "Love you."

"Love you, too. See you in the morning."

Frankie watched her sister walk to the apartment over her garage and waited until she saw the outdoor light extinguish. She walked to the front door and looked out the window as she checked the lock on the door. Just as she started to turn away, she noticed a dark colored SUV parked up the street with its lights out. The light from the streetlamps danced along the chrome bumper and although she couldn't be sure, she thought someone was sitting in the driver's seat. She closed the blinds and made sure both locks were secure. Frankie wondered if she was being paranoid. Why would anyone be watching her house? Stepping back toward the window, with the lights out, she pushed the blinds apart and looked toward the direction where the car had been parked. The SUV had not moved, and the windows were dark. She let the blinds close, turned away from the window, and laughed at herself.

"You're losing it, Thomas," she muttered as she walked to her bedroom.

Moments later the headlight of the SUV turned on. As the car drove away the red glow from a cigar emanated from the driver's seat.

/ # CHAPTER
THIRTY-NINE

FRANKIE AWOKE to the sounds of chaos. Tyler and Dani were arguing over being quiet so they didn't wake her up; Isabelle was barking at their cat Koda who was hissing; and her cellphone was chirping alerting to an unread text message.

"Ugh," she groaned and covered her face with her pillow. She laid there listening to the sounds of her children clamoring in the kitchen for a few more moments before rolling over to look at her phone.

"Mornin' sunshine! Looking forward to tomorrow night. Have a great day. XO."

Derek always knew how to make her smile. She rolled onto her back and thought of him but before she could dial the phone to call him hers began to ring.

"Hello."

"Hey Frankie, it's Jim. Jim Craven. Got a sec?"

"Yeah, what's up?" She sat up and grabbed her notepad and pen from the table on the side of her bed.

"I know you're off today, but I wanted to check and see if you wanted Fitz and I to run out to Stevenson's and do a little snooping around today."

"Why don't we go together on Friday? But, if you have time, maybe you can run out to the dealership in Mission and see if anyone will talk," she replied, impressed and just a bit surprised that he was asking her opinion instead of just taking over.

"Sounds good, Frankie. I'll try to get out there today. Got any big plans for your day off?"

"I'm taking a group of kids to the Ronald McDonald House to cook. Otherwise, not much. Thanks for asking. What about you? Plans for Thanksgiving?" She heard a crashing sound coming from the kitchen. Before he could answer she said, "Jim, I'm sorry but I've got to go before my kids burn the house down."

She could hear him laughing. They said good-bye and hung up the phone.

She sent Derek a quick text then got up to begin her day. After inspecting the noise from the kitchen, she threw a load of laundry in the wash, grabbed her sneakers and phone, and told Dani she was going for a run. Dani was sitting on the sofa eating a bowl of cereal watching a rerun of a Disney program.

"Watch your brother," Frankie said.

Dani didn't look up from the television as she nodded her response.

"I don't need watched, mom. I'm not a baby," whined Tyler.

"I know you're not a baby, Ty, but you're not ready to stay home alone just yet." She ruffled the hair on Tyler's head, grabbed the leash and said, "Let's go Iz. I'll be back in about forty-five minutes."

Frankie had a route plotted in her neighborhood she had been running since they moved there seven years prior. She stretched her legs and arched her stiff back before hitting the pavement on the road in front of her house. With each pounding step she felt the release of the tension in her shoulders. With each deep breath, she felt her mind get a little clearer. The sounds of Daughtry, Nickelback, Journey, and others like them filled her ears as she increased her speed. To her running was not about racing, but about losing, losing the stress and worry that filled her mind the other twenty-three hours a day. Although Isabelle was getting old, she kept pace with her on the five-mile trek, slowing only during the last half mile to cool down and stretch.

Frankie opened the door and was surprised to find the kids had tidied the living room and cleaned the kitchen. Dani was in her bedroom listening to music and reading a teen magazine. Tyler was in his bedroom making a village out of Legos and talking to his guinea pig, Cocoa. Frankie thanked Tyler and Dani for helping out around the house, returned to the kitchen, and grabbed a bottle of water. Isabelle sat patiently waiting for a cup of food and fresh water.

"Good run today, girl." She patted her loyal companion on the head and grabbed a treat from the jar on the counter. "Here you go, Izzie."

While the dog happily chomped on her treat, Frankie filled her food and water bowls. She cooked eggs and toast then jumped in the shower. Letting the water wash down her back she thought about her latest case. She replayed the photographs and crime scene in her mind and could not shake the nagging thought that something was not right.

After she finished her shower, she started gathering supplies for the dinner at the Ronald McDonald House. She was preparing baked spaghetti. It was always a big hit and easy to reheat. As she was putting the jars of sauce into the carrier her phone beeped with an incoming text.

"It's Jim. Craven. Got some names of associates. Following up. Working tomorrow?"

Frankie replied, *"Hi Jim. Craven. Yep. Be in at 1500."*

"Ok. Will stop by."

She sent a thank you message then started loading the Jeep. Once she was finished, she texted the kids she was picking up to tell them to be ready at four. Her vehicle only allowed her to carry two extra kids, so she tried to rotate which of the teens rode with her and which rode with the other parents. She always made sure both the parents and children were comfortable with the arrangement before sharing the load. At about 3:30 she told Tyler and Dani to get into the Jeep so they could leave. After the usual banter of who got the front seat, they were able to back out of the driveway and head to Brooklyn's house.

Frankie had not even put the Jeep in park when Brooklyn came bouncing out of the side door with a grocery sack in one hand and purse in the other.

"Hey Miss Frankie! Dani. Ty." Brooklyn smiled and ruffled Tyler's hair when she said his name.

"Hey Brooklyn," the trio said in unison.

Dani climbed in the backseat with Brooklyn and created a "Tyler sandwich." They started talking of the typical things teen girls discussed

- boys, fashion, gossip, and more talk of boys. During their time together it did not matter that the girls went to different schools in different areas of the city. For a few hours, they were just teenage girls. Frankie smiled listening to their chatter. She was grateful the girls felt comfortable talking in front of her and that Brooklyn had a few hours to be a teen and not worry about her mother.

She drove the ten blocks to the next house and when they pulled in the driveway Tyler let out, "Alright! Carl!"

Just as Tyler finished saying his name, Carl Williams walked out of the house. Carl was fifteen and a freshman at the same school Brooklyn attended. He stood about 5'9" and wore his hair cut close to his scalp. His skin was the color of milk chocolate and his eyes, the color of dark coffee, lit up when he saw the Jeep full of his friends. Unlike Brooklyn, Frankie did not meet Carl because he was in trouble but instead when she worked at one of the school's events.

All of the teens involved in VISION were special to Frankie, but Carl had been there the longest and spent the most time with her family. His father was not around, his mother worked two jobs, and his older brother and sister had moved out and were living their own lives. Carl had a younger brother who occasionally joined the group, but he seemed to be more interested in girls, and she suspected drugs, to join them regularly. She did not push but instead made sure he knew she was there for him. To help fill the gaps in his home life, Frankie regularly invited Carl to various activities she did with her own children.

"Hey Carl," she said as he climbed into the front seat of the Jeep.

"Hi, Miss Frankie," came the soft reply from the boy whose voice had not yet changed to the deep base she suspected it would someday be. He turned in the seat to say hello to the rest of the people in the vehicle and then started chatting with Tyler about Lego's, Star Wars, and any other topics he knew would be of interest to the young boy.

It only took about twenty minutes for the crew to arrive at the Ronald McDonald House and the time went quickly. Frankie recognized two of the cars in the driveway as belonging to one parent and one volunteer mentor. She smiled to herself knowing that tonight was going to be a great night.

AFTER COOKING and cleaning up the dinner dishes, Frankie drove the teens back to their respective homes. The night had been a success and a nice distraction for her but now that it was over the quiet overcame her and her thoughts started to drift back to the case and her adjunct partners. The sounds of Ty's soft snoring and the quiet murmurings of the girls created the background noise to her thoughts.

Jim and Fitz had texted her throughout the day with minor updates but neither had tracked down any smoking guns. Jim mentioned he would drop by the office on Thanksgiving to talk to her about what he'd learned, and Fitz told her he would catch up with her on Friday so they could do some strategic planning. She respected their work ethic and appreciated them keeping her up to date on what they were doing, respecting her lead instead of trying to take over the case.

She began making a mental list of what she wanted to accomplish at work the following day. Brooklyn interrupted her thoughts by saying, "Miss Frankie?"

Returning her attention to the people in the car she said, "Yeah Brooklyn?" She pulled into the driveway at Brooklyn's house and put the Jeep into park.

Brooklyn fidgeted in the seat, tapping her fingers on the strap and zipper of her purse. "Can I talk to you in private for a second?"

She opened the door, "Of course."

She could see their breath in the cold air as they stood in the driveway next to her Jeep. She rubbed her hands together and blew into them, giving Brooklyn time to talk.

"Thank you for finding my momma last night, Miss Frankie. And for, um, taking care of her. She called me and said you were real nice, said you surprised her."

She put her hand onto Brooklyn's shoulder, "It was my pleasure, Brook. I care about you and your family and am happy to help. And when your momma's ready to talk, tell her to call me. I'll do what I can to help her, okay?"

Without warning Brooklyn wrapped her arms around Frankie's waist and squeezed. She nodded her head and said, "Thank you again, Miss Frankie. For everything."

Unexpected tears welled in Frankie's eyes from the embrace. Brooklyn let go without looking up and quickly walked to the door, stopping to raise her hand in a wave and smile. Frankie waited in the driveway until she was sure Brooklyn was inside the house safely and then drove the few blocks to drop Carl off.

"Is your mom home?"

He raised his head from the seat and looked at the clock on the radio. It was 9:00 p.m. "Yeah. If not, she'll be home in about an hour. She said they were closing early today."

"Okay. Do you want to go driving one day next week?"

Frankie had been taking him, Brooklyn, and a couple of the other VISION teens driving to help them prepare for their driver's test. There was a park and zoo near his house and the open lot and surrounding roadways were a great place for the teens to drive without having to worry about traffic or other distractions. He was not going to be sixteen for nine months, but she knew he was not going to get much practice if she didn't take him.

"Yes ma'am," he animatedly said. "What day?"

"I'm working at the school Monday. How about we go right after? We can drive for an hour or so before it gets dark. Sound like a plan?"

Frankie stopped the car in front of his house.

"Yes ma'am. I'll see you then. Thanks for the ride!"

"No problem. See you Monday."

Frankie watched Carl walk to the front door and let himself into the small ranch style home. His family struggled financially but the house and yard were always neatly kept.

Frankie and her children drove the thirty minutes home in relative silence. Dani played with the stations on the radio while Tyler slept. When they began gathering their things to go inside Dani asked, "What time do we have to go tomorrow?"

"We should leave about 9, so let's get ourselves to bed soon. Okay?"

Dani nodded, grabbed the keys from her mother and got out to unlock the front door. Frankie picked Tyler up out of the seat and started to carry him inside the house. Closing the door to the Jeep she noticed the same SUV she had seen the night before, only it was parked on the other end of the block. Like the previous night, the lights were off but this time she was certain she saw the shadow of a person sitting in the driver's seat. The adrenaline began to course through her veins causing her to move with purpose, double locking the house doors behind her.

Once inside her home she took a deep breath and grabbed her phone, not sure if she should call 9-1-1. Her hands were shaking. She suspected she was being paranoid but also believed she should always follow her gut. She picked up her phone to call dispatch as she waked through the house checking the window locks. Before dialing, Frankie peeked through the blinds of her window to see if the SUV was still parked where she had seen it. Through the narrow slits of the blinds, she saw the headlights of the SUV turn on and felt a cold shiver run down her spine as the vehicle drove slowly past her house. She gasped when she saw a red glow, similar to a cigar or cigarette, from the driver's side.

FORTY-ONE

THANKSGIVING MORNING BROUGHT an early rise for the Thomas house. Frankie's mother lived an hour from her house and wanted to have lunch at noon. Tyler was spending the long weekend there and she was planning to drop Dani off at her ex-husband's on the way back to the office. Loading the Jeep, she thought to herself, *"I don't remember the last time I had a lazy Thanksgiving with my family."*

If she didn't work her primary job on Thanksgiving, she worked a secondary job. Some years she did both. Companies paid a premium for officers to work holidays and, as a single mom, there was never a shortage in need for extra money, especially around the holidays. This year she skipped the extra duty so she could have lunch with her family.

After making sure the kids had everything they needed for the long weekend, she backed out of the drive and headed east toward her home-town. She and the kids got to her mother's a little after 10:30. They were greeted with the fragrant aroma of roasted turkey and stuffing.

Frankie went about getting the macaroni started and the rolls on the cookie sheet while texting her dad to tell him she and the kids would come by for Sunday brunch. She worked Sunday evening but would pick the kids up that morning and join her dad, his wife and her siblings for a belated Thanksgiving brunch. She was grateful her family was willing to make adjustments so she could do her job without missing out on family events.

At twelve o'clock sharp the family sat down, said grace and enjoyed their Thanksgiving feast. Dani and Tyler dominated the conversation talking about school, their friends and the latest books they were reading. Once the meal was finished the kids cleared the dishes while Frankie's mother packed up some leftovers for her to take for the weekend. By half past one Frankie and Dani said their good-byes and headed back toward the city.

Before they could get out of the driveway Dani asked, "Mom, what happened to Brooklyn's mom?"

Frankie looked over at her teenage daughter and wondered how she should answer. Unfortunately, Dani and Ty overheard a lot of her conversations and were more familiar with what she did than they should be. It was not that she sat down and openly discussed her work with them, but she would occasionally answer her phone or talk to colleagues and forget the kids were within earshot. She tried to be careful, but she knew she should do better.

A few moments passed before Dani said, "Mom?"

"Her mom was assaulted by a man, Dani. Mia and I took her to the hospital so she could get checked out, that's all."

"Did you get the guy mom?"

"Ms. Jenkins didn't want to make a report right now, so no. But you don't need to worry Dani. This guy's not going to hurt you." Frankie wanted to reassure Dani but was not sure how to help her understand Asia had made decisions that made her vulnerable and that was why the man chose her to attack. She also wanted Dani to understand those decisions did not equal Asia deserving her attack.

"Was she in a bad part of town?"

Frankie nodded her head in response as she thought about the amount of worry her daughter must feel.

"And the man won't be driving around our neighborhood?"

Frankie reached across and patted Dani's leg, "No sweetheart, he won't be in our neighborhood. You'll be okay."

"Okay mom." Dani turned her attention to the radio. She turned the dial up and started to sing along.

Frankie dropped Dani off at her ex-husband's house. As she pulled back out on the highway her phone began to ring, "Thomas."

"Hey beautiful, are we still on for tonight?" Frankie smiled at the sound of Derek's sultry voice.

"Do you want to come to my house, or shall I meet you at yours?"

"Why don't you and Isabelle come spend the weekend at my house?" He inquired.

She and Isabelle loved spending the weekend with him and Bear. She did not get to do it often, so she readily agreed.

"I'll run by and get the dog for you on the way home from my mom's. Do you want me to pick anything else up?" Derek asked.

"No, I have a toothbrush at your house and a change of clothes in my bag. I can pick up anything else I need tomorrow," she replied.

CHAPTER
FORTY-TWO

FRANKIE AND MIA talked good-naturedly for about thirty minutes after they arrived to work then got busy writing reports. The television in the squad room, tuned to holiday movies, was playing softly in the background while both women tapped lightly on their respective keyboards.

The stillness was broken by the sound of Jim's slow southern drawl, "Happy Thanksgivin' ladies."

"Hey Jim, what are you doing working on the holiday? I thought Feds kept banker's hours?" Frankie stood up to shake his hand as he reached her desk. Moving her workbag she said, "Have a seat."

He accepted the chair, "Aw, you know how it is. There's always work to be done and besides none of my family is 'round here. I can only sit around my loft so long without going stir crazy, so I decided to come by and see what you gals were up to."

Mia turned her chair around toward Frankie's desk to join the conversation, "Where are you from Jim?"

His face broke into a slow smile, "I grew up in a small fishing town just across the bridge from Topsail Island, NC, just up from Wilmington. I went to school at University of North Carolina-Wilmington, then moved to Chicago and worked for the police department there. All my family still lives on the coast."

Frankie's face lit up while he talked. "I love that area. I visit the North Carolina coast at least once a year and more often if I can swing it."

"Yeah, me, too. My momma owns a little bookstore on the island. Quarter Moon…"

"I know that store!" Frankie said with excitement. "I go every time I'm there! Is Miss Lolly your mom?"

"Yep. That's her," he laughed. "My daddy has a couple of boats he uses to take tourists out deep sea fishin' and a couple more he uses just for shrimpin'. Heck I was a deckhand before I started kindergarten."

The trio shared personal antidotes for a few more minutes before Frankie pulled out her notepad and pen. She asked, "Guess we should get down to business. What do you have for me, Jim?"

"Now that's a loaded question," He answered, raising his eyebrows up and down at her before turning to Mia and asking, "Does she ever just relax?"

Mia laughed, "Rarely."

"I did a little research into some of the players involved in this mess of a case. Where do you want me to start?"

"Maggio." Frankie's pen was poised over her notepad ready to take notes on what he told her.

"That guy's a piece of work. He's a Kansas City, Missouri native with strong ties to the Northeast neighborhood. He has worked at three different car dealerships in the metropolitan area, all directly tied to either Marzullo or the Dante Group. He worked at the first dealership about ten years and the second two less than a year each. I couldn't find anything on why he left and moved around but his financials revealed some suspiciously large payouts to individuals under the auspices of anonymity. I'm still working on finding out who the anonymous folks are but probably won't have any names until next week. My guess, based on his history, is they are women who worked for him.

"Maggio's wife divorced him after he left the second dealership. She got the house, the kids, and a healthy amount of child support and alimony. He makes a good salary, according to the IRS, but he has to be getting money from another source because in addition to all the money he pays the ex-wife he also pays to send his kids to a pretty expensive, private Catholic school. To top it off he is a high roller everywhere he goes.

"Maggio also has a sidekick that seems to follow him from dealership to dealership, a guy by the name of Craig Midori. I ran Midori's financials, and he has a little money in the bank, drives a nice car, sends his kids to the same private Catholic school Maggio's kids go to and has a house in a very exclusive subdivision; all worth more than his annual salary would indicate he could afford. Ready for the best part?"

Jim paused for effect as he looked from Frankie to Mia and back to Frankie. Both women nodded but like a child waiting to share a surprise, he sat silent for another moment to build the suspense.

"Come on Jim, spill it!" exclaimed Mia.

"I went by Midori's house yesterday. He just happened to be leaving as I was doing a drive by. He's a white guy, probably in his late thirties or early forties. He's not super big, just average. He was wearing a black Burberry leather coat, black gloves and a black stocking cap on his head." Jim paused again before saying, "And he was driving a newer model, dark blue, Mercedes sedan."

He sat back with a satisfied look on his face and crossed his arms.

Before either woman could say anything, Jim added, "Oh, and did I mention his car had a dealer's tag on the back?"

Frankie let the information sink in. Her initial thought was this was going to be easy. Pick Midori up, get him to flip on Maggio, and call it a day. But it seemed too easy, too convenient.

"Did you follow him?"

"Where's your excitement Frankie? I expected more animation. Maybe a 'you're amazing Jim' or 'you're my hero' or something along those lines," he smiled as he teased her. "Yes, to answer your question, I did follow him for a while. He ran a few errands and then picked his kids up from school. Once he had his kids, I quit tailing him. I figured he wasn't going to do anything too crazy with his kids in the car."

"Good deal. This is definitely some good information to work with. I still can't figure out how these goons knew when the girls would be home. I find it hard to believe they were just waiting in the garage for hours with the hopes they would come in – much less come in together."

"You think someone tipped the guys off," Mia stated more than inquired.

"Had to. The question is, who? And when?"

He appeared to hesitate briefly then asked, "At the risk of sounding like an uncompassionate jerk, what do you know about the girls? Is it possible one of them was involved?"

Mia looked to Frankie remembering their conversation at the crime scene and waited while she weighed her response.

"I don't think so, at least not Hannah. I'll be honest though, I'm not sure about Tessa." Frankie tapped her pen on her desk. "But they were both assaulted. Hannah had a slew of injuries. She was bruised, scratched up, got stitches and she was raped. Tessa ended up with a knot on her head, a couple of bruises and she said she was unconscious. And they were both so scared." She rambled as if she were talking to herself. "But it makes sense that one of them was involved. That one of them tipped those guys off so they would know when to be there. I think we should check their phone records."

"Give me their numbers and I'll pull them for you," directed Jim. "It'll be faster than waiting on the phone company to respond to a subpoena."

"Sure. I'm going to have them come in for a follow-up anyway. When they do, I'll download their phones. Can you run down Maggio and Midori's numbers?" Frankie asked.

"Yep. I'll see what I can find for you. Shouldn't be too hard to get their numbers. I'm going to head over to the bureau office when I leave here and see what I can find. You gonna be around for a while?"

"Right here at my desk all night. God willing." Just as she replied, the phone began to ring. "Shit, I think I spoke too soon."

Mia answered, "Sex Crimes, Detective Boden."

Frankie and Jim said their good-byes quietly. He agreed to call her when he found something.

CHAPTER
FORTY-THREE

"WE GOT SOMETHING?" asked Frankie when Mia hung up the phone.

"Naw, it was just Killer. That guy cracks me up. I answer the phone and he asked, 'got any sex?' He did ask about your case, but I told him we couldn't tell him anything."

"Good deal, thanks."

Frankie turned back to the computer to continue writing her reports. A couple of hours later Jim texted her to tell her the computer systems were down but he would work on the phone records when he got to work on Friday. The women worked in relative silence until about 10:30.

Mia had just finished her last report when she asked, "Are you going to Derek's tonight?"

"Yeah. He went by and got Isabelle so I can go straight there. In fact, why don't we head out? I'm on call, so if the phone rings it's coming to me anyway," reasoned Frankie.

"You don't have to tell me twice. I can run by the station and see the hubs on the way home," said Mia.

Mia's husband, Erik, worked as a SWAT officer and was pulling extra duty because of the holidays. The two women walked to the car lot and said their good-byes. Frankie grabbed her cellphone and dialed Derek's number. After two rings she heard a throaty, "Hello there."

"Hey, did I wake you?

"Naw, I'm just lying in bed waiting for my favorite gal to get here."

"Better call her and tell her not to come. I'm on the way."

"I'll text her when I hang up. She'll be disappointed, but I think she'll get over it," he teased.

Frankie laughed, "Yes, she will. Need me to bring anything?"

"Just yourself," Derek replied.

Her call-waiting interrupted their light banter.

"Dammit. I'll call you right back." She clicked over the phone and said, "Detective Thomas."

A quiet, raspy voice said, "Detective Thomas, it's Hannah."

"Is everything okay?" Frankie asked.

"There's a car outside of my house. It's probably nothing but it's been there for a while. I'm worried it might be one of the guys that attacked me."

"Did you call 9-1-1?"

Hannah coughed lightly, "No. I wasn't sure if it was important enough to call 9-1-1."

"Hannah, I want you to listen to me very carefully. Hang up and call the police. After you call the police call me right back. Okay?"

Frankie sat in the Jeep and waited. As her phone began to ring, she pulled out her notepad and pen.

"Hannah, did you talk to the police?"

"Yeah. They're on their way."

"What does the car outside your house look like, Hannah?"

She strained to hear Hannah's soft voice, "It's dark so I'm not sure what color it is. I'm in my room now with the door locked and can't see it anymore. I think it was a four-door sedan, maybe a Toyota. I couldn't really see who was driving the car but I'm sure it was a man."

"Hannah, are you sure you don't want to go to a safe house? I can make some calls and get you a place tonight."

Hannah didn't say anything for a few moments. Frankie waited patiently and let her contemplate her options. The deep sound of a dog barking in the background broke the silence.

"I think I'm okay, Detective Thomas. The security alarm is on. Hold on, I think the police are here."

Frankie waited while Hannah talked to the officers who had responded to the call. After a few moments Hannah said, "The car was gone by the time they got here. The officers said they would do extra patrols in our neighborhood, so I think I'll be okay here tonight."

"Okay, Hannah. If you change your mind, let me know."

Frankie said good-bye and pulled out of the parking lot. After letting Derek know she was finally on the way she put her phone in her bag and began the drive. She turned up the radio to drown out the thoughts racing through her mind as she sped north on I-35. Frankie sang along loudly to every song, changing the station when a commercial came on. The loud music and speed were just the catharsis she needed after that phone call.

When she parked the Jeep in Derek's driveway, she noticed a glow coming through the back door of the house. A folded piece of paper was stuck to the outside of the door. She unfolded the piece of paper and read the words aloud, *"Follow the candlelight."*

Frankie opened the door and observed a path of tea light candles leading down the hallway toward the bedroom. She smiled to herself. She laid her bag, gun, and coat on the table, removed her shoes, sat them next to the door and began to walk quietly down the hallway. The blankets on the empty bed were folded down and the candles created a path on the floor around the bed.

"Derek?" She said with a hint of question in her voice.

"Follow the candles, Frankie," came a deep voice from the direction of the primary bathroom.

She carefully followed the trail of candles around the bed into the bathroom where she found Derek soaking in an oversized bathtub full of bubbles. Additional candles lined the tub and two glasses of chilled wine sat on the edge.

"You."

"Why don't you take those clothes off and relax in the tub with me?" He asked in his deep sultry voice.

Frankie began to slowly remove her clothes one piece at a time playfully, teasing Derek by providing him glimpses of her body, then covering them up. With each piece of clothing, she took a step closer to the tub until finally she had nothing left on her taught, muscular body.

She stepped into the tub and lowered her body into the hot, sudsy water and after kissing his lips leaned into him letting her worries float away like the bubbles in the air.

As they sat in the tub, he took a sponge and filled it with water, trickling the hot droplets down her body. They talked of their day, discussed plans for the weekend, and sat in comfortable silence listening to the sounds of soft jazz coming from the speakers of the radio. When the water started to cool, they got out of the tub, and he followed her to the bedroom.

He stood behind her, put his arms around her waist, and began to kiss her neck. Their bodies moved together in unison much like dancers anticipating one another's moves. When they were both spent, they lay facing one another and talked late into the night. Frankie fell asleep with him gently stroking her hair. As she drifted off he thought he heard her softly say, "I love you." He continued to stroke her hair as he said in a voice so low it was almost inaudible, "I love you, too."

FORTY-FOUR

FRANKIE WOKE to an empty bed and for a moment wondered if the night before had been a dream. Had she really told Derek she loved him? More importantly, had he said he loved her, too? Her thoughts were interrupted by the sound of silverware tapping the side of a ceramic cup. She knew she only had about five minutes before he would be back in the bedroom with a coffee cup in one hand and a glass of diet soda for her in the other. Frankie hopped out of bed, brushed her teeth, and grabbed her running clothes.

When Derek returned, she was dressed and in the process of lacing her sneakers.

"Mornin' counselor," she said as she stretched to give him a kiss.

"Mmmm. Morning," he responded after returning a kiss filled with satisfaction and a hint of longing. After setting his coffee cup on the nightstand he grabbed her around the waist and pulled her close. "Where are you headed? I thought we'd spend a leisurely morning in bed."

"I need to get a few miles in before I go to work. Want to join me?"

"I can think of a better way to get your cardio in," was his reply. Derek started to kiss her neck, pushing his hands up her shirt.

Frankie moaned and arched her body as his hands caressed her breasts and his tongue traced her slender neck from her collarbone to her ear. When he began to nibble her ear, she pushed back and said, "After my run. Grab your sneakers and the dogs." She winked at him and added, "If you can keep up, I'll let you wash my back in the shower when we finish."

Derek groaned, fell back on the bed, and said, "Fine you win. Give me a minute to get dressed."

Derek, Frankie, and the two dogs climbed into Frankie's Jeep and headed to the police academy. The four ran for about an hour on the Trail of Heroes. The tree-lined path that wound its way around the grounds was dedicated to those who wore the badge and paid the ultimate sacrifice and was just wide enough for the two runners and their dogs. Derek let Frankie set the pace and gradually their footfalls and breathing fell into a harmonious rhythm.

Each let their thoughts drift, Derek to his upcoming murder trial and Frankie to the Waldo investigation. She replayed Hannah and Tessa's statements through her mind, wondering what she was missing. She had attended enough training and read enough books to understand how trauma impacted memory. Frankie knew it was possible after a few nights of rest there could be additional memories surface so she should consider doing another interview. She also knew the latency in the recollection could be difficult to explain but could be done if the prosecutor called in an expert to testify.

Frankie had finally resolved to call the women when she returned to work when the sound of Derek's voice broke into her thoughts, "Ready to head back to the house? It's been an hour and I'm starving."

"Now that you mention it, I'm famished."

They walked the final quarter mile to the Jeep. Frankie was glad she had thought to bring their water bottles, drinking half of hers before they pulled out of the parking space. They talked about their respective cases during the drive and while preparing breakfast. Derek shared the details of his witness interviews with her and when he finished, she shared some of the basic lawsuit information from her case.

At the mention of the name Maggio, Derek perked up and asked, "What's his first name? Nicholas or Anthony?"

"Anthony. Why? Do you know him?" Frankie inquired.

"Yeah. I went to school with both. Anthony was a year or two older than me. I'm pretty sure he married a girl from my class. Christine - Christy Salvo. I played ball with Nick; his brother and Christy rarely missed a game. Tony was always kind of a dick, but Nick and Christy were cool. I always thought those two had a thing for each other but there was no way Nick would cross Tony and act on it. No one did."

"Really? Why do you say that?"

"Rumor had it Tony's dad was connected to one of the big, organized crime families. Before Tony graduated, he started working with his dad. Nick didn't want anything to do with it and left home right after graduation. Nick used to come home for Christmas. I ran into him occasionally at one of the local markets but when his mother died, he stopped coming back." Derek looked out the kitchen window while he talked, seemingly lost in thought. "I haven't thought of him in years. I wonder where he is now?"

Frankie touched his arm, drawing him out of his memories, breaking the spell.

"Any ideas on how you want to spend the next hour before I go into work? We could always curl up in bed and watch a good movie…or football…or…"

With that Derek turned and reached for Frankie's hand, which she happily gave him. "I have a better idea," he said seductively. With that he led her back to bed.

FRANKIE LEFT DEREK'S house a little after two with the promise of returning later that night. As she pulled out of the driveway her cellphone rang.

"Thomas."

"Hey Frankie! You on your way in?"

"Hey Jim. Yeah, I just left the house. You still working?"

"Depends. What are your plans for tonight?"

"I was thinking about taking a trip down to Stevenson Automotive."

With a half laugh he said, "I was hoping you'd say that. I'll be at your office in twenty. Oh, and Frankie?"

"Yeah."

"I'm drivin'."

Frankie laughed as she hung up the phone. She had planned to ask Mia to go with her to the dealership, and still would, but had to admit she was a little excited about Jim going along. There was something about this man that really intrigued her, and his instincts matched hers.

Mia was already at her desk when she arrived.

"Hey girl, you're here early," Frankie said.

"The hubs is working tonight so I figured I would catch up on some paperwork."

Frankie said, "Jim is on the way in and we're going to go to Stevenson's. Want to join us? We could use an extra hand talking to people."

Before Mia could respond Jim walked into the office with a box of cookies and a big grin. With the most southern charm he could muster he said, "Afternoon ladies. I've got some of the best cookies you'll ever taste right here in this box. I suggest the Kiss by the way, it's my favorite," Jim locked eyes with Frankie on the word kiss. "After you try one, we can go try to nab a bad guy or two."

Frankie did not miss his long, lingering stare - and neither did Mia.

"Jim, where'd you get these?" asked Mia, breaking the moment. She moaned while devouring the first cookie.

Jim looked to Mia allowing Frankie to turn away.

"This little shop in Northtown. I stumbled upon it one day when I was there getting some new boots. I went in for a cup of coffee and the owner was working the counter. She offered me a free Kiss. Cookie, that is. I've been a loyal customer ever since."

"Thanks for thinking of us, Jim. Are you ready to head out?" Without waiting for him to answer Frankie asked, "Mia, are you coming?"

She did not miss the almost imperceptible look of disappointment on Jim's face when Mia answered, "Yep. Let me grab my coat."

The trio chatted amicably on the drive to Stevenson's. They decided to divide and conquer, talking to anyone who would give them five minutes. Each of them knew if they were going to get anyone to talk, they would have to convince them they were not on anyone's side. They were just there to gather facts.

Frankie scanned the parking lot as Jim pulled his dark colored government-owned SUV into Stevenson's Automotive. The dealership was two stories of solid glass on three sides. Unlike a traditional dealership that housed hundreds of models of vehicles of varying expense, she estimated there were less than a hundred on the lot and all the vehicles were top of the line. A maintenance bay was located on the east side of the building, with three garage bays. The doors to one of the bays were open and Frankie thought to herself, "*You could eat off that floor.*"

About fifty yards from the dealership was a small gazebo with a sign that read, "*Smoking Allowed.*" Standing under the gazebo were two men, about 30-40 years old, wearing dark colored suits and smoking cigars.

One of the men watched her get out of the SUV and began walking toward the dealership's entrance. A chill ran down her spine when she turned her back to the men.

The lobby of the dealership was busier than Frankie expected. There were three salesmen, all dressed in black suits, starched white shirts, and red ties assisting couples wearing clothes that she estimated cost more than her monthly salary. A young woman with long raven-colored hair stood behind a shiny, modern, black desk that stood at pub height just inside the door. She wore a black mini skirt, starched white blouse a size too small with the buttons opened to reveal her ample cleavage, and 5" shiny black heels. As they walked in the door she said, in a singsong voice, "Welcome to Stevenson Automotive. How may we help you drive home in a new car today?"

Frankie smiled at the girl who could not have been much more than twenty-one years old. She showed the girl her detective shield as she looked at the nameplate and said, "Hi Candie we won't be buying a car today, but I bet you can help us. We'd like to talk to the general manager."

The smile on Candie's face froze as stumbled with her response. "Mr. Whiting is not in. He's in Chicago visiting his family. Can someone else help you?"

Jim leaned on the black lacquered desk, his hand inches from her own. He smiled and locked eyes with Candie. His words dripped with a Carolina accent as he asked, "Who's runnin' the place while Mr. Whiting is gone? Is it you?" He drew out the sound of the word "you" with a wink.

Color rose up Candie's neck face and moving from pink to red as she shook her head no. Biting her lip, she stared at him and said, "Mr. Midori is covering in Mr. Whiting's absence. He might be able to help you. Would you like me to call him for you?"

"Darlin' if you would, I would really appreciate it," he responded, gently caressing her hand.

Mia and Frankie looked from the scene unfolding in front of them to one another and mouthed, "Can you believe this?" and tried not to laugh.

Candie picked up the desk phone, twirled the cord in her hands, and stared into Jim's eyes. "Yes sir. Okay, I will tell them, sir." She placed the phone on the receiver, looked at him and said, "He will be out to get you in a few moments. Can I get you a sparkling water, glass of wine, or maybe something a little stiffer?" She punctuated the syllables of the word "stiffer," never taking her eyes off him.

Jim smiled at her as he responded, "Thanks darlin' but my partners and I can't drink while we're on duty. Now if you want to write down your number, I might be willin' to buy a beautiful lady a drink after she gets done workin' her poor fingers to the bone."

Candie did not hesitate to put her phone number on a business card and hand it back to Jim. He lightly caressed the outside of her hand as he took the card. Placing it in his shirt pocket Jim patted his breast and said, "I'll keep it right here. By my heart."

Before Candie could say anything in response, the men from the gazebo walked inside the building. One of the men, with a booming voice, and a hint of a Brooklyn accent, extended his hand and said, "Agent Craven, Craig Midori."

Jim shook Midori's hand and gestured toward the women, "These are my partners, detectives Thomas and Boden."

Mia noticed the color drain from Frankie's face as she muttered, "Nice to meet you. Thank you for taking the time to talk to us."

CHAPTER
FORTY-SIX

MIDORI ESCORTED the trio to an office at the back of the building. Frankie took note of the framed advertisements hanging on the walls. Photos of Hannah and Tessa with high end luxury cars lined the hallway. Both women were wearing what she suspected was the official Stevenson Automotive uniform - black miniskirts, starched white blouses a size too small with the buttons undone to reveal ample bosoms, and spiked high heels. Tessa and Hannah stood in front of the cars with their arms folded under their breasts and seductive smiles on their faces. The sex appeal of the women eclipsed the vehicles they were trying to sell.

Midori walked behind his desk and motioned for two of them to sit on the leather wingback chairs in front. Jim nodded to the women to take the chairs as Midori asked, "How can I help you?"

Jim knew his charms would have no effect on this man, so he stood back and let Frankie speak. "Mr. Midori, we would like to talk to you and some of your fellow employees about Ms. Reitzell and Ms. Kemp."

He guffawed, "Are you still investigating that nonsense from a few weeks ago? I thought that was over."

Frankie did not answer his question directly but instead asked, "Do you know anyone who might have a bone to pick with Hannah?"

He looked at her and leaned forward to rest his elbows on the desk.

"The only person I can think of that would have a beef with that sweet, little piece of ass is T-E-S-S-A." He punctuated each letter as he spelled out Tessa's name.

Ignoring his 'little piece of ass' comment, she asked, "Why do you think Tessa has a beef with Hannah?"

"That bitch got both of them fired and Tessa has made some, let's just say questionable, financial investments lately and really can't afford to be out of work. Plus, I think that dyke wanted more than friendship from Hannah."

She let the information sit in silence before asking, "Can you think of anyone that would want to hurt Tessa?"

With that he laughed out loud. "She has made a few enemies but if you're coming here looking for suspects you're wasting your time. Tessa was always very well liked here. The beef those girls had was with Maggio, not anyone else here. And if you ask me, Tessa wasn't the one with the beef. Only Hannah seemed to have any problem with him."

Jim used the mention of Maggio as an opportunity to insert himself into the conversation, "How well do you know Maggio?"

Midori leaned back in his chair, placing his clasped hands in his lap. He was not quick to answer. He locked eyes with Jim and, in a voice that indicated the subject was not open for discussion he replied, "Well enough."

Jim was not ready to reveal the hand he held, so he let the conversation drop and instead stood up and said, "Thank you for your time, Mr. Midori. Would you mind if we talked to some of the folks that worked with Hannah and Tessa?"

Midori gave his consent adding, "Please use discretion. I would hate for our customers to feel uncomfortable or intruded upon. I believe you can find your way out." With that he nodded toward the door then toward the computer screen, signaling the end of the conversation.

Frankie, Mia, and Jim walked away from the office in single file. Once they got to the lobby Jim headed to talk to the saleswoman he had seen as Midori escorted them to his office.

Before Frankie could pick out a target Mia pulled her aside and asked, "Are you okay? You went completely ashen when you saw Midori's face."

Frankie sighed heavily and gestured for Mia to step outside the building. After looking around to be sure no one was listening she said, "It may be nothing, but I think I've seen him before." She paused, "Down the street from my house."

"What?" exclaimed Mia so loudly a woman walking in the lot glanced up from the sticker on the car window.

"I'm not 100-percent sure Mee, it may not have been the same guy. But the other night a guy that looked a lot like him was parked about half a block from my house. At first, I thought it was nothing but now I'm not so sure. Plus, he matches the description Hannah gave of the guy at the mall."

"Shit! Did you tell Sarge?"

Frankie shook her head.

"Frankie, you have to tell him. Seriously. That's your house. Your home. Where your kids are. Did you at least tell Derek? Or Fitz. Or Jim?"

She shook her head, "You're the only person I've told. I don't want to make a big deal out of this. Maybe it was just a coincidence."

Before Mia could say anything, Jim walked out of the building and said, "Ready to go ladies? We can talk to the other employees later."

Mia looked to Frankie who was a bit surprised with Jim's abrupt desire to leave but answered, "Yep. Let's head out."

CHAPTER
FORTY-SEVEN

ONCE JIM PULLED AWAY from the business, he let out a large sigh and said, "Aren't you going to ask me what I found out?"

Frankie looked over at Jim, whose face looked like the proverbial cat that ate the canary.

"It must be good for you to have that look on your face," Frankie said with a laugh.

"Well, the lady salesman, Christina, she had a lot to say when I was able to get her away from the finance guy. Quite a lot, in fact."

He stopped for effect, not readily volunteering any additional information, whistling. He tapped his fingers on the steering wheel as he drove.

"Spill it, Jim," said an exasperated Frankie.

He laughed.

"I wondered how long it'd take before you'd say something. Ten seconds. You sure are impatient, Frankie. Well, according to Christina she and Tessa used to be tight until Hannah came along. Christina and Tessa started working at the dealership at the same time. Since they were the only women in sales, Christina said they knew they could either be competitors or friends. They chose to be friends. They attended work functions, parties, and hung out at that guy Kristof's house in Brookside. They even went on a few trips together.

"Christina said Tessa told her she was a lesbian early on in their friendship. Christina was single so she figured less competition, right?"

Mia and Frankie nodded and gave a half shrug while he continued.

"Tessa eventually started to date a doctor, so it went from Christina and Tessa to the three of them doing things together. Christina said there was some teasing about her being Tessa's other girlfriend or work wife but both girls just laughed it off. Occasionally they played along with the teasing just to see people's reactions.

"When Hannah was hired things changed with all of them. Tessa took an immediate liking to Hannah and invited her to join their little group. Christina thought Hannah was whiney and basically said she got on her last nerve. Before long Tessa and the good doctor broke up and suddenly Tessa and Hannah were inseparable. Christina wondered if the two were dating but when asked Tessa said Hannah was straight. She continued going on social outings with the women until Maggio took the job as GM.

"Christina referred to Maggio as an 'egotistical, sexist, pig.' She couldn't say enough bad things about him. He came on to her the first day he was there, but she quickly told him to 'shove it where the sun doesn't shine.' Maggio took the rejection in stride and turned his sites toward Hannah and Tessa, quickly and efficiently ignoring Christina. She was still getting internet referrals and making sales, so it didn't faze her. Christina thought he was a jerk so initially she didn't mind when he didn't invite her to happy hour or other after-hours events, but eventually the other salespeople stopped including her, so Christina started to feel exiled and excluded.

"The final straw for Christina was when Maggio started working with Hannah and Tessa on marketing ads. She said she went to him and pitched a few ideas using the trio but he just smirked, looked her up and down and told her she had 'too much' of what he was looking for."

Frankie and Mia both groaned.

"What an ass. What is she a size 8?" asked Mia.

Frankie asked, "Did you get the name of the doctor girlfriend?"

"Of course, I did. I can't believe you doubt me, Frankie. Her name is Dr. Veronica Padgett. She has an orthopedic practice over in Mission."

Turning to Mia, Frankie said, "Maybe we can run out there next week."

Mia nodded in agreement.

"Did you sweet talk anyone else while you were there."

"Well, now that you mention it, I did talk to that sweet little receptionist Candie. She was more than happy to engage in conversation with this ole boy."

Under her breath Frankie said, "I bet she was."

"What was that, Frankie?"

She blushed, shrugged her shoulders and looked at him as if to say, "I don't know what you're talking about."

"I stopped by to chat with her on my way out and it was just starting to get good when Midori came out and told her he needed her in the back. I made a point of letting Midori know my interest in Candie was purely social by kissing her check and telling her I'd see her at The Brooksider at 7. Something tells me she's going to have company - if she even shows up."

Mia laughed and said, "Oh, I don't think you have to worry about her showing up, Jim. Frankie, what do you think about dinner at The Brooksider?"

Frankie's cell phone dinged with the sound of a text message. As she unlocked her phone to read the message a distracted Frankie said, "Sounds good to me."

FORTY-EIGHT

WITH A COUPLE of hours to kill before Jim's "date," Frankie suggested they go do a secondary area canvas. As they approached the neighborhood her phone began to ring.

"Thomas."

A female voice spoke so softly she could barely hear, "Detective Thomas?"

"This is she."

"It's Hannah. Hannah Reitzell. Do you have a second?"

Frankie turned the radio down in Jim's car and motioned for them to be quiet. Putting her finger in the ear opposite her phone she asked, "Sure. What's up, Hannah?"

Hannah cleared her throat then stated, "I think I'm being followed. I'm at work and I think there's someone watching me. What should I do?"

"Hannah, where are you? Are you alone?"

"I'm at my part-time job on the Plaza. A red BMW is parked across the street with a guy sitting in the driver's seat looking in the direction of the business. I'm scared, Detective Thomas."

"Hannah, can you see the license plate on the vehicle?"

She could hear rustling in the background while she waited for Hannah to respond. After a few moments Hannah said, "It looks like a

Missouri plate, but I can't say 100-percent for sure. The first three letters are WF3. I can't see the last part."

"Hannah, hold on for just a minute, okay? I'm going to call dispatch." She didn't wait for Hannah to respond before using Mia's phone to call the dispatcher. A familiar voice answered after the first ring. "Hey Stace, it's Thomas from Sex Crimes. Can you dispatch a radio car to do a car check for me?"

The dispatcher collected the address, vehicle description, and partial plate before asking, "Do you want them to call you when they stop the car?"

"Yes. Tell them to call me before releasing the driver."

"You got it. Stay safe."

"Thanks, Stacey," switching phones Frankie asked, "Hannah, are you still there?"

"Yeah. Is somebody coming?"

"Dispatch is going to send a marked car to check on the vehicle. They will call me when they I.D. the person driving. Is it still there?"

"Mm hmm," she replied. "He's just sitting there smoking. A cigar, I think."

"Okay Hannah. It's not uncommon for high-end vehicles to be on the Plaza, why did this one stand out to you?"

"The man is just sitting there watching my business. Not moving. Something just didn't feel right. Do you think I'm overreacting?"

"No. Always listen to your gut, Hannah. Do you feel safe where you are?"

"I think so. Will you call me back?"

Frankie assured her she would call her back then hung up the phone as Jim pulled into the neighborhood to do the canvas.

"Jim, why don't you and Mia see if the people that live in the house behind the garage are home? I'm going to walk around the garage while I wait for the officers to call me back then go see if Dr. Vergara is home and get a statement from her."

Mia hopped out of the backseat of the SUV and said, "You got it, Frankie. Come on, Jim, let me show you how we do it in KC!"

Mia winked at her then led Jim to the neighboring house.

Frankie laughed and shook her head and walked the opposite direction. She knew Mia was not flirting as much as she was letting Jim know local law enforcement knew how to get the job done. She walked the perimeter of the garage. When she reached the back, her phone began to ring.

"Thomas."

"Detective Thomas, this is Officer Stickler from Center Zone. Me and my partner were dispatched out to do a car check on that BMW."

"Have you made contact?"

"We did. The driver is Frank Lincoln with an address out of Chicago. He said he was waiting on his wife who was shopping. While we were talking to him a woman approached and identified herself as his wife. Do you have any reason for us to detain him?" inquired the officer.

She was not sure if she should be relieved or frustrated.

"Get all their contact information both local and in Chicago. Then I need you to write a miscellaneous information report using the case report number dispatch put on the call. Include a sentence in the report saying you contacted me in regard. Please document any anomalies on the car - things you observed on the car, the driver, or his wife."

"You got it. I'll have it done before I go home tonight."

Frankie thanked the officer and hung up. She called to update Hannah then began to walk across the street to Dr. Vergaro's house. She knocked with purpose when she reached the front door of the house. Just as she was prepared to walk away a meek, female voice asked, "Who is it?

"Detective Francesca Thomas, KCPD, ma'am. I'd like to talk to you about the incident that happened across the street if you have a moment."

She could hear the deadbolt and chain being disengaged and then the door slowly opened.

"I'm sorry, after the other night I am a bit nervous about just opening the door," said Dr. Vergaro.

"Please don't apologize for being safe. Do you mind if I come in?"

"Of course, where are my manners? Please come inside and have a seat," replied Dr. Vergaro.

"Doctor, I know you spoke with an officer and a detective the other night, Detective Boden I believe? I was wondering if you'd mind talking to me. I would like to record your statement," explained Frankie.

"Sure, Detective Thomas. Can I get you a cup of tea?" asked Dr. Vergaro. She gestured for her to sit at the table located in the kitchen. "It'll only take a moment I've already put a pot on to boil."

Frankie smiled at the kindness of this woman. Sensing a rejection would disappoint the doctor she said, "No thank you, Dr. Vergaro. I'm fine but I would be grateful for a glass of water if it's not too much trouble."

"Sure. And please call me Katie."

The water on the stove warmed while Katie removed a glass from her kitchen cupboard filling it with ice and water, setting it down in front of Frankie.

"Thank you, Doctor," Frankie corrected herself, "Katie."

The teakettle started whistling, to indicate the water was boiling. Katie placed her teacup, teakettle, and a container of teabags onto the table. Once she was finished, she sat in the chair positioned diagonally from Frankie and said, "I can't believe this happened. Our neighborhood is normally so quiet. The last couple of months, though…it's been crazy."

Frankie nodded. She removed a notepad and digital recorder from her bag. As she started making notations on the notepad she asked, "Tell me what has changed in your neighborhood."

FORTY-NINE

"A FEW WEEKS AGO, Hannah came over to my house and asked me if I had noticed anyone hanging out in the neighborhood. She said some guy had jumped the fence by her garage and held her up at gunpoint. That was when she told me about the lawsuit. She said she didn't think it was random. She thought it was related."

"Did she tell you what the lawsuit was about or who was involved?" inquired Frankie.

Katie pulled a teabag from the container and after unwrapping it placed it in the teacup.

"Hannah told me some guy had sexually harassed her at work and there were rumors her company was connected to the mob. She didn't get into any more details."

"Had you seen anything unusual in the neighborhood since Hannah told you that?"

Katie sat quietly for a moment, lifting the teabag in and out of the steaming cup. She slowly lifted the teaspoon and teabag, pressing the teabag into the spoon over the waiting cup. Once all of the liquid was expelled, she laid the spoon and teabag on the saucer and looked up at Frankie.

"At the time I didn't think there was anything but now I'm not so sure."

Frankie watched Katie stare into the teacup. "What do you mean?"

"In hindsight, there have been a lot of high-end cars in the neighborhood lately. With the holidays and all I just assumed they were visiting someone, but last weekend I could have sworn there was someone sitting in an SUV facing Hannah's house. It was dark so I probably wouldn't have noticed but there was a red glow coming from the driver's side. Like someone was smoking."

An involuntary chill ran down Frankie's spine. She hoped the expression on her face did not betray the thoughts racing through her mind. Was it possible it was the same person that threatened Hannah at gunpoint? Was it possible it was the same man she had seen outside of her house?

"What can you tell me about the SUV you saw the other night?"

Katie picked the spoon up from the saucer and began stirring the lemon she had placed in the teacup.

"I don't really know cars very well. Like I said, it was dark, but I don't think the vehicle was black. I actually think it was red or maroon. The light hit the front in a way that made me think it was a color in that family. It might have been a Range Rover, but it could just as easily have been a Lexus or BMW. It was definitely high-end and new."

"What about it made you think it was new?"

Katie closed her eyes. She looked as though she were trying to catch a glimpse of an image in her memory.

"The exterior was in good shape but that's not what made me think it was new. There was something on the window and from where I stood it looked like a new car sticker. Now as I think about it, it could just as easily have been one of those sunshades parents put on their windows when they have babies in the backseat. I just know there was something in the window."

"Had you ever seen that vehicle, or one like it, in the neighborhood before this past weekend? Or since?"

"I don't think so and the house he was sitting in front of – that's the other thing that stood out. The house belongs to Judge Harvey, and she's been out of town."

"Could it have been someone there to look in on her home, get the mail, take care of pets, etcetera?"

Katie shook her head.

"Judge Harvey travels a lot. She doesn't have any pets and her mail goes into her house through a mail slot in the door so no one will know if she has picked it up unless they go to her door and look. She has her television and lights on timers and always parks her car in the garage so unless she told you she was leaving, you wouldn't know for sure she was gone. She usually lets me know so I can keep an eye on things and this week she is in San Diego visiting her brother."

Frankie laid her pen down and stretched her hand, which was cramping from note taking. She was thankful Katie was willing to talk. She had provided some valuable background information but now it was time to get to the hard stuff.

"Katie, can we talk about the other night?"

CHAPTER
FIFTY

KATIE STARED at the teacup as though the answers might somehow lie in the tea leaves. She lifted the cup, sipped from the edge, then returned it to the saucer.

"How about you start with when you got home. Did you notice anything unusual? Talk to anyone?"

"I saw Tessa's car parked on the street but didn't notice any other cars. I'm not even sure the girls were in Hannah's house."

"Did you know Tessa's car before all this happened?"

"No. I mean yeah. I recognized the car as being one that visited Hannah a lot but didn't know it was Tessa's."

"Katie, can you please talk about what happened the other night? The night Tessa came to your door?"

Katie took a deep breath before answering. "I got home from work around 3:30 or 4:00. My sister Maria lives with me, but she wasn't home yet. She's going to medical school and was at the hospital doing rounds 'til after 5. When she got home, we ate the takeout she brought us and started watching television.

"I'm not sure exactly what time it was but out of nowhere I heard something at the backdoor. At first it sounded like something scratching the door, then it became more of a pounding. By the time I got to the door I could hear a woman's voice saying, 'Help me.' I pushed the curtain aside and saw Tessa standing on the porch." Katie choked on the last word and her eyes filled with tears. The two women sat quietly for a few moments before she said, "I'm sorry. I…"

Frankie assured Katie her reaction was normal and to take her time explaining what she saw.

After taking a moment to collect herself Katie said, "She had duct tape on her hands and around her head. It looked like the tape had gone across her mouth, but she had somehow gotten it down and was able to talk."

"What did she say to you," Frankie inquired making a note to ask more about the duct tape.

"While I was cutting the tape from her hands, she told us she and Hannah had been attacked in the garage. Hannah was still in the garage, so I went back to the living room and grabbed my phone while Maria and Tessa ran across the street. Thank goodness I wasn't far behind them. Poor little Hannah. She was lying on the cold floor with tape on her hands, legs, and around her head covering her mouth. I was on the phone with 9-1-1 when I walked in."

"Describe what you saw as you crossed the street."

Katie closed her eyes, recalling the scene from memory.

"The garage door was open, and a light was on. Hannah's car was parked in the garage and both car doors were open. I think the car was running but I'm not sure. Hannah was lying on the floor by the driver's side door and her skirt was pushed up and twisted around her waist. Her panties were pulled down around her knees and her sweater was pushed up and twisted like someone had been holding on to it. And there was blood. Blood on her legs. Blood on the floor. I checked her vitals, and she was tachycardic but breathing. She was unconscious so I gave her a sternum rub to try to rouse her. I pulled her skirt down to try and cover her and had Maria get a blanket from the house to keep her warm until the ambulance could get there."

Frankie took notes as Katie described the scene, mentally comparing it to what she had observed.

"Did Hannah say anything while you were trying to help her?"

"The police got there pretty quickly; I had just covered her up when they arrived. Hannah was moaning. I pulled the tape down off her mouth so she could breathe." Katie took a sip from her teacup. Her hands trembled as she returned it to the saucer. "Tessa. I think she said Tessa. I figured she was wondering about her friend, so I told her Tessa was okay and she was going to be okay, too."

"Had you ever been in Hannah's garage before that night?"

"No. I've driven by when she was coming or going, and the door was up but I can't say I had actually been in the garage prior to that night."

"Okay. I just have a few follow-up questions. You mentioned Tessa's hands were bound together. Can you show me how her hands per positioned?"

Katie thought for a moment and then said, "I thought they were behind her back but now that I think about it, I think they were in front of her. I remember thinking it was odd that she did not remove the duct tape from her head."

Frankie made notations on her notepad, "What about Hannah? How were her hands bound?"

"They were behind her back. She also had tape on her ankles."

Frankie scanned her notes before asking, "Is there anything else you can think of? Anything that maybe didn't seem important? Anything you would like to add?"

"Should I be scared, Detective Thomas? Maria and I live here alone. Should I be worried about our safety?"

Frankie looked up from her notepad and caught the earnestness in Katie's gaze. She wanted to be honest with the woman, but she knew there were no guarantees, and she did not believe in making promises she couldn't keep.

"Dr. Vergaro, I will tell you what I tell all women who live alone. You need to be careful and cautious. Keep your doors and windows locked, but I don't think you need to worry about these guys. You didn't see anyone and don't pose a threat to them." She handed the woman a business card with her work and cellphone numbers and said, "If you remember anything, if you need anything, if anything unusual happens, you can call me. If you feel in danger, call 9-1-1 but otherwise call me. Okay?"

As she took the card Katie said, "Thank you, Detective Thomas."

Frankie stood up and gathered her things, "Thank you for your time and for helping those women the other night."

Katie walked her to the door and asked, "Detective Thomas, do you think you'll find the men that did this? Do you think you'll catch them?"

With one hand on the doorknob Frankie turned around and said, "Yes, I do. We have a great team working on this case and I'm not known for giving up. I promise to do everything I can to get to the bottom of what happened the other night."

With those words Katie nodded. Frankie said good-bye and walked out the door. She knew she had a long road ahead of her but what she told Katie about not giving up was true. As she approached Jim's SUV, she saw he and Mia were walking back with looks of victory on their faces.

"Hey guys! You two look pretty pleased with yourselves."

Jim and Mia updated her on what they learned during their area canvas. No one had seen or heard anything the night of the attack; however, two different neighbors reported seeing an SUV parked facing Hannah's house a few days before the attack. One neighbor thought it was red while the other neighbor was unsure of the color. Both were certain it was a BMW or a Mercedes. One of the neighbors saw someone sitting in the vehicle, most likely a man, smoking a cigar. Neither neighbor got a license plate number but thought it was a dealer tag. One of the neighbors said there was a sticker or shade on the backseat window.

Frankie was pleased with the information they had. It went right along with the rest of the witness statements they had obtained. She looked at the clock on the car radio and said teasingly, "Hey Jim, isn't it about time for your hot date?"

He guffawed as they pulled away from the curb and headed to meet Candie at the Brooksider.

CHAPTER
FIFTY-ONE

WHEN THE TRIO arrived at the restaurant Mia and Frankie grabbed a table while Jim sauntered over to the bar where Candie was already sitting talking to a man wearing a suit with a loosened tie. Frankie scanned the room. She was about to think Candie had not been followed when she saw a man sitting at a table. Frankie was certain the man had been standing in one of the dealership bays earlier that day. She picked up the menu and touched Mia on the arm and pretended to show her something as she gestured toward the man. Mia nodded slightly and laughed, letting her know she understood.

When Jim reached Candie, he leaned in and whispered hello causing her to blush and giggle.

"Who's your friend?" He asked, gesturing to the man on her left.

"Where are my manners? Agent Jim Craven this is Alexandre Kristof. He does the marketing for the dealership. Since I was a little early, he offered to keep me company until you arrived."

Jim extended his hand, "Nice to meet you Alexandre, but if you don't mind, I'd really like to spend some time alone with the lady." He drew out the last words allowing his southern accent to come through stronger.

"Not a problem, I was just leaving. I'm meeting a lovely school-teacher for dinner at Kona Grill on the Plaza. Enjoy your cocktails.

Candie, I'll see you at my house Saturday," Kristof winked at her then walked away.

Candie let out a nervous giggle and said she would see him there. She offered to Jim, "He's having a party Saturday night. He has a party most Saturday nights. I usually go... unless someone makes me a better offer."

Jim picked up on her hint and replied non-committedly by saying, "We'll just have to see about that. Tell me a little bit about yourself, Miss Candie. Where'd you grow up? How'd you end up working at Stevenson? What are your hopes and dreams darlin'?"

Candie told Jim about growing up in a small town east of Kansas City with dreams of leaving and making something of herself.

"I graduated high school a couple of years ago and moved to the city. I started attending classes the community colleges but was having a hard time making ends meet. One of my friends invited me to work with her one night at the Shady Lady on 12th Street. The money was good, and the hours were flexible so one time turned into two and eventually a part-time job.

"One night while I was dancing, Anthony Maggio approached me and asked if I had ever thought of leaving the club and doing something better with my life. I told Maggio I was in school and studying business, so he offered me a job at the dealership as a receptionist. He told me it was just a start. I've only been working at Stevenson's for about a year. They paid me well and I no longer had to dance to make ends meet.

"When Midori took over, he continued to make promises, telling me if I kept doing a good job, I would get a chance to work where the real money was – in sales or finance. I don't really want to work in car sales but I was trying to do a good job so I can build my resume and someday do something else besides answering phones and greeting customers all day."

Jim asked Candie to tell him about the people she worked with. She was happy to oblige and rambled on with gossip of the business as they sipped their drinks. By her second Cosmopolitan, she opened up even more, sharing stories about Tessa, Hannah, and Christina. She seemed miffed that none of them included her in their social outings but chalked it up to jealousy. Candie had a high opinion of herself and made sure

Jim knew she frequently had men falling all over themselves to ask her out.

"That intimidated those little bitches," she hissed.

Candie continued talking about the parties and store politics but never mentioned Maggio.

Jim waited until she was taking a drink out of her third Cosmo before he asked, "What do you think of Mr. Maggio? How was he to work for?"

A shadow came over Candie's face and the easy smile quickly vanished. She played with the swizzle stick resting on her glass before saying, "I think I should call it a night. I have an early day tomorrow."

Jim knew he'd hit a nerve and wanted to explore it a bit further so he turned up the southern charm and said, "Aw baby, it's still so early. Can't we at least finish this drink before you go?"

He let a slow, easy smile cross his face. Frankie was watching from the table she shared with Mia. She didn't know what had happened, but she knew whatever it was Candie was going to be putty in Jim's hands with that smile.

Candie smiled and answered, "Okay, but this has to be the last one."

CHAPTER
FIFTY-TWO

SIGNALING to the bartender Candie asked, "Can I get a glass of water please?"

As the bartender placed a glass of water in front of her, Jim touched her hand with his right and raised his left and said, "Scout's honor." Candie didn't need to know he had never been a Boy Scout, he thought. "Now, darlin' where were we? Oh yeah, you were telling me what it was like to work for Maggio."

"There really isn't much to say. He hit on anything in a skirt. The 'uniform' we wear is all because of him. He frequently told us, 'Sex sells, so you need to look sexy.' I don't even sell freaking cars. I just answer the phones, but he doesn't care. 'It's an image,' he said. 'A branding.' As much as it pissed me off to say it, he's right. He had Hannah and Tessa do all those billboard and magazine ads wearing the 'uniform' and within a week of the ads being launched we had an increase in foot traffic. More men came in to buy cars – either for themselves or their wives. Nobody cared why they came in as long as they sold cars."

"Did you ever have any run-ins with Maggio?"

Candie fidgeted in her seat, stirring the swizzle stick, and looking anywhere but at him.

"He was always a bit too friendly to me but for the most part he kept his hands to himself. The only comments I ever heard him make were about Hannah and Tessa; he was obsessed with those two. He thought they were a couple and he made it obvious that he wanted to watch them do…stuff."

Candie stopped and looked back at her drink. He placed his hand on her arm waiting for her to continue.

"I made a point of not ever being alone with Maggio. He gives me the creeps."

He spoke softly when he asked, "Why's that darlin'?"

Candie continued to look at her drink, moving the swizzle stick from side to side. When she finally looked up, she had tears welling in her eyes.

"One night I was at Kristof's for one of his killer parties, I think it was the 4th of July, and Maggio showed up. There was a live band playing, everyone was swimming and dancing, and, of course, drinking. I saw Maggio walk in, but I was hanging out with one of the guys from the repair shop, Josh, so I waved hello and went back to doing shots with Josh.

"Josh got hammered. I mean stupid hammered. Kristof has a rule about not letting people drive home after drinking at his house so when he saw how lit Josh was, he helped me take him to one of the guest rooms to sleep it off. When we laid him down Kristof touched my ass and told me I could stay with Josh or if I wanted to, I could sleep in his room with him. I just laughed it off and told him I'd be back down to the party after I went to the bathroom." Candie took the last drink from her Cosmo and asked, "Jason, can I get another glass of water? This time with lemon please? Thanks.

"When I came out of the bathroom Maggio was standing in the hall. I told him 'It's all yours' and gestured towards the bathroom. He reached over and grabbed my waist and said, 'Really?' I pushed on his chest and told him I was referring to the bathroom, but he kept a hold of my waist and started trying to kiss my neck. I told him to knock it off. I was about to use the heel of my shoe to stomp on his foot when he let me go. I walked away and went back to the party. Maggio waited upstairs for a couple of minutes and then came back to the party.

"After everyone left the party, I was trying to decide if I wanted to go back upstairs to Josh or catch a cab home. I knew I couldn't drive but wasn't sure about staying at Kristof's since I'd never stayed there before. Maggio came up to me again and this time asked if I liked my job and if I thought Josh liked his. I told him we both liked our jobs, why was he asking? He took his finger and traced it along my shoulder blades and told me I should think about how much we both like our jobs before I start running my mouth off about the 'misunderstanding' in the hallway. I told him there was no misunderstanding and I had no intentions of saying anything if he left me alone. He offered me a glass of wine and said, 'truce?'"

Candie took a long drink of water.

"I accepted the glass of wine and before I could call a cab Kristof came in and asked Maggio and I if we wanted to join him and his girl-friend - the schoolteacher he said he was going to meet tonight - in the hot tub. That's really the last thing I remember about that night. When I woke up the next morning I was in bed with Josh; naked and sore." Tears were trickling down her cheeks as she said the word naked. "I didn't think I drank that much but I guess the wine really pushed me over the edge."

Jim squeezed Candie's forearm, "What happened when you woke up?"

She brushed the tears from her cheeks and gave a half-hearted laugh, "What do you mean? I got dressed and went downstairs. Kristof cooked me a gourmet breakfast, gave me a tall glass of water and a shot of tequila along with a couple of ibuprofens. When Josh woke up, we both left."

Jim watched as she composed herself and downed the glass of water.

"Josh and I talked later and both of us are pretty sure nothing happened. He was out of it and, well, I was, too. I probably took my own clothes off when I got back to the bedroom. I mean after all I was drunk. I never did figure out why I was sore though."

Jim wasn't sure who Candie was trying to convince that nothing happened, him or herself. She wiped the remaining tears from her face and tried to laugh it off. Candie started to apologize, "I cannot believe I told you that. I haven't talked to anyone about it since that night."

"I'm glad you did," Jim said.

The two talked for a few more minutes before she told him she really had to leave. Jim stood when Candie did and kissed her lightly on the cheek.

"It's been a pleasure talking to you, Miss Candie."

"It's been a pleasure talking to you, Jim. Thank you for the drinks. Perhaps we can do it again sometime?"

He let a smile stretch across his face and into his eyes, "Perhaps" and watched her sashay out of the bar.

CHAPTER
FIFTY-THREE

JIM TOLD Frankie and Mia the full story on the drive back to their office. Frankie looked to Mia and asked, "Are you thinking what I'm thinking?"

"Yep," responded Mia.

"Well do you mind filling me in?" asked Jim.

"Frankie thinks Candie was drugged and raped," answered Mia. "Probably by Maggio but Kristof could have been in on it, too. The way you describe her loss of memory and her waking up naked is consistent with her being given something so she wouldn't remember."

"Hmm. Do you think we should call her in and talk to her some more?" Jim asked.

Frankie paused briefly before replying, "No, I don't. I don't think she realizes she was drugged and probably raped. After this much time has passed there is no physical evidence and no forensic examination to pull from. Add to that the most important fact - she doesn't identify herself as a victim. As horrible as this is, I'm not sure it would help her to see what happened through a different lens. But something tells me this isn't the last we've heard of Kristof and when we catch another case with his name attached, we will call her in and see if she will give us a full statement. If the facts are substantive, we can send it to the prosecutor's and let Lady Justice do her thing."

The trio drove for a moment in silence, each lost in their own thoughts. Frankie had retrieved her cell phone and was texting as Jim was grappling with what to do with this newfound knowledge. He wanted to do something for this young girl and the more he thought about it, the angrier he got.

"So, what you are saying is we have to wait for another victim. How many victims will be enough? How many cases do you have to have before you put your fucking phone down and do something?"

Jim slammed the palm of his hand hard against the steering wheel as he drove. His jaw was clenched in anger and his mouth twisted in frustration. The vein in his neck pulsed harder as his blood pressure rose.

Frankie took a deep breath. She finished her text and turned her body in the seat to face him before she said, "Jim, I know how frustrating this is. Believe me – it pisses me off, too. But we are fact finders, not judgers of fact. We cannot open a case or arrest a person based off a conversation you and Candie had over drinks. A conversation, I might add, where she did not say she was raped or ask for a report to be taken. Based on her body language and disdain for Maggio I would say she has a pretty good idea something happened, but she isn't ready to talk about it – yet. She may not be ready to admit it to herself – yet. Mia and I won't forget about the conversation, and we will follow up if his name comes up again. We just have to have more before we do. As for my phone, I was texting one of my buddies in the drug enforcement unit to see if they had any info on Maggio or Kristof. I wanted to see if they have any drug cases linked to those guys."

Jim began to say something but then stopped. He was frustrated with himself for losing his cool. He had let his history impact his present. Jim was passionate on the worst of days, and this hit a little too close to home for him.

FIFTY-FOUR

AFTER DRIVING a few more blocks he pulled over to the side of the street and put the SUV into park. Jim turned to face Frankie.

"I'm sorry for losing my shit." Mia tried to interrupt to say it was okay, but he held up his hand and said, "Let me finish. I should have trusted you all. I've seen enough to know you both care and are damn good at your jobs. This just hit a little too close to home for me.

"Candie reminded me of my younger sister Jocelyn. She followed me to college and in the middle of my senior year I got a call from the hospital. Jocelyn had been brought in, high and barely conscious. She had gone to a fraternity party with one of her friends and they got separated. One of her friends found her half naked in a hallway on the second floor of the house. Instead of calling 9-1-1 she half-drug, half carried, Jocelyn to her car and took her to the hospital. She found my number and called me so the hospital wouldn't call mom and dad. They tested her urine, and it tested positive for GHB. I don't know if she had a forensic exam, but I know she never made a police report. Joc was so different after that. I'm mad about what those guys did to Candie, but I think I'm madder at myself, mad that I didn't pick up on what she was telling me."

"Dang Jim, that's rough. How's your sister now?" asked Mia.

Mia saw tears in his eyes when he turned toward her.

"She struggled the rest of that year but she's doing a lot better now. She got married and bought a house across the bay from mom and dad."

Frankie smiled and winked at Mia, "Jim, you know your accent gets thicker when you're mad. It's kind of sexy."

Jim laughed. He put the car back in drive and pulled away from the curb. The three chatted amiably about the weather and football as they drove back to police headquarters. He dropped Frankie and Mia off at the garage entrance. Frankie was preparing to exit the car when Jim reached across the console and grabbed her arm. His stare bore into her, "Call if you need anything, okay?"

Frankie returned his stare, captivated by his penetrating gaze. She nodded and replied, "Sure thing, Jim." Her nod broke the spell causing him to release her arm as she finished, "I'll let you know what the Drug Enforcement Unit comes up with."

THE REST of the evening went by quickly. Frankie and Mia worked on reports while the sound of holiday movies played on the television. The two did not feel the need to fill the silence with idle chatter when there was work that needed to be done.

The sound of the phone ringing pierced the silence, "Sex Crimes, Detective Thomas."

"Got any sex?" asked Gary Kinder from the local news station.

"Got nothin' for you, Killer."

"How's your Waldo case coming along, Frankie?"

"It's coming," she was intentionally vague.

"Can you tell me anything?"

"Now Gary, you know better than to ask me that. You know I can't talk about open investigations."

"Alright, Frankie, but I want the scoop when you can give it."

"Sure thing, Gary. Have a good one." She hung up the phone, turned and asked Mia, "You about ready to call it?"

"Mhm. Give me a second," she said with a pen clinched between her teeth. She stared intently at the computer and typed. When she was finished typing, she scribbled something on her notepad and put a thin file folder back inside her desk drawer. "Let me grab my gun and coat."

Frankie and Mia made small talk as they walked to the elevator. Once inside Mia turned to Frankie and asked, "What's up with you and Jim?"

Frankie blushed. She looked at Mia and answered her question with a question of her own, "What do you mean? There's nothing 'up' with Jim and I."

"Hm. Whatever you say, Frankie. I think that guy has got a thing for you."

The elevator door opened in the basement of the building and the women walked toward the exit in silence. When they reached the door to go outside Mia put her hand on Frankie's arm and said softly, "Just be careful."

Frankie opened her mouth to respond but before she could say anything her cell phone rang, "Thomas." Frankie stood at the door and listened to the person on the other end of the phone, reached into her bag and grabbed her notepad and pen and said, "Mhm hm. Where are you? Okay. Give me fifteen minutes and I'll be out. Have you called Crime Scene yet? No, I'll call them. Okay. See you then." She disconnected the phone and said, "Fuck me."

"What do you have?"

She began to take inventory of her bag while she answered, "Attempted rape at 24th and Bellefontaine. Straubel has a woman who said a guy tried to rape her. They have a possible crime scene in the alley but no suspect in custody so hopefully I can get a statement from her while crime scene takes some photographs and collects whatever they can. Then I can make my way north."

"Want some help?"

She looked up from her bag and answered, "Thanks Mia, but go on home and spend some quality time with Erik. This shouldn't take long. Are you working tomorrow?"

Mia nodded, "Yep. I'll see you then. Call me if it turns into a cluster and you need help."

As they began walking to their cars she answered, "You know I will. Thanks Mee."

While Frankie let the unmarked police car warm up, she called the Crime Scene Unit and asked them to meet her at 24th and Bellefontaine to process a possible crime scene. After hanging up, she made the dreaded call to Derek.

After only one ring he answered with a smile in his voice, "Hey Frankie, are you on the way?"

She hesitated before answering, "I wish. Unfortunately, I have to go out to 24th and Bellefontaine first. Hopefully it won't take long. Wait up for me?"

"I'll try but if I don't make it feel free to wake me up when you come in," he answered with a hint of disappointment in his voice.

Frankie told Derek she would be there soon then disconnected the call. She listened to the air traffic on the police radio as she drove. A couple of car checks, 9-1-1 calls and a house alarm that was disregarded before the cars arrived. *"Quiet for a Friday night in the city,"* she thought. *"Hard to believe it could all change in an instant."*

When Frankie approached the scene, she made a mental note of what she saw. There was an ambulance parked on the side of the street facing Bellefontaine with a patrol car parked slightly in front. Standing outside of the ambulance door was a young officer listening to an animated young woman talk. She was flailing her hands about as she paced two to three steps in each direction. After putting the car in park Frankie grabbed her notepad and walked toward the scene wondering who was in charge, the officer or the woman.

FIFTY-SIX

THE WIND WAS COLD, causing Frankie to suck in her breath as she walked toward scene. The closer Frankie got to the woman the more obvious it became that she was not only traumatized but possibly a little inebriated. The officer was exercising patience, letting the woman move about. She was complaining that she wanted a cigarette and was not planning to wait all night for a "damn pencil pusher" to come and talk to her.

"Good evening, ma'am. My name is Detective Thomas and I'm with the Sex Crimes Unit. Thank you for waiting for me to drive out here."

"It's about damn time. I've got things to do. I already told this guy what happened. I'm not sure why the hell I had to wait on you anyway. Can't he write a report or something?"

The woman's voice was deep and gruff, like that of someone who has smoked for many years. As she talked, she continued to pace with a nervous energy that reminded Frankie of a caged wild animal.

"Miss…I'm sorry, can you please tell me your name?"

"Lorelei Rain."

"Miss Rain, would you mind if we sat in my car while we talk? It's a bit warmer and we'll have a little privacy."

Before Lorelei could answer the paramedic opened the back door to the ambulance. "Miss Lorelei." The sound of Bruce's voice caused

Frankie to look up from her notepad. "Are you sure we can't give you a ride to the hospital to be checked out?"

Lorelei smiled at him and coughed her smoker's cough, "I told you I'm fine. I'm not going to any damn hospital."

Bruce's voice was soft, and his tone told Lorelei he genuinely cared. He explained the paperwork he needed signed and handed her his clipboard directing her where to sign.

"Okay, Miss Lorelei, I'm on all night so if you have any trouble breathing, I want you to call 9-1-1 so I can come get you and take you to get checked out."

Lorelei nodded, smiled at him, and then turned to Frankie and said with a gruff voice, "Can we get this over with?"

Frankie looked over her shoulder at Bruce and mouthed the words "thank you" as she opened the door of her car and directed Lorelei to have a seat.

When Frankie sat down inside the car, she turned down the police radio, pulled out her audio recorder, and told Lorelei she would be recording their conversation. Frankie started to gather basic demographics but quickly learned Lorelei was unhoused, so she started asking about her family and daily routine.

"I usually have breakfast at the mission. When they make me leave, I go to the park and read if the weather is nice. If it's raining or cold, I go to the library. I love to read and always have a book in my bag.

"I try to go to the Shower House on 10th Street for lunch because they let me shower and do laundry a couple of days a week. If the weather's really bad, they let me stay until closing as long as I help out with chores. For dinner, I go to whatever church has their soup kitchen open. I usually sleep in abandoned buildings or abandoned cars in the bad weather and under the stars in the park in good weather. Once a week I go to my mother's house to see my daughter and take her to church on Sunday. I never miss a week."

Frankie listened intently while Lorelei described her routine and life on the streets. She suspected she was being used in prostitution but wanted to hear what had transpired that night before asking. If Lorelei trusted her, she would divulge any illegal activity she may have been involved in.

When she finished talking Frankie said, "Miss Lorelei, before you tell me about what happened tonight, I want you to know it is very important that you tell me everything. I've been doing this job a long time and sometimes people leave things out. It's not always intentional. Sometimes they forget or are worried about what I'll think, or they are worried they will get in trouble. I'm a good investigator and I always find that thing they left out – whatever that thing was – and it looks like, to the prosecutor, that the person lied. Even though I know it wasn't intentional, that there were reasons the person didn't tell the complete truth, the prosecutor will often refuse to take the case. So, I'll make a deal with you. I'll be 100-percent honest with you, but I need you to be 100-percent honest with me. If there were drugs or prostitution involved, I want you to know I will not arrest you. I just need you to tell me because we can work with it if we know about it up front."

LORELEI LOOKED out the windshield of the car into the dark night. The crackling of the police radio could be heard faintly and, just as Frankie was about to say her name, Lorelei looked over at her with tears welling in her eyes.

"I was standing on the corner of 39th Street and Prospect trying to make a date, so I could score some crack, when this guy pulled up. I haven't been out much lately because I've been trying to kick this habit. I mean, I used to have a couple hundred dollar a day habit and I've gotten it down to about $40 a day, so I've been doing pretty good. Anyway, this guy driving a nice car and seemed nice. When he stopped, I got in and asked him what he wanted. He asked me how much for head and all I could think of was I wanted a rock and a cheeseburger, so I told him twenty bucks. He agreed and started to drive up Prospect. He drove around and ended up in the alley over there."

Lorelei pointed toward the alleyway near the ambulance.

"When he pulled down the alleyway, he got really weird. Suddenly he was agitated. He had this look in his eyes and I decided I needed to get the hell out of that car. When he stopped, I tried to open the door, but it was locked and wouldn't open. I told him he better unlock the freaking door but when he put the car in park, he pulled out a gun. He told me I was nothing but a stupid whore and forced me into the backseat of the car."

Tears flowed down Lorelei's cheeks and her fingers tapped the dashboard of the police car.

Lorelei paused for a moment to compose herself and then said, "He couldn't get it up at first. That made him angry, so he hit me, and started choking me. I started gasping and pulling at his hand until he stopped. Then he slapped me again. After he slapped me the second time his dick got hard, and he raped me. When he was done, he unlocked the doors and told me to get out. He threw my clothes at me and drove off with my bag in the car."

"What can you tell me about the car?"

"It was gray or white. Four doors. Had leather interior with a nice stereo. It was a Honda or something like it. I couldn't get it all, but I think the first two numbers on the license plate were 8A."

"What about the man? What did he look like?"

"He was a black guy. Kind of big. Not fat, just muscular. Like a football player. He was strong. He had a fade haircut and was dressed nice. He was probably about forty."

Frankie took notes on Lorelei's description, which sounded all too familiar.

"What does your bag look like?"

"It's blue and white. It has my change of clothes, toothbrush, wallet, and my book."

"What book are you reading, Miss Lorelei?"

"To Kill a Mockingbird," she replied rather demurely.

Frankie smiled to herself, admittedly surprised at Lorelei's choice of literature. "One of my favorites. Is there anything else you can remember?"

"No. Dammit, if I lose that book the library is going to make me pay for it and I won't be allowed to check out anymore."

Frankie saw Lorelei's eyes begin to well up with tears again. She reached over and patted her hand and said, "I'm going to go look for your bag tonight. Will you wait around for a bit while I look?"

"Can I stay in your car?"

Frankie nodded. She got out of the car and gestured toward the patrol officer. Once she was out of Lorelei's earshot she said, "Would you mind keeping an eye on my car for me? Miss Lorelei is going to sit there while I look for her bag."

The officer nodded in agreement. She walked toward the alley just as the crime scene van pulled up. They quickly mobilized after she filled them in on what she wanted photographed. After the photographs were captured, they began walking the alleyway. As they walked Frankie decided if they didn't find the bag she was going to go to the library and pay for the book. She knew books were the only true escape Lorelei had from her hard life and was probably part of what kept her from going insane.

About three quarters of the way to the end of the alley she saw a flash of white out of the corner of her eye. Upon closer inspection, she realized it was the blue and white backpack. After the crime scene technician photographed it, with her gloved hands she picked up the bag and looked inside. The bag held a wallet, some clothes, and a copy of To Kill a Mockingbird. She smiled to herself, closed the bag and turned to walk back to her car.

Frankie finished at the scene and then headed to Derek's. As she drove, she thought about Lorelei and the look on her face when she handed her the book, then the bag. It was a combination of surprise, joy, and relief. Lorelei took the book from Frankie and grinned when she saw the bookmark was still where she had left it. Frankie offered to take her to a shelter, but Lorelei declined as she slung the bag across her back and said she had a place to stay nearby. Frankie was pretty sure Lorelei was lying but didn't push the issue. Instead, she made sure Lorelei had her business card then stood by the car and watched her walk down the dark road and disappear into the night.

CHAPTER
FIFTY-EIGHT

DEREK WAS asleep when Frankie got back to his house but he had left the back porch light on so she didn't trip up the steps when she walked to the door. A note was taped to the inside of the door. After she closed the door, she placed her bag on a chair and gun on the table, removed her work shoes, and turned the light on over the sink so she could read the note.

The moment she read the words she felt her heart push its way into her throat at the thoughtfulness the note contained.

Frankie, I'm sorry I couldn't keep my eyes open. I opened a bottle of your favorite wine and left it to chill in the fridge. Your glass is on the counter and bath salts are on the side of the tub if you want a hot bath. Or you can always wake me up and I'll do what I can to warm you up and help you relax. D

She grabbed the glass and bottle of wine and went to the living room where a few lonely embers still glowed in the fireplace. She sat in Derek's chair and when she leaned into the cushion, she smelled the fresh scent of his cologne. As she sipped the wine, she felt the tension in her neck and shoulders lessen. With each sip, she put the thoughts of Candie and Lorelei and their stories into separate boxes in her memory bank. By the time she was halfway through the second glass the embers had almost completely died and her thoughts had turned to Derek and his note. She pulled herself out of his chair, put the cork in the bottle, and made her way down the hallway.

Derek woke when she climbed into bed and without a word the two communicated their desires. When they lay spent in one another's arms he asked her about her day. She told him about Candie and all the things she had learned. He agreed with her that it could be more traumatizing to go after Kristof based on the bar talk; however, he made a mental note to see if they had any information on him in their office.

She then told him about Lorelei and the book.

"I want to do something for her. I don't know what, but I want to do something."

"Frankie, you can't save them all. She is out there for a reason and if she wanted to help herself, she would," said a jaded Derek.

Frankie rose from the pillow and propped her head on her hand. The moonlight shown through the window onto his face.

"If you had met her you would understand. This girl is smart. You can tell she doesn't want to be on the streets and doesn't belong there. She hasn't quite kicked the crack habit and doesn't want to go to rehab. You should have seen her face when she realized I found her book. And it was a damn library book. Can you imagine how she'd be if she had one of her own?!"

Her voice rose slightly, and the words came more quickly as she defended Lorelei. The compassion she felt was punctuated by each word she said.

Derek reached across the bed and brushed a strand of hair from Frankie's face. He listened intently as she spoke. He loved how much she cared but worried about her getting hurt. Derek knew she aspired to save the world but also knew it put a lot of pressure on her shoulders to try. Instead of reiterating what he had said earlier he asked, "What did you have in mind?"

She took a moment before responding. She knew there wasn't much she could do for Lorelei unless she was willing to help herself. She didn't want to enable any behavior but wanted her to believe in herself.

"I was thinking a book or two and maybe a pair of gloves. I don't know what kind of coat she has but I may have an extra one at the house I could give her."

"I think that sounds great, Frankie."

Derek leaned in and kissed her on the mouth, gently pushing her back onto the pillow. He looked deeply into her eyes and listened to the hum of the ceiling fan above them. Frankie pulled him back to her waiting lips and softly replied with a kiss full of longing.

The rest of the weekend passed quickly and Sunday morning she started gathering her things together so she could drop Isabelle off at her house, pick up the kids, and meet her dad for brunch before her shift.

Derek walked her to the door, put his arms around her waist and said, "It's going to be awfully quiet around here without you."

Frankie touched his cheek and smiled slightly, "Something tells me you'll manage just fine but for what it's worth, I'm going to miss sleeping next to you, too." She winked at him, "Miss Iz just isn't the same."

Derek leaned down and kissed her on the lips, then hugged her tight. He rested his cheek on her head and without saying the words he let her know just how he felt when he said, "Be safe out there tonight."

"Always," was her reply. She released the hug and walked out the door.

BEFORE FRANKIE COULD GET home to drop the dog off her cellphone started ringing. "Thomas."

"Hey Frankie, it's Jim. Did I catch you at a bad time?"

"Nope. Just heading to the house to drop my dog off and then to brunch at my dad's house before my shift. What's up?"

"Not much. I had to go into the office and thought I'd see what you had on the agenda for tonight."

"I think I'm going to call the girls and see if they'll come in and let me download their phones," she answered. "I've requested the phone records but that can take a while."

"Is Mia in tonight?"

"No, I'm flying solo."

"Want some help?"

"I should be good but thanks."

With a hint of disappointment in his voice he said, "Okay, give me a call if you change your mind."

Frankie assured Jim she would call him if she needed help before disconnecting the phone. She had brunch with her family and then dropped her kids at the house before going to work. After getting briefed by the day shift detective, Frankie pulled out the case file to get Hannah and Tessa's phone numbers. She called Hannah first and had to leave her a voicemail, but Tessa answered on the second ring.

"Tessa, it's Detective Thomas."

"Hi, detective. Do you have news for me?"

"Unfortunately, no. I was wondering if you would be willing to come to my office this evening."

Her request was met with silence.

After a few moments Tessa cautiously asked, "What do you need, detective?"

Frankie was quick on her feet, "I've been working all weekend and just had a few follow-up questions. I'm working tonight and thought it would be a good time to meet since you wouldn't have to mess with downtown traffic."

She could hear a tapping sound through the phone. It sounded like Tessa was either texting or typing on a computer. After a moment of silence Tessa said, "What time would you like me to come in, detective?"

"Would 5 give you enough time to get around and get here?"

"Is Hannah coming, too?"

She was not surprised Tessa asked about Hannah and would be even less surprised if she found out she had been messaging her as they talked.

"I've left her a message but if you talk to her would you mind mentioning that I would like to talk to her, too?"

Tessa perked up noticeably, "Of course. We'll see you at 5. Will Olivia and Beth be there, too?"

"I haven't contacted them; would you like an advocate? Since it's Sunday I can't guarantee they'll be the ones to respond."

"No, I think it will be fine. See you soon!"

As Frankie hung up the phone she thought about the brief conversation and wondered how she would get Tessa to let her view the phone. She was not sure she even knew what she expected to find. Was it possible Tessa had sent a text to someone telling him or her when she and Hannah were on the way?

CHAPTER
SIXTY

TRUE TO FORM, the women arrived together and on time. Frankie escorted them to the interview room and instead of trying to divide them, she allowed them to sit together. Once inside the interview room she asked the women, "How have you two been the last few days?"

Before Hannah could speak Tessa said, "It's been stressful. I am so nervous all the time. I mean, what if they try to do something even worse?"

"Has anything unusual happened since the attack? You've been staying at your house, right?"

"I'm staying at home. Nothing odd has happened since last week," replied Tessa.

Hannah sat quietly and waited for Tessa to finish before saying, "That car was back again last night. And I think someone was following me earlier today."

Frankie turned to Hannah and asked, "Since you called me the last time?"

"Yeah, it was late last night but I didn't want to bother you. I went to dinner with my parents and when we got home, the same car from the other night was parked on my block. I called the police but when they got there the car was gone again. Then today I was driving to get my paycheck and I swear this guy was following me when I left. I was going to go by my house but when I saw him following me, I headed straight to my parent's house. Eventually he turned off."

"Hannah, what did the car from last night look like?"

"Same as before. Dark sedan. Guy smoking in the driver's seat. It was too dark to get much else."

"What about the car from today?"

"It was a few years old. American made but higher end. Maybe a Lincoln?" Hannah said with a hint of question in her voice.

"Have you ever seen any vehicles like these around your house before?"

Before Hannah could answer Tessa said, "I think Maggio's buddy has a Lincoln Town Car. He usually drives a car from the dealership, but I've seen him in the Town Car a few times."

"Who's Maggio's buddy?" Frankie asked, wondering if she was referring to Midori.

Tessa perked up slightly, "His name is Craig Midori. If Maggio's around, Midori's not too far behind. Maggio hired him as soon as he took over as the GM, but it was very apparent there was a long history with those two. They're very close."

"Did either of you ever have any run-ins with Midori?"

Tessa quickly said, "The guy's an ass. It was obvious he didn't like me and didn't like the attention Maggio gave Hannah and I. I think he was a bit jealous."

Frankie looked at Hannah and asked, "What about you? Did you ever have any run-ins with him?"

Hannah was thoughtful in her response, choosing her words carefully. "He could be gruff, but he was always nice enough to me. He treated Tessa kind of shitty though."

Frankie took notes while the women talked. "Did either of you exchange text messages with Maggio?"

Hannah looked at Tessa then to Frankie before saying, "He texted me a few times. Every now and then he would call but after a while I stopped answering the phone when I saw it was him calling."

"He messaged me, too," said Tessa. "He finally stopped when we got an attorney."

Frankie produced a consent form and asked each woman if they would be willing to let her review their phones. She wanted to hook it up to a device and copy all the data from each phone. Although the harassing texts could be a great tool for their lawsuit, she was hoping the information on the phones would either support her theory that one of them alerted the attacker or it would put it to rest.

After a few moments of chatter amongst the women, they both agreed to let her review their phones. She brought the device into the room and completed the download while the women watched. As she was working on the phones, she continued to talk to them in the hopes additional information might surface.

When the phones had downloaded, Frankie escorted the women to the lobby and returned to her office to finish her shift.

CHAPTER
SIXTY-ONE

"WHAT THE FUCK? Why'd they want to look at your phone?"

"I don't think it's that big of a deal. The detective just wanted to see if we had any harassing text messages from Maggio or his attorneys. She isn't going to find anything other than texts from Roni trying to get me to come back to her," answered Tessa.

"Are you sure there is nothing else on your phone? Emails or anything?"

"No. I told you. Relax, there's nothing on my phone. I used a pre-paid phone the other night and threw it away at the hospital. I don't think she suspects anything anyway. I'll call you if anything comes up. In the meantime, back off Hannah. Every time you go by her house, she calls that detective. It's only a matter of time before they catch you over there."

"I'm just following orders and, if you know what's good for you, that's what you'll do too."

"I've done everything they've asked me to do," she said in exasperation.

"The boss is getting impatient. He wants his money."

"He'll get it. Once this damn lawsuit is settled, I'll be liquid and when I get my cash, he'll get his. The more you freak Hannah out the more likely she's going to drop the suit."

"You better make sure she doesn't. If the boss gets wind, she is even thinking about it he's gonna give different orders."

Tessa's voice trembled, "I'll make sure she doesn't. She's just scared. If you back off, I think I can keep her in line."

The gruff response she received sent a chill down her back. She just wanted money. Tessa didn't want Hannah to get hurt but she had to figure out a way to keep her from running scared.

CHAPTER
SIXTY-TWO

FRANKIE FINISHED her shift and made her way to her Jeep. Her shoulders ached and her eyes burned. It was her last night on call and she hoped it would be a quiet one. She was supposed to be off the next day but had made plans to meet Fitz to do some interviews.

As she entered her neighborhood, she thought she saw a high-end SUV following her. She wondered how long it had been behind her. She drove out of her neighborhood to see if the SUV followed her or if she was just being paranoid. The SUV stayed a reasonable distance behind, but it was definitely following her. When she slowed, it slowed. When she drove faster, it drove faster.

Frankie's heart pounded in her chest. She pulled onto the highway and headed south. The SUV pulled onto the highway and stayed about two car lengths behind her. There was a gas station at the next exit, so she quickly pulled off without signaling her direction. The SUV followed suit. Instinct took over and Frankie pulled her Jeep into the first gas station in sight; a gas station frequented by law enforcement. Before exiting the vehicle, she made sure her firearm was on her hip and her phone was readily available.

The SUV did not pull into the gas station but slowly passed by. It stopped at the traffic light, so Frankie grabbed her phone and zoomed the camera and tried to get a photograph of the license plate. After she was certain it was gone, she went into the store, showed her creds, and asked to see the surveillance video. The store cameras reached to the street allowing her to get a still photo of the SUV and a glimpse of the driver's profile. She had the clerk run a copy of the video for her, then sat in her car before heading back to her house.

She was happy Sophie had decided to stay at the farm with their brother and Keith and Bruce were at the house. Sophie could handle herself, but it was one more person Frankie would worry about. Frankie debated on calling Derek but knew he was probably already in bed. They were picking a jury in the murder trial the following day and she didn't want to worry him. As she sat in the parking lot, with trembling hands she pulled out her cell phone and placed a call.

"Cr…" Jim cleared his throat then said, "Craven."

Frankie wasn't sure why she called him except she knew she needed to talk to someone about what happened. "Hey Jim, it's Frankie. Sorry if I woke you."

"Hey Frankie! What's up? I was just lying in bed watching TV. Are you okay?"

Just as she began to think she had overreacted Frankie saw the SUV backed into a parking spot across the street. She couldn't be certain, but she thought she saw the glow of a cigar coming from the driver's seat. "Jim, I think I'm being followed."

He sat up in his bed and asked, "Are you sure? Where are you? Did you call dispatch?"

"I'm sitting in a gas station lot on Armour Road in Northtown. And yeah, I'm sure. I didn't go home because I noticed the SUV tailing me. I've seen it near my house before but thought I was being paranoid. I was able to get pictures of the vehicle from the gas station surveillance camera. I thought it was gone but then when I was getting ready to go home, I saw it again. It's backed into a lot near where I'm sitting." She hit the steering wheel of her Jeep. "Dammit! This is my house, Jim. My kids."

"I can be there in five. We can car check him."

"Alright. I'm going to call dispatch and get a radio car over here, too." Frankie texted Keith and told him something had come up but she would be home soon.

CHAPTER
SIXTY-THREE

FRANKIE HUNG UP WITH DISPATCH, waited, and watched. After a few moments, she saw the vehicle start to move. Frankie put the Jeep in first and prepared to follow the SUV.

"Let's see how you like being followed, asshole."

The SUV pulled out and headed west on Armour Road. Frankie waited about thirty seconds and then pulled in behind. Her chest tightened. Frankie tried to stay far enough back so she wouldn't spook him.

As she drove, Frankie called Jim, "I'm following this guy. We're heading west on Armour Road towards Burlington. Where're you coming from?"

"Frankie," he started to chastise her and then realized she was going to continue following the SUV regardless of what he said so he needed to offer to help her. "I'm at 18th and Burlington now. What cross street are you at?"

"We are coming right towards you. We just turned south onto Burlington towards the River Market," she answered. She was grateful he was jumping into action. "I'm in a red Jeep Wrangler. The SUV is about two blocks ahead of me. Once you intercept it and get behind it, I'll call dispatch so they can tell the radio where we are."

"Call off the radio car. It might work to our benefit if we can see where this guy is going."

"Copy. Once we cross the bridge, I'll try to parallel you guys or at least hang back."

"I've got 'em, Frankie. Hang back. Turn off in case he's seen you." Jim could see her when she turned left. "Great. Drive a few blocks and then pull out behind me. Keep my vehicle in sight but try to stay out of his."

"Copy. I'm going to call dispatch and then I'll call you right back."

Frankie disconnected the phone and called dispatch. She told them to cancel the radio car and told them she and Jim were in the area doing surveillance; she left out the fact they were tailing a car and were off duty. Frankie drove about three blocks south and then made the necessary maneuvers to get back behind Jim. Two blocks away she dialed his number.

"Hey, Jim. I'm about two blocks behind you. What do you think this guy's up to?"

"Looks like he's heading to the northeast area. We just turned east on the avenue. Why don't you hang back? I'll try to get a little closer, see where he's going, and then I'll rally back up with you."

Frankie was exasperated. She wanted to be part of what was going on but at the same time she knew Jim was right. He had a better shot at getting closer and gathering more intel if she hung back. So, she drove back to the old police academy at 13th and Agnes and waited.

"Frankie, where'd you say you were parked?"

"13th and Agnes, why?"

"After cruising Independence Avenue and Prospect this guy just parked at 12th and Chestnut. Wait, he's getting out. Looks like he's going inside a strip club across the street. Why don't I come pick you up and we'll watch this guy for a while?"

Frankie and Jim sat about a block away from the club making small talk for about thirty minutes before they saw the guy walk out.

"Does that guy look familiar to you, Jim? I feel like I've seen him somewhere before."

Jim watched the guy walk to the SUV, climb in, and pull away. He waited until the SUV passed them and was a block away before he pulled out, turned the lights on, and began to follow him. They didn't have to drive long before the SUV pulled into the driveway of a historic home off 3rd and Lydia. They watched the man grab his coat and head in the backdoor of the house.

Jim was about to pull up to get an address when Frankie touched his arm and said, "Wait. Watch for the lights. Make sure he's inside."

The pair watched as the various lights illuminated then extinguished until finally a light stayed on in a room on the second floor. Jim looked at Frankie and said, "I think he's in for the night. You ready?"

Frankie let out the breath she didn't even realize she was holding. "Yeah. Drive by and I'll get the house address."

After getting the address they drove back to her car in silence. Frankie believed Jim was going to chew her out when they got back to her car but when he parked all he said was, "Thanks for calling me. Do you want me to follow you home? Just to be sure?"

Frankie shook her head, "No. Thank you though. I'll be fine."

As she exited the vehicle Jim reached over and grabbed her hand, "Be careful, Frankie. Watch your six."

She nodded. Jim released her hand so she could get out of the car.

Frankie hands were still shaking during the drive home. Why had someone followed her? Was it this case or one of the others she was working on? Should she call Sergeant Baker? Should she tell Derek? Sophie? Keith and Bruce? Were her kids in danger? In the ten minutes it took her to get to her house she decided it was best if she didn't tell anyone. She and Jim had an address and a name - Joseph Westin. Dispatch couldn't find anything other than a couple of traffic violations when they ran the name and the vehicle, but she had a few other databases she wanted to check. She was certain there was something out there and she would find it.

CHAPTER
SIXTY-FOUR

FRANKIE WAS STILL a little unnerved when she got home and stood in her door at the ready while Keith walked the short distance to his house. After scanning the neighborhood and double-checking the locks on the doors and windows she had finally gone to bed only to find sleep elusive. After what seemed like only minutes the alarm went off and a tired Frankie rallied and got her kids up to go to school.

She dropped Tyler at school first and then drove Dani to her school. Before pulling into the carpool lane, she looked at Dani and said, "Meet Ty at the bus stop today and walk home together."

"Ugh, why mom? He walks home by himself all the time. I'm usually doing my homework by then."

"Just do it Dani," Frankie paused then added, "Do it because I asked you to."

Something about the look in Frankie's eyes made Dani pause before launching an argument.

"Okay mom," was Dani's only response.

"Call me the minute you are both home and inside. Don't let Ty play outside today either. I should be home by dinner."

Again, something about Frankie's look made her answer "Okay" without any argument.

"I love you Angel-girl," she said using the nickname she had coined when Dani was just an infant.

"Love you too, mom. Be safe today."

"Always," was her reply as Dani got out of the vehicle. Frankie returned home, donned her running attire and grabbed the dog leash. "Come on Iz. Time to burn off some of this nervous energy."

Frankie was debating on whether to grab her gun when her phone began to ring.

"Thomas."

"Hey, Frankie. It's Jim."

"Hey Jim. I was just about to go for a run, what's up?"

Frankie looked at her watch. She only had an hour before she would have to start getting ready to go meet Fitz. She didn't have time for small talk or mindless chatter.

"Want some company? We can talk while we run," he said.

She looked at her watch again and said, "How long will it take you to be ready?"

"I'm dressed and about a block from your neighborhood now," he replied with a smile in his voice. "All I need is your exact address."

Frankie gave him her address and true to his word he was only about two minutes away. They walked the first block making small talk and then she broke into a slow jog. It only took a few moments for the two to find an easy rhythm and matching stride. As they jogged, they discussed the evening before and the plan for that afternoon. Frankie was angry and, although she wouldn't admit it, a bit frightened.

"Do you mind if I join you and Fitz today? The three of us can knock it out quicker and maybe you can be home in time for dinner with the kids."

Frankie couldn't think of any reason to decline so she said, "Sure" and looked at her watch, "I think we should head back. I need to shower before heading in."

The two jogged back to her house and the conversation turned to other things. Jim entertained her with stories of growing up in a small town on the coast while she shared stories of her own small-town upbringing.

Back at her house Frankie told Jim she would see him in an hour and went inside without asking him if he wanted to come in. Her phone rang before the locks on her door clicked. Without looking down, she knew who was calling.

"How's voir dire coming?"

"I think we are almost finished. We have about twenty people to question after lunch and then hopefully the judge will issue his instructions so we can begin our opening statements," replied Derek. "How are you doing? I missed you last night. I was surprised you didn't call."

With just a pang of guilt she said, "I'm sorry. I got stuck out late on something and knew you needed your sleep, so you'd be fresh for today."

They talked for another five minutes while she gathered her things to shower. After they hung up Frankie justified to herself that she was protecting Derek by not telling him what had happened. He would worry and he needed to focus on the trial. She told herself if anything else happened she would tell him.

CHAPTER
SIXTY-FIVE

FRANKIE WALKED into the empty squad room about an hour after Jim left her house. She was slightly relieved no one else was there. She wanted to run a background on Westin without having to answer a bunch of questions about the case. Before she could start her search, she received a text from Jim saying he wasn't going to be able to help her and Fitz after all. She was surprised at how disappointed she was that he wasn't coming.

Frankie checked every database she had access to and scanned the Internet for any open-source information. Westin owned his home and had lived there at least ten years. He was married and had three children. According to his Facebook page, his children attended the same private school as Midori and Maggio's children. Beyond that there were no other obvious connections. She was unable to find any employment information. Frankie thought it a bit odd but not completely unheard of. She would have Fitz or Jim see if they could locate any tax records. She suspected he worked off the books and the lack of records on the Internet supported her theory.

The sound of the dinging elevator broke her out of her trance. Frankie quickly put the files and notes in her bag and began to gather her things to leave. As she slung the bag over her shoulder Fitz stepped through the doorway and asked if she was ready.

"Yeah, just gathering my things now."

"I just got off the phone with Jim. He said he poked his head into Dr. Padgett's office today. You know, Tessa's old girlfriend. He thinks we should start there today. Said she has some information we would be interested in."

"Really?" She asked. Jim must have gone to Dr. Padgett's immediately after he left her. "We went for a run this morning and he didn't mention it. When did he tell you?"

With one eyebrow arched he answered, "I got the impression he just left there. He was going back to his office to work on another case when he called but said the doc had some interesting insight."

Frankie followed him to his car, waiting while he moved his equipment bag to the backseat before jumping in.

"Where is Dr. Padgett's office located? And what makes you think she'll talk to us? Or that what she says will be helpful? Tessa made it sound like she was a disgruntled lover."

Fitz laughed and said, "From what Jim said I think Tessa might be the disgruntled lover. The office is in Overland Park, about twenty minutes from here. As far as talking to us, Jim said she wanted us to come out. Dr. Padgett told him we would benefit from some background on Tessa and Hannah."

Fitz and Frankie chatted good-naturedly as he drove. Frankie and Jim exchanged text messages and by the time they arrived at the office, through his messages, she understood why he thought they should talk to Dr. Padgett as well as a plan of how she wanted to direct the interview. Fitz dropped her at the door while he parked the car. As he backed into the parking spot, he caught a glimpse of a black SUV passing by slowly. Jim had told him about the SUV following Frankie, so he waited until he was sure the SUV did not return before getting out.

Frankie checked in with the receptionist and about ten minutes later she and Fitz were escorted to the doctor's private office. Frankie introduced herself and Fitz as the doctor invited them to sit in the chairs across from her desk.

"Dr. Padgett, thank you for taking the time to talk to us today. I know you're busy," Fitz said.

Dr. Padgett smiled. She looked from Frankie to Fitz. When she spoke, there was a hint of New York or Boston in her accent.

"It's my pleasure. And please, call me Roni. Smart move sending the special agent over this morning! The ladies in my office were more than happy to talk to him. Cravey, Crave, Craven, whatever his name is. The girls are still talking about his smile, his charm, and his uh, shall we say, other attributes?"

Frankie had to fight the smile that was trying to form on her face. She knew exactly what "other attributes" the ladies liked. She, herself, found them quite distracting. Throw in the southern accent and women were like putty in his hand. Well, most women.

"Ji...uhm Agent Craven mentioned you might have some valuable information on this case."

"Yes, as a matter of fact I do think I might have some information you will find helpful. First, I just have to say I don't think you have the full picture on these women. In fact, I think you are missing a lot."

Frankie looked to Fitz, surprised at Roni's candidness.

"What makes you say that?" Frankie asked.

Roni placed her elbows on her desk, clasped her hands together, and leaned forward. She looked from Fitz to Frankie and once she was sure she had their attention she said, "I'm betting your first impression of Hannah was she is a sweet, young, innocent girl."

"Are you saying she's not?" asked Frankie.

"I have spent a lot of time with that girl, and I think Hannah is a whiney, manipulative little bitch."

Frankie stifled a laugh that was building as she thought to herself, *"Don't hold back, tell us how you really feel!"*

Instead, she waited until she was sure Roni was finished talking before asking, "How long have you known Hannah?"

"I'm not sure. We met shortly after she started working at Stevenson's. Tessa had taken her under her wing and Hannah was always around. Everywhere we went Hannah either rode along or met us there. At first, I really didn't mind. She was fun to be around. But then her immaturity started to show. It did not take long before her being around all the time got old. Tessa and I rarely got any time alone and when we did it seemed like Hannah either called, texted, or just showed up. That *child* was so damn needy. Mind you, Tessa is needy, too, but I was used to her. What made it untenable was the two really fed off each other."

"How long have you known Tessa?" Frankie asked.

"We met a couple of years ago during happy hour, right after she started working at Stevenson's." Roni stared out the window of her office, lost in her memories. "Tessa was a force to be reckoned with. She had just gotten out of a long-term, serious relationship so for the first few months we were just friends. Eventually one thing led to another, and we started dating. We started to talk about moving in together but then things changed."

Frankie watched Roni stare out the window, giving her a moment. When she looked back toward her and Fitz, Frankie asked softly, "What changed?"

Roni took a deep breath, looked back toward the window, and let out a sigh. "It wasn't really one thing; it was a series of things. I would like to blame it all on Hannah, but she was just a symptom of much larger problems. Problems that were there long before she came along."

She waited a moment to see if Roni would say anything more. When she did not, she asked, "Like what?"

Roni sat quietly and appeared to be considering whether she should share the intimate details of their relationship and potentially betray Tessa's confidence. With a deep sigh she said, "I guess you'll find out eventually so I might as well be the one to tell you. Tessa liked to gamble and spent a lot of time at the casino in Riverside. I mean *a lot* of time. She did not do anything small.

"At first it wasn't a huge deal. She was pretty good and most of the time came out on top. Sometimes only a couple of hundred but a few times she won thousands. I was busy with my practice so didn't really think much of it at first. The wins always seemed to outweigh the losses, but then she started asking to borrow money. The first time it was just a hundred dollars and she paid it back right away. A few weeks later she asked again. This time the amount increased. Then it became a regular event – especially towards the end. At first, she made sure she paid me back immediately but then it started taking days, then weeks, for her to pay. It became a pattern. I really didn't care about the money as much as I was worried she was getting in over her head.

When I would ask her about it, she would get angry, and we would fight.

"A couple months after Hannah started working at Stevenson's we were all out at the casino celebrating the sale of my condo. Tessa surprised me and asked me if I would move in with her. I was going to have to rent a place until I decided what I wanted to do nest, so it seemed like a good fit to move into her house. We got as far as talking about how we would share expenses. In her rationale, it would help us both save for our futures. We could travel, do upgrades on her house, and all the things couples do. I told her I would think about it. And I did. I loved her and thought maybe it would be a good move. I thought it would bring us closer. Then a few days later she asked me for five thousand dollars. This time she didn't even pretend that she was going to pay me back. Initially she said the money was to pay to have work done at her house. Then she said she needed help paying some bills because her commission was late. Then she made up some other bullshit excuse. I found out later the reason she wanted the money was to go to the casino. When I learned that I started to rethink moving in with her. Suddenly sharing expenses did not seem like a benefit to me. By that time, she had borrowed over $30,000, most of which she had not paid back. I was certain if I moved in, I would never get a penny back. I did a little digging and discovered Tessa had gambled over $70,000 that year. I realized she had a problem and began to pull away from her.

"The more I pulled away from Tessa the more pressure she put on me about moving in together. By this time, she and Hannah had filed the lawsuit against Stevenson's, and I was pretty fed up and decided I'd had enough. Enough of Hannah, enough of the casino, and enough of Tessa borrowing money from me. So, I ended it."

FRANKIE AND FITZ let the information sink in. Once she was certain Roni did not have anything more to add Frankie asked, "How often did Tessa go to the casino?"

"It varied but no less than twice a week. If Christine asked her to go with her, then it might be more frequently."

Frankie wondered who Christine was.

"Did she have friends or people that she spent a lot of time with when she went?" Frankie asked.

"Christine. But Tessa knew her prior to going to the casino. In fact, Christine is who turned her on to the whole high-rolling lifestyle. Christine didn't know how to bet small. She would throw down a couple of hundred on a hand without blinking an eye. Some days she would lose thousands and other days she would be up thousands. Then there was this guy, Geoffrey. Finnegan, I think. Geoff was another high roller. He played blackjack almost exclusively and had even created a game he planned to sell to a casino in Vegas. Christine is okay, snooty but okay. Geoffrey, he's another story. Something about him is just... I don't know. Off."

"Can you elaborate?" Frankie asked.

Roni began tapping her fingers on her desk as though the rhythm might generate the answer. Finally, she asked, "Have you ever met someone that just seemed like a bad guy, but you couldn't articulate what it was specifically that was bad?"

"Mhm hmm."

"That's Geoffrey. He tries to act like a nice guy, but you can tell it's just that - an act. He's married but I'm pretty sure he and Christine are screwing. He's always leering at women and seemed to take a special interest in Hannah when she was around. Geoff doesn't have a job but always has wads of cash. He does okay at the casino, but his winnings don't seem to match the rolls of money he carries around."

"What's Christine's last name?" asked Fitz.

Roni held up a finger as if to say, "wait a minute" and began typing on her computer. "We are friends on Facebook. Here it is, Salvo. Christine Salvo."

"What about Geoffrey? Do you know his last name?" inquired Frankie.

"Finnegan. Geoffrey Finnegan."

Frankie felt a chill go down her spine at the sound of that name. Was it a coincidence that Tessa's gambling buddy had the same last name as the Marzullo family's rival? She didn't believe in coincidences.

"What did you hear about the attack?"

"All I know is what Tessa has told me and what I read in the paper and saw on the news. Tessa told me two goons hid out in Hannah's garage then jumped them when they got back from shopping. Tessa seemed pretty shaken up initially. She even asked me to come stay with her so she wouldn't have to be alone."

"And did you?" asked Fitz.

"No. I was, shall we say, otherwise occupied…with my current girl-friend. I went over the next day, and she told me all about it. Tessa said she played dead during the attack."

Something about the way she said it made Frankie say, "You have doubts."

Roni sat quietly behind her desk. She no longer looked out the window but instead looked at her hands. She began to play with the diamond tennis bracelet on her wrist. She looked up from her bracelet and locked eyes, first with Fitz then with Frankie.

"Maybe. Something doesn't feel right about the whole situation. But what do I know? Tessa asked me to conduct a follow-up physical examination on her a couple of days after the attack. Based on her injuries something happened in that garage. I'm just not 100-percent convinced it happened like Tessa said it did."

Up to this point Fitz had been quiet, "Do you have any theories?"

"Not really a theory, per se, just an idea. Is it possible one, or both, of them are involved in this? Like maybe it was a set up. Or that maybe it has nothing to do with the lawsuit? Could this have been a random attack? Are you sure Hannah and Tessa were the intended targets? Are you sure Tessa wasn't just in the wrong place at the wrong time? Maybe Hannah was the real target and Tessa just got in the way."

"We are still gathering evidence and statements currently. It's too early in the investigation to speculate." Frankie was measured in her response, careful to remain impartial although she was starting to have theories of her own. "You mentioned you did a follow up examination on Tessa. When did you do the exam and what, if anything, did it show?"

Roni turned to her computer and with just a few keystrokes she pulled up Tessa's chart. "She had a few bruises all in different stages of healing. It is hard to tell definitively how old they were. She also had a knot on her head and complained of general back pain. She said she had been kicked and attributed the pain to that but..." Roni stopped mid-sentence.

Frankie could tell Roni was holding something back. "Roni, what are you not telling us?"

Roni, who had been looking directly at Frankie as she talked, turned toward her office window, and looked out wistfully.

"This is not the first-time Tessa has come to me complaining of back pain or knee pain and asked for pain killers. That was another red flag. A few months ago, she told me she was having some knee pain and asked if I would prescribe her something for it. I didn't think a lot of it. I did an exam and she indicated tenderness in all the right places. A few weeks later I asked her how her knee was doing, and she said it was doing better but then referenced the opposite knee. Love really is blind, isn't it? If it wasn't I would have called her out on it but instead I just let it go."

"You think she's abusing pain killers?" inquired Fitz.

Roni gave him a look that said, *"No kidding,"* but she reined herself in and said, "Think? No. Know? Yes. After I refused to prescribe her any more pills for her knee, she went to visit her parents at their house at Lake of the Ozarks. When she came back, I was at her house and went to get the toothpaste out of the medicine cabinet and found a bottle of pain pills prescribed to her mother. Her mother who has cancer. I think Hannah is abusing prescription medications, too."

"What leads you to believe that?" asked Frankie.

"Well, she all but admitted it. We were all out to dinner one night after they filed the lawsuit. Hannah was upset about something their attorney had told them. She was really worked up. That girl – she had a way of getting Tessa all worked up, too. Anyway, eventually she was talking about how stressed and anxious she was and wanted to know if I would prescribe her something. I told her it wouldn't be appropriate for me to treat her since we were friends but referred her to another doctor in our practice. Then after the first attack," Roni chortled as she said the word attack, "she was even more high strung that normal. She told me she finally went to see the doctor I recommended. She claims they prescribed her a 'bar' of Xanax. Detective Thomas, doctors don't prescribe Xanax that way. She had to have gotten it off the street. I didn't ask her about it, but I did ask my colleague and Hannah never saw him. I probably should have confronted her, but I didn't. I decided it was none of my business."

CHAPTER
SIXTY-SEVEN

"WHAT THE FUCK is going on? What was that nosey ass detective and her partner doing in Padgett's office?"

"I don't know. Maybe she's just getting my medical records. Roni did a follow-up exam after..."

"They were in there way too long for that, Tessa. Retrieving records should take five minutes, ten tops. They were in there over an hour. You know it wouldn't take two of them to get a few records. You better take care of this, Tessa."

Sweat began to collect on Tessa's brow as she fidgeted on the other end of the phone. Her heart pounded and her mind raced as she scrambled for a response. Trying to sound calm and self-assured she said, "I'm not sure what you are worried about, Joe. Roni doesn't know anything."

"If you don't know what I'm worried about you are even more stupid than I give you credit for," was the gruff response.

"Look, I'll call Roni tonight and invite her to dinner. A glass or two of wine and she'll talk. She always does."

"Give it a day or two before you call her. If you call her today, she'll be suspicious."

"Okay."

CHAPTER
SIXTY-EIGHT

FRANKIE AND FITZ sat in the SUV at Dr. Padgett's office, each processing what she had just told them. Fitz broke the silence, "Alright Frankie, what do you think? Is Roni a disgruntled lover or could there be some meat to what she said?"

Frankie scanned the area surrounding the business as she contemplated her response. Her scan stopped when she observed a dark colored SUV parked just beyond the office building. She was unable to see who was in the driver's seat and just as she was about to say something to Fitz the vehicle pulled away.

"I think we need to check it out. I'll ask Jim to pull Tessa and Hannah's financials. If Tessa is spending a lot of time at the casino and borrowing money, there should be a record of large withdrawals and/or deposits to her account. I bet the casinos have records as well. I'll reach out to one of my contacts there and see what they can pull. As for the drugs... I'm not sure what to think of that. I don't get addict from either woman, but crazier things have happened."

Her phone began to ring before he could comment.

"Thomas."

Fitz started to put the vehicle in gear but Frankie placed her hand on his elbow and gestured for him to wait for a moment. She pulled her notepad out of her bag and began making notes.

"What makes you think someone has been in your house, Tessa?"

At the sound of Tessa's name Fitz put the car in park. Frankie put the phone on speaker so they could listen as she explained.

"I went out to run some errands this morning. Normally I park in the garage, but since… well, I have started parking in the driveway. When I got home I went in through the front door and got the feeling something wasn't right. It was like someone had been in my space. Then I realized Mika, one of my dogs, didn't come and greet me like she always does. I walked through the kitchen and saw the back door was ajar. Thankfully Mika was right outside but it made me look around some more. I don't use the back door so it wouldn't have been left open. When I started looking around, I realized I had been robbed."

"What's missing?"

Tessa began to cry, "My gun, my grandmother's 3-karat diamond solitaire, and my Rolex. I also had some cash in my bedroom, but I haven't looked in the safe yet to see if it's missing."

"Tessa, have you called the sheriff's department?"

Sniffling Tessa said, "No, you were the first person I called."

"Tessa, I need you to call the sheriff's department. They will take a report and process your house for possible evidence. When they are finished, I want you to call me back with the case number. If they give you the name of the detective who is going to be investigating the case I want their name, too."

"Okay," was Tessa's quiet response.

Frankie hung up the phone and turned to Fitz, who had been listening with a hint of skepticism.

"Do you think it's related?" he asked.

"I don't know. My guess is it's just a coincidence, but I'll follow up with the sheriff's department later today."

"Where to now, Frankie?"

He put the car in reverse as she suggested, "Lunch?"

CHAPTER
SIXTY-NINE

"HEY DANI, DO YOU HAVE HOMEWORK?"

"Working on it now, mom. What time will you be home?" Dani was used to being home alone after school. "Can you bring pizza for dinner?"

"Don't forget to meet Tyler at the bus stop. He should be getting off the bus in about ten minutes." Frankie could hear Dani tapping on a computer and immediately said, "Danielle Elizabeth, get off the computer and go meet your brother."

With a huff Dani agreed, hollering at the dog to go to the door. "I don't understand why I have to walk him home. He's not a baby, mom."

"Just do it Dani. Text me when you guys are inside. Don't let him play outside today either."

"Fine."

"Love you, Angel girl!"

Dani grabbed her iPod and the dog and headed to the bus stop. She was irritated she had to walk to meet Tyler. She scanned through the songs on her iPod looking for something to sing along to as she walked up the block. Dani glanced up just as her neighbor, Miss Mary, stepped out onto the porch. She waved and let the dog lead her to the corner.

While Dani waited for Tyler a chill ran up her spine causing her to glance over her shoulder. Not seeing anything out of the ordinary she turned her eyes back to the road and laughed to herself. Her mom had planted the worry in her mind. Just as Dani was certain it was all in her head Isabelle began to growl, causing her to jump. She looked around a second time. At first, she didn't notice anything out of the ordinary, but Isabelle continued to growl. When the bus pulled up and Tyler climbed off with his friends, Dani saw a black SUV drive by slowly. Once the SUV passed Isabelle stopped growling.

"Come on Ty, we need to get to the house. Let's race!" Once inside she locked the doors and fixed him a snack. After he was settled with a snack and cartoons, she called her mother. "Mom, when are you coming home?"

"I'll be there in about an hour. Are you guys, okay?"

"Yeah, I just miss you mom," she said, her hands shaking. She tried not to let her mom hear the fear in her voice.

"Miss you too, kiddo. I'll be there soon, and we'll order pizza. Love you."

"Love you too, mom." Dani decided not to tell her mom about the SUV, figuring it was probably nothing.

True to her word, Frankie got home within the hour and ordered pizza. While the trio ate dinner, the kids talked about their day. Dani shared the latest middle school gossip while Tyler made them laugh. While they ate and cleaned the kitchen the rest of the world disappeared. No phones. No emails. No text messages. Frankie focused on her children and for a few brief moments forgot about the case.

Once the leftovers were put away and the dishwasher loaded, Dani went to her room to study for a test and Tyler sat in the living room playing with his Legos. Frankie sat on the couch and flipped through a home improvement magazine. She tried to read the words on the page but her mind kept drifting to the case. Frankie picked up her phone but before she could text Jim her phone beeped with an incoming message.

"Got financials."

Frankie told Tyler she would be right back and took her phone and went into her bedroom. Jim answered on the first ring, "I wondered how long it would take you to call. Sixty seconds, not bad."

"Would have been quicker but I had to leave the living room," she said with a laugh. "What did you find out, Jim?"

"What, no foreplay?"

She felt her face turn red as she laughed out loud at his response. "Not tonight."

"Well damn." He chuckled. "In that case, I guess I'll just tell you what I know. I pulled Hannah and Tessa's financials like you asked. There were no surprises in Hannah's."

Jim paused and waited.

Exasperated Frankie said, "But?"

"Well, Tessa's were a different story. She made about $90,000 last year. Owns a house in Kansas and in Sunrise Beach, Missouri. I think that might be by the Lake of the Ozarks."

"It is."

"She has mortgages on both houses but owns her vehicle outright. It's valued at about $50,000. She has a couple of credit cards that she used to pay off monthly but about three months before the lawsuit was filed, she started making just the minimum payments on her credit cards and has run up about $45,000 in debt. Until a month ago she was able to keep up the payments, but she has fallen behind and her cards are getting close to their credit limits. Now here's where it gets interesting. Tessa has made huge withdrawals from her retirement fund and savings account, which now only has about $100. None of the money has gone to her debt from what I can see. I'm betting, no pun intended, that it has gone to the casino."

"So, what you are telling me is she really needs this lawsuit to end well."

"It would seem so. At the very least I think you're going to find that she has a gambling problem."

"Thanks for working on that, Jim. I'm back in the office tomorrow afternoon and will work on casino records. I'll run by and get those financials after I check in with Sarge."

"Want to go for a run in the morning?" Jim asked with trepidation.

The question took her by surprise, but she quickly recovered and said, "Sure. I drop the kids off at 8 and can meet you after. Riverfront Park at 8:15?"

"See you there," he responded with a smile in his voice.

THE NEXT MORNING Frankie met Jim at Riverfront Park and after a good run they had breakfast at the City Diner. Over pancakes and eggs Jim regaled Frankie with his exploits as a police officer in Chicago. As time passed and Frankie marveled at how similar his experiences were to hers. She couldn't help but think how crime in big cities was alike.

"Do you ever miss it?"

Jim laughed lightly and winked at Frankie, "Sure, but this job has its perks too."

Frankie lowered her eyes. Color filled her cheeks as she turned away. The ringing of her phone broke the spell of the moment.

"Thomas…What? What happened? Where is he? I'll be there in ten."

Frankie grabbed cash from her wallet and threw it down on the table and told Jim she had to leave.

"Is everything okay? Is there anything I can do?"

With tears welling in her eyes a distracted Frankie answered, "No. Thanks though. I'll talk to you later."

"Okay. Call if you…need…anything," said a confused Jim. Frankie nodded as she quickly made her way to the car.

Once inside the vehicle Frankie dialed her cellphone and called Mia.

"Tell Sarge I'm going to be late. I'm heading to the hospital. I'll call him when I know more," Frankie's voice trembled as she talked.

"What? Are you okay?"

"I don't know. It's my dad. Sophie just called. They think it's his heart."

Tears streamed down Frankie's face as she explained the situation to Mia.

"Want me to come to the hospital?"

Frankie paused before answering, "No, but thanks for offering. Sophie and Jake are on their way with Jody."

"Okay, call me as soon as you know anything."

Frankie assured Mia she would as she parked her Jeep in the parking garage of the Emergency Room. Throwing her phone in her bag, Frankie locked the door to her Jeep and ran to the Emergency Room door.

"Frankie," said Jody, enveloping her in a hug. "Jake is parking the car."

"What happened?" inquired Frankie.

Jody wiped tears from her face. Her voice cracked, "Frank had gone down to the park for a walk after breakfast. About an hour after he left, I got a phone call from the police saying he had been found on the ground by a jogger. He was grabbing his chest and saying he couldn't breathe. The jogger called 9-1-1 and an ambulance rushed him here. Jake was at the house working on Sophie's truck. He drove us here."

Frankie hugged the woman who had been a part of her life for as long as she could remember. Sophie embraced them both. Just as the women were preparing to sit and wait Jake's broad frame filled the door.

"Any news?" Jake's deep voice resonated in the small room.

Jody shook her head.

"I'll be right back," Frankie said and stepped away to call Sergeant Baker.

"Take the night off, Frankie. Take whatever time you need. If something major comes up, I'll text you. Focus on your family."

"Thanks Sarge," Frankie said.

Frankie leaned against the wall, tears welling in her eyes. Her next call was to Keith.

Frankie explained the situation and said, "So obviously Soph won't be home to watch the kids tonight. Can..."

"I'll go to the house and sit with the kids until you get home. I'll just tell them Sophie had to work late. You can explain when you have news. We've got you."

"Thanks Keith. I'll text you when I know more."

Frankie began to walk towards the waiting room and decided to send Derek a text message. She knew he was in court and was not surprised when he didn't immediately respond.

Frankie sat next to Sophie on the hard bench and flipped through the pages of a magazine. She stared at the words as they swam across the page. Frankie was more frightened than she had ever been. She couldn't imagine a life without her dad in it, even with the possibility staring her directly in the face.

SEVENTY-ONE

EVERY MINUTE FELT like an hour as Frankie and her family sat in the waiting room. She gave up the magazine for staring out the window but instead of a parking lot full of cars she saw an old country road. Frankie watched as her childhood memories floated past the window. She was 5 years old sitting on the back of a motorcycle clinging tightly to her father's waist as they made their way through the curves by her grandpa's house. She was a little girl lying on a blanket staring into the dark night listening to her father point out the constellations. A teenager on a four-wheeler riding through the woods trying to catch up as her father blazed the trail. A young woman graduating from college hearing her father say he was proud of her. Frankie let herself get lost in the memories of the countless hours spent riding in a car rambling while her dad listened and offered advise; learning to drive a 5-speed car and being told *"if you can drive this you can drive anything."* Frankie recalled hours sitting on a stool in the garage while her father worked on her car and talked to her about life, always careful not to tell her what to do. The memories were endless.

Frankie looked around the room letting her gaze pause on Sophie, then Jake. The look on their faces mirrored hers as they were lost in their own memories. Jody was bereft. Frankie could imagine the decades of memories filling her thoughts. Frankie was the oldest and felt a responsibility to take care of her family; she had to be strong for them. Just as she was about to ask if they needed anything from the snack machine, she heard someone call her name. She looked up to see Jim walking through the door.

"Jim? What are you doing here?" asked a confused Frankie. She stood and walked towards him.

"I stopped by the unit and Mia told me what happened. What do you guys need?"

After thanking him for coming and assuring him she didn't need anything, Frankie introduced Jim to her family. She had just invited him to sit down when a doctor walked out and called, "Mrs. Moretti?"

Jody and the rest of the group stood up quickly as she answered, "Yes?"

"Would you and your family like to come with me?"

"Dr. Wilhelm, I didn't know you were working the ER today," said Frankie. They followed the doctor to a consultation room where they were invited to sit. Dr. Michael Wilhelm was the chief of trauma in the ER as well as the coordinator for the forensic program at the hospital. Over the years, Frankie had teamed up with him to teach multidisciplinary groups about sexual assault for various community events. She trusted the doctor and had come to consider him a friend.

"Frankie, I didn't realize Mr. Moretti is your father. I'm sorry you all had to wait so long. It was touch and go for a while. We ran a series of tests and discovered a blockage. He was rushed into the Cath lab where they were able to eradicate it. With some medication and lifestyle changes he should be just fine."

"When can we see him?" asked Jody. Tears of relief streamed down her face.

"He's being moved up to the CICU for observation. Give it about thirty minutes and then you can go in two at a time for about five minutes each."

"Thank you, Michael," said Frankie.

Dr. Wilhelm squeezed her shoulder and nodded as he walked out of the room.

Jim accompanied Frankie and her family to the CICU where they took turns visiting. When it was Frankie's turn, she went into the room by herself where she sat and held her father's hand while he slept. Tears trickled down Frankie's cheeks as she stared at the man who always seemed larger than life but now appeared so frail.

Frankie spoke quietly, "You really gave us a scare dad. The doc said you have to make some lifestyle changes but then you'll be back to your old self before you know it." Frankie's voice became more urgent as she said, "You have to be okay, dad. I still need you. We all do. I don't know what I'd do without you!"

Frankie laid her head next to her father's hand and wept quietly. After a few moments Frankie kissed her father on the cheek, wiped her face, and said, "I love you dad."

The sun was just beginning to rise when Jim walked Frankie to her car. He made her promise to call if there were any changes or she needed anything. Once inside the Jeep Frankie grabbed her phone expecting to see a missed call from Derek. Instead, she had a text that read, "Court ran late. Working on closing. Sorry to hear about your dad. I'll text later. DK"

With those words, the dam broke. All the stress, anxiety, and fear Frankie felt erupted. She sat in the dark parking garage of the hospital, laid her head on the steering wheel, and sobbed uncontrollably.

Spent, Frankie pulled herself together. She was about to pull out when her phone rang. After checking caller ID, an exasperated Frankie answered the phone, "Thomas."

Meekly Derek asked, "Hey Frankie, how's your dad?"

"He's stable. Should make a full recovery. I'm heading home from the hospital now."

"Sorry I didn't call you last night. Co-counsel and I worked late on our closing, and I didn't want to wake you up when I headed home."

Frankie didn't immediately say anything in response. After a moment of silence, she said, "I just pulled into my driveway, and I'm beat. I'll talk to you later. Good luck on the trial."

Frankie ended the call, grabbed her bag, and walked inside her house to try and sleep.

CHAPTER
SEVENTY-TWO

FRANKIE HAD NOT BEEN ASLEEP MORE than an hour when her phone rang. A heavily breathing Tessa was on the other end of the phone. "Detective Thomas, I'm so scared!"

Frankie sat up and grabbed her notepad. "What happened?"

"I just got a call," Tessa's voice trembled. "A man. He threatened me. Threatened my family. He said they know where my parents live, and no one is safe. He said if we don't drop the lawsuit, he's going to kill my parents. He said he knows where Hannah's staying."

"When did you get the call, Tessa?"

"Five minutes ago. He called my house phone. Normally I don't pick that phone up, but my mom's been sick, and I thought... what should I do?"

"Have you called the local police?"

"No. I called you and I called my parents to make sure they're okay. Dad is putting the school on lockdown."

Frankie remembered Tessa saying her father was the dean of a private school in the Ozarks. "Okay. Do you have caller I.D.?"

"It showed up as a private number."

"Do you want me to try to secure a shelter for you, Tessa? I'm sure I can find somewhere for you to stay and be safe."

"I'm not sure what to do, Detective Thomas." Frankie heard a beeping on the phone. Tessa said, "That's my father, can I call you back?"

"Of course. Please consider what I suggested regarding the shelter." Tessa told Frankie she would and disconnected the line.

Frankie immediately dialed Jim and told him about the call. Tessa had called her from her land-line telephone, the same one she said the threats came in on, so she was able to provide Jim with the number.

"Do you think it's legit, Frankie?"

"Jim, she was in a panic. If she was faking it, she's one hell of an actress."

"Okay. Let me run a trace on the number and I'll call you right back. By the way, have you heard anything about your dad? Did you get any sleep at all?

She was touched Jim asked about her dad, "I slept about an hour. I'm going to call Jody when I hang up with you. And Jim?"

"Yeah?"

"Thank you for staying at the hospital last night and for asking about him today. It really means a lot to me."

"That's what friends do, Frankie. I'll call you in a few." With that he disconnected the call and went to work on the trace.

While she waited for him to call her back, Frankie talked to Jody.

"Your dad is awake and already asking to go home," Jody said.

Frankie laughed knowing her father was not one to lay in bed for long.

"I'll drop in later today and bring you some lunch. Text me with your order."

"You don't need to do that. I can run down to the cafeteria," Jody said.

"I know I don't need to. I want to. I'm coming by to see dad so I might as well bring you something to eat."

Jody reluctantly agreed. When Frankie hung up the phone she laid back on her pillow and waited.

As luck would have it, her wait was not long. Within five minutes of hanging up with Jody her phone began to beep with an incoming text message from Jim.

"Meet me at your office as soon as you can. And bring your vest. We have some residence checks to do tonight."

"I'll be in after I run by the hospital."

Frankie thought to herself, *"This is going to be an interesting night."*

Residence checks meant they would be going out and knocking on doors of possible suspects, hence the direction to bring her bullet proof vest. Maybe they would be able to finally get some answers in this case.

CHAPTER
SEVENTY-THREE

"DID THAT BITCH BUY IT?"

"She bought it. She wants me to go to a shelter," laughed Tessa.

"Maybe you should. Might make your call a little more believable."

"Maybe. I'll think about it. For now, I think the call bought us some time. Did Adam go where I told him to make the call?"

"Don't insult me like that, of course he did. That little pipsqueak would dance on his roof naked if I asked him to. Everything will check out if they trace the call."

"Great," answered Tessa. "And Geoff?"

"What Tessa?"

"Do you think this is going to work? Do you think they'll finally pay out?"

"You better hope so, little girl. If not, you better have a back-up plan for the cash. Or those fake threats to your family will no longer be fake."

Tessa assured him she was good for the cash before ending the call. Her hands trembled as she put the phone back on the receiver and leaned against the wall.

"This better fucking work," she said out loud to the dog who looked up at the sound of her voice.

CHAPTER
SEVENTY-FOUR

IT TOOK Frankie less than an hour to get her gear together. She called to update Sergeant Baker on the drive to the hospital. Keith and Bruce would be at her house as soon as they got off work. Dinner was in the crockpot and snacks were on the counter. With her family cared for she could focus on the night ahead.

Frankie took Jody her lunch and spent a few minutes talking to her dad on her way to the office. Frank was restless but in good spirits. Sophie and Jake were bringing in dinner, but he was hoping to go home the following day.

"Can't get a bit of sleep in this place. Nurses in and out all night. I need my own bed."

"Don't rush it, dad. I need you to be okay."

Frank patted his daughter on the hand and said, "It's going to be okay Francesca. I'm going to be around for a long time."

Frankie smiled through the tears and said, "You better be dad."

Frankie kissed her dad on the check, gave Jody a hug, and left the room a little lighter.

Fitz and Jim were waiting for Frankie when she got to the office. The three walked into the conference room and began discussing their strategy. Jim began writing on the whiteboard.

"The call Tessa received was traced back to a cellphone in the name of

Adam Santini. The call hit off a cell tower at 83rd and Mission on the Kansas side."

"The same exit as the car dealership Maggio went to after he was moved from Stevenson's," chimed in Frankie. "Where does Santini live?"

"Lee's Summit. I thought we'd start with his house," said Jim.

"What does Santini's record look like?" She asked as she tapped her pencil on the notepad lying on the table in front of her.

"He's clean. Not so much as a traffic ticket. I pulled his financials. Looks like he is married. He and his wife own their home and two vehicles. He doesn't appear to have a job, but his wife is a doctor. I looked at his phone records. Most of his calls and texts go to a phone number out of Chicago. Neither his nor his wife's number are Chicago area numbers."

"Do we have a name that goes with that number?" she asked.

"Gina West." Jim answered.

Frankie reviewed the printout of the call records before saying anything. "Do we know who she is? A lot of these calls are late at night."

Jim winked at her. "I thought the same thing. I did a little digging on Gina West. She is employed by a local nanny service."

"The time and frequency of the calls aren't consistent with someone checking on their children," Frankie said.

Fitz laughed and said, "So you think maybe the nanny is taking care of more than the children?"

"Could be good leverage to get him to talk." Frankie tapped her pencil nervously as she scanned the paperwork Jim brought with him. Nothing unusual stood out on paper. Could this guy really be the one making the threats? If so, why?

"Is there any connection between him and Maggio or the Marzullo family?"

"Nothing that I could find," Jim conceded. "However, his last few jobs were in the finance departments at a couple of car dealerships in Lee's Summit."

"Can you get someone to dig a little deeper and see if any of his previous employers were owned by Marzullo?"

"On it." Jim picked up his cell phone. Within seconds he was providing detailed instructions to an analyst from his office.

The door to the conference room opened and broke into Frankie's thoughts.

"Hey, Frankie!" Mia's voice echoed in the room.

"Hey, Mia. Do you and Coleman have anything going on tonight?"

"Trying to identify the car from last week. But that's about it. What's up?"

She proceeded to update Mia on the latest developments.

"Would you mind staying close to the office? We're going out to do a residence check and I may need some help on this end."

"No problem, Frankie. I'll text if I get called out."

Frankie and Jim grabbed their flashlights, jackets, and bulletproof vests and headed out the door. By the time they hit the streets the November sun was setting on the horizon. The air was cooler and held a hint of moisture. Frankie felt a shiver run down her spine. She was unsure if it was the cold air or a premonition of what was to come.

CHAPTER
SEVENTY-FIVE

"I DID IT," Santini said breathlessly. "I did exactly as you asked."

"Calm down, Adam," Geoffrey barked. "All you did was make a damn phone call."

"When do I get my money?"

"As soon as that bitch pays me. If that fucking detective has half a brain, she'll arrest Maggio. Then Marzullo will be ready to settle."

"You really think that phone call will be enough? I'm no lawyer but..."

"That's right, you aren't. Everything points to Maggio."

"Unless it comes back on me," whined Adam.

"Did you use the courtesy phone in the lobby?" asked Geoffrey.

"What courtesy phone? I didn't want to be caught on camera, so I pulled into the lot and used my cell phone."

"You dumb motherfucker. Don't you know they can trace your cell phone?"

Adam's hands began to tremble with fear. He looked at the cell phone he held in his hand as Geoffrey continued to scream obscenities and make threats. Adam threw the phone down, grabbed a bag, and started to throw clothes inside. The last thing to go in the bag was a loaded .40 caliber Glock.

SEVENTY-SIX

FRANKIE AND JIM drove in silence, each immersed in their own thoughts. As they pulled into Santini's subdivision the hair on the back of her neck began to rise. She could not put her finger on it, but something didn't feel right.

"Hold on, Jim. Let's make sure we're all on the same page before we pull up to the house. I've got a funny feeling. This whole thing just seems too easy. Like a set up."

Jim pulled into the the clubhouse, turned the car lights off, and turned toward Frankie.

Frankie took a deep breath then said, "Standard tactical approach. Black out. Park half a block away. We don't know how deep this guy is with Marzullo and his crew. He doesn't have any history with weapons or any registered in his name. All that means is he hasn't been caught."

"Frankie..."

"I know, Jim. I trust you. Really, I do. I guess I just needed to say the words out loud."

"Let's suit up." Frankie and Jim stepped out of the car, pulled their jackets off, and put their vests on. He reached over and grabbed the vest on her shoulders with both hands then tugged to ensure it was tight. Their eyes locked, neither wavering.

She finally broke the silence and said, "Let's do this."

Jim drove the two blocks to Santini's house. Just as he was about to turn the car lights off, he saw a red sedan run a stop sign. The tires screeched as it pulled away. "What kind of car does Santini drive?"

"Red Audi." She turned to see the direction the car went as Jim whipped the SUV around. "He just turned right. Want me to call it in?"

"Hold on. I can catch him. I'll hit the lights as we get closer."

"Do you think he knew we were coming? He's driving like the devil himself is chasing him."

He shook his head in a negative response. Frankie held onto the passenger door as Jim took the corners sharp and fast.

Santini exited the neighborhood and headed east on I-70. Once he got onto the highway Santini seemed to relax and slowed down slightly. As the margin of distance decreased, Jim said, "I'm going to follow him for a few minutes. See where he's going."

Frankie grabbed her cell phone to call Mia.

"Sex Crimes, Detective Boden."

"Mia, it's Frankie. I need you to pull all known associates for Adam Santini." She gave Mia his name, birth date, and social security number. A few moments passed before Frankie started writing. "Thanks, Mia. I'll message you in a bit."

"Did Mia give you anything to help us figure out where this guy's heading?"

Jim kept two cars between them and Santini.

"Nothing in this area. Closest relative is in Iowa. He's heading east. I don't think he's going there."

Jim was about to ask her how long she wanted to follow Santini when he pulled off the highway, into a hotel parking lot, and stopped.

Jim pulled behind the car and turned his emergency lights on. They jumped out of the SUV and began their approach. Before Frankie could clear the front of the SUV Santini exited the driver's side of his car. The illuminated parking lot light reflected on the steel of his Glock just as he raised it and pointed it toward Jim. The silence of the night was broken as Frankie yelled, "Gun!"

Jim sought cover and yelled, "Drop the gun!" He and Frankie identified themselves and continued to yell orders in unison as they retreated for cover.

"KCPD. Put the gun on the ground, Santini!" Frankie had the sights of her weapon trained on his chest. "Drop the gun. Now. Show us your hands. Do it now!"

Santini appeared frozen as he looked down the barrels of the two guns pointed at him. "Don't shoot. I'm putting my gun on the ground."

Frankie and Jim kept their weapons trained on Santini who lowered the gun and laid it on the ground.

"Put your hands in the air and keep them where I can see them."

Frankie continued to give orders as she moved toward Santini. By the time she reached him he was on his knees away from the gun. Frankie swiftly applied the handcuffs and searched him for any additional weapons. When she was finished, she got him back on his feet.

JIM OBTAINED Santini's consent and searched through the red Audi while Frankie called Fitz.

"Hey, Frankie. I'm out at the dealership. Maggio and Midori were both gone when that phone call was made to Tessa. In fact, both were in Detroit, most likely meeting with Marzullo. They had surveillance video, but the secretary was reluctant to let me view it."

"Did you sweet talk her, Fitz?"

Frankie knew Fitz would not have given up easily.

"Never doubt me, Frankie. I flashed her my pearly whites and convinced her to show it to me, but she wouldn't give me a CD...yet."

"What did you see on the video?" Frankie was beginning to get impatient.

"Nothing really. About the time the call was made a red Audi pulled into the parking lot. Looked like a white guy driving. He parked and just sat there for a few moments. Looked like he was texting or doing something with a phone. Less than two minutes later he pulled out and left.

"Red Audi. Are you sure?"

"Yeah, why?"

"We just stopped Santini. Damn near shot the little bastard..."

"Whoa, Frankie! What?"

"Stupid guy jumps out of his car with a gun. Fortunately for him he listened to orders and dropped it. I had him in my sites. Finger on the trigger."

"Are you and Jim, okay?"

The playfulness in Fitz's voice was gone. He was suddenly all business.

"We're both fine." Frankie looked down and noticed the slight tremble in her hands. "He was driving a red Audi."

"No kidding? Are you guys heading back to HQ soon?"

"Jim is searching Santini's car then we're going to leave it here and head back. Do you want to watch the interrogation?"

"Yep. Heading there now, Frankie."

Fitz and Frankie said good-bye just as Jim extricated himself from the car.

"COUNT ONE. Murder in the 2nd. How does the jury find?"

The foreman spoke loudly for the court reporter, "Guilty, your honor."

"Count two. Armed criminal action. How does the jury find?"

"Guilty, your honor."

The last three counts yielded the same verdict. Derek was on cloud nine. He had delivered a powerful closing argument and made sure the jury saw photos of the smiling four-year-old just before she was murdered. The images were a sharp contrast to the photographs from the crime scene. He knew he would never be able to erase the image of the crumpled body of the child lying in a pool of her own blood. The trial was over, and justice was served for the child and her family.

"This is Frankie. Leave me a message."

Derek turned away from the door and stared out his office window. He was disappointed she didn't answer. He wanted to share his success. With her. At the sound of the beep he said, *"We did it, Frankie. Guilty on all five counts. Sentencing will be in thirty days. No guarantees but I expect him to get life. Good guys win for a change. Call me when you can."*

"Hey counselor, want to celebrate?"

The sound of Jessica's voice startled him.

"Hey, Jess. I thought you'd left already. What'd you have in mind?"

Jessica Moon had been his co-chair during the murder trial.

With her hands on her hips and pursed lips Jessica replied, "Harry's Country Club or The Peanut? Raise a glass?"

Derek looked at her as though he were seeing her for the first time. Her suit was tailored to flatter her long legs and slim body. Jessica had kind eyes and a sexy smile. Ignoring the alarms sounding off in his head he smiled and asked, "Have you ever been to The Levee?"

Jessica shook her head.

"You will love it. I'll drive."

The pair locked their offices and made their way to their cars. As they walked across the dark lot neither noticed the blacked-out SUV sitting across the street. Derek paused to open the passenger door of his car just when the sound of the first bullet pierced the air. He reached out to catch Jessica as her body lurched forward. The force of the bullet piercing her body thrust her into his arms. Adrenaline coursed through his body as he tried to shield her and felt the bullets tear his flesh. Seconds later their bodies lay crumpled together on the cold, hard ground.

CHAPTER
SEVENTY-NINE

FRANKIE EXITED Jim's vehicle in time to hear him yell. "Watch out, Frankie!" She jumped back as a blacked-out SUV sped past them on the street.

She grabbed her phone to call dispatch and provided the dispatcher with a description of the SUV, including a partial license plate number. By the time she walked Santini across the street she could hear sirens heading in the direction the vehicle fled.

She left Santini sitting in a locked interview room.

Jim asked, "Got any coffee?"

"Head up to the jail. They usually have a fresh pot. I'm going to grab some water. Meet you in five."

Before Frankie could put her stuff down on her desk Fitz started firing questions. Mia was quiet as Frankie answered. "That punk is lucky to be alive," was his response to the detailed account of Santini's car stop.

"Half a second later and he wouldn't be. I..."

Jim interrupted her. "She saved my ass from getting shot. Ready, Frankie?"

She led him into the interview room where Santini sat cradling his face in his hands.

Tears streamed down his face and his quiet whispers could barely be heard.

"Fuck. Fuck. Fuck."

Frankie sat down and placed a bottle of water in front of Santini. After advising him of his legal rights she asked, "Ready to talk?"

Santini looked up and said, "I swear I had no idea you were cops."

"The lights didn't give us away?" Sarcasm dripped from Jim's words.

"I thought you were someone else. I'm not stupid. I wouldn't point a gun at a cop. That shit will get you killed."

"Just about did, Adam." Frankie didn't try to disguise her annoyance. "Who'd you think we were?"

"They're going to kill me. I'm dead. Seriously. I'm dead."

"Tell us who they are. Maybe we can help." She worked to make her tone one of concern, not contempt. "Who were you running from?"

"Can I get a cigarette?"

"Normally they won't let you smoke in here. Talk to me and maybe I can work something out." Frankie kept a pack of cigarettes in her desk just for this purpose, but she was not ready to give him any privileges. She asked, "Do you have any idea why we pulled in behind you?"

"No." He paused. "Maybe."

She pulled a photograph from the folder sitting in front of her. "Do you know either of these women?"

He looked carefully at the photograph of Tessa. After a moment, he picked up the photograph of Hannah. He seemed to carefully consider his answer. "No. I may have seen this one," lifting Tessa's photo, "with my buddy Geoff but I've never actually met her. I've never seen the other one."

"Who's Geoff?"

"He's my neighbor and poker buddy. I think that one girl came to a game at his house a couple of months ago. Why?"

Santini's expression was open. He appeared to be telling the truth.

Frankie considered Santini's answer. Together she and Jim continued to question him. After identifying Geoff's full name and address they dove into questions about Santini's whereabouts earlier that day.

"I was home all day. I didn't leave the house until right before you stopped me."

"Cut th...."

Frankie interrupted Jim to take the questioning a different route. Inching slightly closer she tempered her tone and asked, "What does your wife do, Adam?"

Adam and Jim both seemed slightly shocked at the question.

Santini said, "She's a pediatric oncologist."

"That must be hard. I bet she works a lot of hours."

"It is and she does. Since I've been out of work, she's been the primary breadwinner."

Santini wore a puzzled look.

"You must get lonely. Being home alone with three small kids. Especially during the day when they're at school."

Frankie doodled on her notepad as she talked.

"Nathan is the only one in school. The other two are home all day but I manage. I have a nanny and that helps."

"That's nice. What's her name?" Frankie glanced at Jim. She could tell he had caught where she was going with the questioning.

"Gina."

Santini started to fidget uncomfortably in his chair.

"I looked at your phone records. I couldn't help but notice there are a lot of phone calls and text messages to a number belonging to a Gina West. Is she the same person?" Frankie was leading up to what she hoped would be her bargaining tool.

"Yeah. We talk a lot when I have to be away from the house," Beads of sweat formed on Adam's forehead.

Frankie leaned in toward him, "Looks to me like the calls and texts were late at night. Times when the children would most likely be in bed. Now Adam, I don't care if you're having an affair with Gina, but I'm sure your wife does. I may have to point out this information when we talk to her – that is unless you are willing to help us out."

Santini didn't skip a beat. He looked from Frankie to Jim and said, "My wife and I are both with the nanny."

FRANKIE TOOK a drink of water to hide her shock at Santini's response. Jim took the opportunity and changed the line of questioning.

"Alright, Adam. Let's talk about today. You said you were home all day. We have your phone records. We know you're lying. What we don't know is why."

Santini's hands trembled as he glanced from Jim to Frankie. He cradled his face in his open palms. Frankie was about to say something when she heard him mumble, "It was supposed to be easy money. A phone call. That's it. Just a phone call."

She looked at Jim who winked at her as if to say, "We've got him now."

Santini took a deep breath. The words came out in his exhale, "About a month ago I was at Geoff's for a poker game. That girl from the picture, I think she said her name was Tessa, was there, too. She was bitching and moaning about a sexual harassment lawsuit she had filed. She was frustrated because it was taking a long time to settle. She said it should have been settled quickly but their attorneys were fighting everything. This went on all night. Bitch wouldn't talk about anything else."

"What does that have to do with today?" Jim was becoming impatient.

"Keep your pants on. I'm getting there. A couple of days later Geoff told me the other girl involved in Tessa's lawsuit had been attacked. He said something about the girl being held up at gunpoint in her yard or something. Anyway, Tessa thought after that happened the lawsuit would get settled."

Santini scoffed then waited.

Jim nodded as if to say, "go ahead."

"Yesterday I was outside messing around in the yard when Geoff pulled into his driveway. He waved me over and asked if I was interested in making an easy $10,000. I thought he was messing with me because he knew I was out of work – so I laughed. But he was serious. He said all he needed me to do was make a phone call, then once this lawsuit settled, he'd pay me $10,000."

"Didn't that seem a bit too easy to you?" inquired Frankie.

"Sure, it did but look, Geoff's not the kind of guy you say no to. He gave me a phone number and told me to drive out to Mission to the car dealership. I was supposed to go inside and use the courtesy phone in the lobby. Geoff said all I needed to do was dial the number, wait a couple of minutes, and then hang up."

"Did you know who you were calling?" Frankie asked.

"I assumed it was Tessa but to be honest I didn't ask."

"Did you go inside the dealership like Geoff told you to?"

Frankie knew the answer but wanted to hear his response.

Santini looked down at the table and paused, "No. I pulled into the lot but didn't go in. I used my cell phone. I dialed the number and waited for a few minutes then hung up."

"Did you say anything to the person on the phone?"

"No. I just sat there. I think I heard a woman say hello but that's it."

The questioning continued for another hour until Frankie and Jim were sure they had all they needed from him.

"What do you think, Detective Thomas?" Jim was anxious to finish up so they could pick up Geoff.

"Is there anything else you think we need to know, Adam?"

Santini shook his head at Frankie.

CHAPTER
EIGHTY-ONE

DEREK COULD HEAR the officers talking.

"223. We have shots fired at 13th and Oak. Two down. Send me a couple of cars and a bus."

The officer began firing questions at him. Where did the shots come from? Did he see the driver? Did he see the license plate? Derek answered the questions as well as he could and listened as the officer sent the information over the air waves to the other patrol officers.

The first paramedics arrived quickly and immediately called for a second ambulance. While Derek and Jessica were being tended to the officer was putting crime scene tape around the empty lot. He gave updates to the other officers as they arrived on the scene. Within minutes of the first paramedic's arrival, they left with Jessica. Lights and sirens pierced the silent night.

The second set of paramedics arrived just as the first ambulance left.

"How's Jessica?" Derek was hungry for any information they could provide him.

"I'm not sure sir. They're taking good care of her though. Is that your wife?" The paramedic talked while he prepared to take him to the hospital.

"No. She was my co-counsel on a murder case. We're prosecutors. We were going out to celebrate."

The words came out in a staccato as Derek struggled to speak.

The first responding officer walked up when he finished his sentence, "Wait, are you the prosecutor that handled the gang shooting where the little girl died? Joaquin Jackson was the shooter."

"We got...a... guilty...verdict," Derek said in a staccato voice and gave a half-nod of agreement.

The officer immediately keyed up his radio, "223."

"*Go ahead 223.*"

"*Can you have a car drive by 5106 Agnes and check for a black SUV? It should have Missouri plates. Partial plate is possibly Charles Henry 2. If the SUV is there have them sit on it and call me. Do not approach. I repeat. Do not approach.*"

"*Copy 223.*"

Derek looked at the officer with a question in his eyes. "Why that address?"

"Me and my partner patrol that area. Joaquin's best friend, and soldier, Jamel Cason lives there. I figure if he found out about the guilty verdict he'd be pretty pissed. Maye even be out for blood."

Derek blacked out as the paramedics loaded him into the ambulance.

CHAPTER
EIGHTY-TWO

FRANKIE RAN a background on Geoffrey Finnegan and printed two copies: one for her and one for Fitz. She grabbed the printouts, her gun, vest, and cellphone and headed for the door. On the elevator ride she noticed a missed call from Derek. Instead of calling she fired off a text.

"Major break in the case. Call you later."

"Ready to get him, Frankie?" asked Jim.

Jim and Fitz were checking their gear.

"Damn straight. Let's do this."

Frankie noticed the lights and crime scene tape at the courthouse and suddenly she felt her stomach drop.

Reading her mind, Jim asked, "I wonder what's going on over there."

Frankie felt a chill run down her spine. She debated on listening to the voicemail she had from Derek, but Fitz's voice interrupted her thoughts.

"Finnegan is a piece of work. He has owned a couple of small-time car dealerships but nothing major. In fact, his assets don't really speak to the money he has in his accounts. And it looks like he has made a lot of significant deposits in the last nine months."

While Frankie was scanning the documents, Fitz continued, "He owns his house outright. Two cars. Four kids. Two out of the house. Two presumably still at home…"

"We've got him. Page 4. Bottom of the page," Frankie interrupted.

"You've got to be kidding me!"

Frankie and Fitz fist bumped and laughed out loud.

Jim looked to Fitz, "Care to include the driver?"

With a smile in her voice that Jim could not see in the dark car Frankie said dramatically, "Midori. His wife's maiden name is Midori. She's listed on the house as Elizabeth Midori Finnegan. Her next of kin is the one and only Craig Midori."

Jim slapped his hand on the steering wheel as he mumbled, "Got you now."

He pulled into the parking lot of the subdivision clubhouse and put the car in park. Frankie leaned forward. He and Fitz turned in their seats to face her. With game faces on, they discussed their strategy.

"I'm going to see if Bobby's squad is working. It would be nice to have some back-up." Frankie began dialing the number. "I know we are bringing Finnegan in but what about his wife? What if Midori is there? Want to snatch him up, too?"

"Let's bring 'em all..." Jim paused to listen with curiosity at the banter between her and the officer on the other end.

"Hey Bobby, I'm going to put you on speaker phone. Watch yourself, okay?" Frankie laughed, "Okay you're on speaker. I'm with Scott Fitzmeyer from Intelligence and Special Agent Jim Craven from the FBI. We could use your help if your squad's working."

"Are you all working on that case from Waldo?"

"Yeah. We're getting ready to do a residence check and want some back up."

Frankie provided Bobby with the rally point information.

"I'll brief you when you guys get here."

"You got it, Frankie. Give us twenty. Hoff and I'll meet you there."

Bobby LeGrande and Frankie had been friends since she was in the academy. While she was attending the police academy, she did road along with him and his partner almost every week. When she went to patrol, they worked in the same zone and occasionally enjoyed one another's company outside of work, but then she went to investigations, and he went to the Tactical Response Team. The years passed, he got married and their paths crossed less frequently - and usually only in high-risk situations like this.

True to his word, Bobby and his partner pulled into the lot twenty minutes after Frankie disconnected the call. When she saw them pull in, she jumped out of the car. The cold wind cut through her like a warm knife through butter. She reached back into the car to grab her jacket and when she turned around the men were standing in a semi-circle around her. With the help of Fitz and Jim, she briefed the team on what Santini had told them.

After Frankie finished her brief, Bobby began issuing instructions. "Hoff, you and I will take the back. I'll call Tim and Chris to see if they can start heading this way. Just in case."

CHAPTER
EIGHTY-THREE

JIM STOPPED ABOUT HALF a block from Finnegan's house. Bobby parked in the darkness directly behind the unmarked SUV. The house was a two-story colonial with a brick front. The light above the front door was dark. Quietly they made their way to the front of the house. Frankie nodded to Bobby as he and Hoff went to the back of the house and she, Jim, and Fitz continued toward the front door.

Jim approached the door from the right while she approached on the left with Fitz slightly behind her. Frankie looked at both men, took a deep breath, and firmly knocked on the door.

"Kansas City Missouri Police Department."

Frankie waited thirty seconds before knocking again. The second time slightly harder. Fitz's booming voice repeated, "Kansas City Missouri Police Department."

They heard footsteps. Instinctively Frankie placed her hand on her on the top of her holstered weapon. The door opened just enough for Jim to put his foot on the threshold. The face meeting Frankie's was a younger version of Finnegan. The boy, not more than sixteen years old had glazed, bloodshot eyes. The pungent smell of marijuana emanated from his body.

"Can I, uh. Can I help you?"

"Where's your dad?" Jim sternly asked.

"I, uh, I don't know."

"What's your name son?"

"Greg."

"Who's here with you?"

Greg fidgeted as he looked over his shoulder. "Uh, just my little, uh, brother."

Already halfway through the door Jim asked, "Mind if we check for ourselves?"

"Uh, yeah. I guess."

Greg stepped aside to allow him to finish walking through the door. Frankie stayed with Greg in the foyer as Fitz and Jim checked the main floor and Bobby and Hoff checked the second floor. Jim shook his head at her when they returned.

Frankie gently asked, "Where's your dad Greg?"

"He and mom went to some party. I don't remember where."

"Did they tell you when they'd be back?"

"Probably any time. They usually get back before Trey has to go to bed. He goes to bed in, like, thirty minutes."

As if on cue they heard the garage door rising.

"What the hell is going on here?"

Geoffrey Finnegan's voice boomed in the hallway.

Frankie walked toward Finnegan and said, "Mr. Finnegan, I'm Detective Thomas with the Kansas City Missouri Police Department. This is Detective Fitzmeyer and Special Agent Craven. We'd like to talk to you about a case we're working on. Would you mind coming with us back to our office?"

"Am I under arrest?"

"No. We just need to talk to you."

"Do you want me to call our attorney?" asked Elizabeth.

Finnegan looked from Frankie to Fitz to Jim. A half-smile, half-smirk crept to his mouth when he said, "No. I don't think I'll need him. I'll call you when I'm done so you can come and get me."

Finnegan sat in the front seat with Jim on the drive to police headquarters. Frankie noticed she had a couple of missed text messages. She checked the ones from her daughter first.

"Home from school and working on homework. Ty's with Keith. Love you mom. Be careful."

She responded, *"Love you both. XOXO"*

The next message was from Derek. *"At the hospital. Call me when you can."*

"Are you okay?"

Frankie's stomach tightened as memories of the scene at the courthouse flashed through her mind. Her hands trembled and the color drained from her face as she hit the send button on her phone.

Fitz sat next to her and whispered, "Are you okay?"

"Yeah. Just learned a friend is in the hospital but I'm not sure why."

She checked her phone multiple times on the drive, but Derek never answered. She and Fitz listened while Jim made small talk with Finnegan. They exchanged a look as Finnegan bragged about making his living gambling and how he paid cash for his house. He said his wife did not work because their son Trey had special needs and required full-time care. Jim was careful not to ask any questions but just let him talk. Twenty minutes later he and Frankie knew what was important to Finnegan. And more importantly, they knew where his weaknesses were.

"YOU BETTER DO SOMETHING, Craig. This has gone too far. The FBI was just here with some female detective. They arrested Geoff. What the hell is going on?"

The volume of Elizabeth's voice increased with each word. She took a drag from her cigarette and held her breath waiting for an answer. She stared out the kitchen window into the dark night and slowly exhaled.

"Don't worry Lizzy. I'll take care of it. Did you call Tessa?"

"Hell no I didn't called Tessa. I called you. You told me it was under control. You told me Tessa could manage Hannah. You told me they would never connect this back to my house."

"Calm down Lizzy…"

"Don't tell me to 'calm down.' The feds weren't at your house!" Elizabeth's face contorted in anger, "I would never have let Geoff help that bitch if I thought it would come back on him like this. What the hell am I supposed to do if he goes to prison?"

"It won't come to that, sis. I'll take care of it."

"You better, Craig. If you don't things are going to get ugly."

Midori parked his car on the side of the road and stared at the blank screen of his cell phone. During the short conversation he had with his sister he had driven to Frankie's neighborhood. He broke his gaze from the phone and stared at the house. Midori watched through the window as Dani typed on her laptop and bobbed her head to a beat only she could hear.

Midori scanned the area looking to see if anyone was outside. Not seeing anyone he stepped out of the car and walked toward the house. *"This should be easy,"* he thought to himself. Midori stepped down the side of the house softly, using the darkness to shield his movements. His breaths came in short bursts as he made his way to the back door and slowly turned the knob of the sunroom door. Just as he expected the door opened with just a slight creaking noise. Midori waited and when he was certain he had not been detected he stepped inside. He gently turned the knob of the inside door and waited for the barking of the dog, but no sounds came from inside the house. Midori stepped lightly across the kitchen floor, then through the dining room until he was directly behind Dani. In one swift movement, he had an arm around her tiny body with the gun barrel buried in her rib cage. His other hand covered her mouth to silence any screams. Danielle squirmed and kicked but she was no match for Midori's strength.

Gruffly he said, "We're going to walk out to my car. If you so much as peep I'm going to put a bullet through your heart. Do you understand?"

Tears welled in her eyes. Dani nodded slowly.

Midori half-walked, half-carried her to the front door. He removed his hand from Dani's mouth with a reminder, "If you scream, I will shoot you!"

Softly she said, "Okay."

They stepped onto the front porch. Dani walked tentatively. Quietly. She moved slowly and scanned the neighborhood for Keith or Bruce. Midori nudged her to move more quickly. As they reached the car, she heard Bruce say, "Dani? Hey Dani!"

Dani screamed "Help! Bruce! Help!"

Midori spun to the right allowing Dani to break away and start to run toward Bruce. Midori aimed his gun and fired.

Bruce yelled to Dani, "Run!"

One shot. Two shots. Three shots. Bruce collapsed on the ground.

Dani screamed "Help!" repeatedly.

Midori scrambled to get into his car and sped away frantically.

EIGHTY-FIVE

DEREK DIDN'T WANT to tell Frankie he'd been shot via text. He wasn't sure how to respond to her *"Are you okay?"* message and was trying to figure out what to say when the doctor walked into his room.

Dr. Wilhelm introduced himself to him then said, "You are going to need surgery, Mr. Kensington. We have confirmed you took at least two bullets. One is lodged about two millimeters from your spine. The other is near your liver. We need to get both out. The sooner the better."

"How is Jessica?"

"Who?"

The nurse explained Derek was brought in with a woman who had also been shot.

"Oh. I believe she is in surgery. She lost a lot of blood. It's been touch and go since she was brought in. We need your permission to take you to surgery."

Derek took a deep breath and slowly exhaled. He could be paralyzed. Jessica could die. As he was trying to process the information Officer McClendon walked into the room, "Hey counselor, you may not remember me but…"

"Aren't you Frankie's old partner? You were at the courthouse, right?"

"Yeah. I have some photos to show you." McClendon laid six photos in front of him, "Do you recognize any of the men in these photos?"

Derek studied the photos and said, "It's like I told you earlier, I couldn't see the shooter." Derek was frustrated. He wanted to pick someone out of the photo array. "It was dark. It happened so fast."

"Is there anything about the car that stood out?"

Derek suddenly realized what the victims he worked with must feel like. He wanted to give the officers answers, but they just weren't there. He was suddenly ashamed of the times he thought victims were being deceitful because they couldn't give enough details.

The doctor interrupted before he could say anything more, "We need to get you to surgery. Now." He put emphasis on the word "now."

The nurses wheeled Derek from the room. McClendon gathered the photographs and promised him they would do all they could to find the men responsible. It was a promise he hoped he could keep. He didn't know what he would say to Frankie if he failed.

AT POLICE HEADQUARTERS Frankie asked Jim to take Finnegan up to the fourth floor. She pulled out her cell phone and tried to call Derek but before she could dial the number, she noticed a text message from Mac. *"Call me, Frankie. It's urgent."*

Her hands trembled as she dialed the number from memory, "What happened, Mac?"

He didn't mince words, "Derek and another prosecutor were shot. It's bad, Frankie. She may not live. Derek may be paralyzed. They're taking him into surgery now."

Her voice broke as she asked, "What happened?"

"They were found on the south side of the courthouse. Looked like they were getting in his car when a blacked-out SUV drove by and fired about a dozen rounds from an automatic weapon. I was on my way to HQ when I heard the call come out but by the time I arrived they were loading the woman up. I recognized Derek and talked to him at the scene. When I realized they were the prosecutors on the Joaquin Jackson case I had a car go sit on Jamel Cason's place."

"I remember him. We arrested him a few times for possession and burglary, I think."

"Yeah, that's him. I'm pretty sure he was the shooter, but Derek couldn't identify him in a lineup. It might have been one of his soldiers.

It smells like his work. Millsap's squad is working on a warrant for the car and house."

Frankie was silent as she processed the information. She was conflicted on what to do. Should she go to the hospital? Go do her interview?

McClendon read her thoughts and said, "Frankie, there's nothing you can do here. Go finish your interview. I'll let you know if anything changes."

"Thanks, Mac. Text me with any updates. I'll call you when I get off."

She put her phone in her pocket and took a deep breath. Frankie mumbled quietly to herself and pushed the elevator button, "Shake it off, Thomas."

Jim was waiting for her in the squad room. Seeing the strained look on Frankie's face he asked, "Are you okay?"

"Yep. Which room is he in?"

"This one," he gestured toward the hall. "He's nervous as hell. Do you need a minute?"

"Nope. Let's do this." Frankie grabbed her notepad and started toward the door, "Mia, can you watch on the monitor? Text me if you notice something."

"You got it, Frankie."

Frankie nodded her thanks and opened the interview room door.

CHAPTER
EIGHTY-SEVEN

FINNEGAN SAT in a chair facing the door. He tapped his fingers rhythmically on the table. His shoulders curved inward, his eyes were bloodshot, and his face scarlet. The nervous tapping of his foot fell in time with his fingers.

"It's about damn time," Finnegan's voice cracked and his attempt to sound gruff failed.

Frankie took her time organizing the paperwork. She had a system and was not going to allow his nervous, impatient behavior dictate her pace. Once she had everything in order, she began asking questions to build rapport with him. With each question, he slowly began to relax. His shoulders lowered and he began to lean back in his chair. When she was confident he was at ease her questions turned to the reason they were there.

"Geoffrey, where were you the Monday before Thanksgiving?"

He fidgeted as he answered, "How should I know where I was? Can you tell me where you were?"

She didn't take the bait. Instead, she laid a photograph of Hannah's garage in front of him and asked, "Do you recognize this building?"

"No, uh, I mean it looks familiar, but I can't say I recognize it."

"Have you ever been to this garage?"

"I don't think, uh, I mean no. Um, where is it?"

Frankie didn't answer his question. She laid a photograph of Hannah in front of him and asked, "Do you know this woman?"

He touched the photograph. Finnegan traced the bruise on Hannah's face lightly with his fingertips then said, "I met her a couple of times. With another friend of mine. At the casino."

Frankie noticed he didn't ask how Hannah got injured. "When was the last time you saw her?"

"Week or so before Thanksgiving."

She laid a photograph of Tessa in front of him and asked, "Do you recognize this woman?"

"Yeah." Finnegan pushed the photographs toward her. "What's this all about?"

Frankie didn't react but asked, "How do you know her?"

He fidgeted in his seat, "I guess you'd say we're friends."

"When was the last time you saw her?"

"Week or so before Thanksgiving. She and Hannah were at the casino." Finnegan began to pick at an invisible thread on his shirt sleeve. "We had a few drinks. Tessa and I gambled and had dinner."

"What about Hannah?"

"She left. She was whining about it getting dark and being afraid to go into her house at night. Apparently one of the goons they're suing held a gun to her head a couple months ago. They jumped her one night when she left her house. She tried to get Tessa to leave with her, but she and I had plans."

Jim interjected, "What kind of plans?"

Finnegan looked at Jim as though he had forgotten he was there then said, "We were going to discuss a possible business partnership. I've been working on a card game and Tessa was going to help underwrite the cost."

Frankie leaned forward in her chair and made eye contact with him, "Where was Tessa going to get the money?"

"The lawsuit."

FINNEGAN LOOKED from Jim to Frankie. He opened his mouth to speak then hesitated.

Frankie inched her chair closer to him and asked, "Tell us what you know, Geoff. Tell us what happened to those girls."

Finnegan looked down to his knees, looked up with a smirk and said, "Those girls? Those girls? Ha! You don't get it. This is so much bigger than you realize."

"Help us understand."

Finnegan took a deep breath then slowly exhaled, "A few months ago, I started working with this guy on a new game for Vegas. I invested about $70,000 of my own money and we are still a few months away from the launch."

Impatiently Jim asked, "What does that have to do with Hannah and Tessa?"

"For Christ's sake, man. I'm getting to it. About a week before Thanksgiving I was at the casino waiting on my brother-in-law when Tessa and Hannah showed up. Hannah was bitching about that lawsuit. Again. After Hannah left Tessa told me she really needed the lawsuit to settle quickly. She's gotten in deep and owes money to some scary people."

He took a drink from the bottle of water.

"Geoff, who's your brother-in-law?"

"Craig Midori. Anyway, we started talking and Tessa asked for my help. She thought if something more serious happened to them then the dealership would settle the lawsuit. She said something about possibly faking an attack. At first, I thought she was kidding so I played along. I told her I'd get a buddy and we'd kidnap them, put them in the trunk of the car and leave them on some railroad tracks. Tessa got off on the idea but said she wasn't going to get into the trunk of a car. It was then that I realized she was serious. Initially I told her I wasn't going to have any part of it but then she offered me a cut. She said if I helped her, she would pay me $75,000. I've been living on my credit cards while I've been working on this game launch, so her offer was tempting. I told her I'd think about it.

"When my brother-in-law got to the casino Tessa took off. When Craig saw I was with Tessa he was all over me asking, 'What the hell was I doing talking to that bitch?' 'What was I thinking hanging out with the enemy?' Craig ranted like that for several minutes. Apparently, Tessa had some bad debt with his boss.

"Without thinking I told him what Tessa wanted me to do and Craig perked up. Next thing I know he had Maggio on the phone, and they are offering me $200,000 if I did something."

"What did they want you to do?"

"Craig is a crazy mother. He wanted me to kill Hannah and really mess Tessa up. I told him I wasn't going to kill anyone, but I'd scare them enough that they'd drop the lawsuit. I convinced Maggio and Craig to let me do it my way. I told them I'd use my friendship with Tessa to set them up. It would be clean and easy and never come back on them."

Jim, who had been listening quietly asked, "What happened next Geoff?"

"What the fuck do you think happened? I called Tessa and set up a meet. The next day she met me at a park near Hannah's and we came up with a plan."

Finnegan picked up his bottle of water, finishing it in one drink.

"What was the plan, Geoff?"

"Do I need a lawyer?" Finnegan asked as he played with the lid on the bottle of water. Twisting it on and off.

Frankie and Jim exchanged a look. They needed him to confess but if he got an attorney, they knew Finnegan would shut down. Silence would work in their favor.

Finnegan ran his fingers through his hair and said, "Fuck it. When I met up with Tessa, I told her what Craig wanted me to do. I thought if she knew maybe she'd offer me more of a cut but instead she freaked out. She yelled and screamed at me. Called me every name in the book. Then she got quiet. Tessa told me she wanted half. She said she'd help me if I'd give her $100,000. She would help set everything up."

"What exactly did Tessa do?"

"Can I get some more water?"

Jim stood up and said, "I need to stretch my legs. I'll grab a bottle."

"Thanks," Frankie said, "So, what did Tessa do, Geoff?"

"She coordinated the whole thing."

FINNEGAN RUBBED the palms of his hands down his jeans and continued, "Tessa got Hannah to go shopping then left the garage unlocked for me so I could get in. Tessa put duct tape and a rose in one of the plastic bins inside the garage along with a fake bomb. Two empty beer bottles were left next to the door.

"I called Craig. Told him I had been following Tessa and tailed them to Town Centre. I asked him to watch them so I could set up and wait for them in the garage. I told him to let me know when they left. I knew I needed an alibi just in case Craig got caught and tried to pin everything on me, so after he got to Town Centre I went and bought a movie ticket. Then I drove back to Waldo, went to a bar, and had a beer. When I got Tessa's text saying they were on the way back I went to the house and hid in the garage. Craig called as I was driving to tell me they were on the way. He told me he wanted to come help, but I was afraid he'd kill them. I didn't want two dead women on my conscious, so I told him I had it all under control. As far as I know he went home.

"About five minutes after I got situated in the garage, I heard the door go up. I was hidden in the corner by the garage door so they couldn't see me when they pulled in. After the garage door went down Hannah turned off the car and jumped out. I was behind her before she had a chance to clear the door. I hit her on the head with one of the beer bottles and watched her fall to her knees. She didn't immediately pass out, so I hit her again. Once she was on the ground I put duct tape on her mouth, hands, and ankles."

"Where was Tessa?"

"She took the fake bomb and put it under Hannah's car. Then she moved behind me and started giving me orders. After I duct taped Hannah, I looked over my shoulder at Tessa. She was almost… smiling. I did what I did then went to get the rose so I could lay it on her body." Suddenly he stopped. His face began to pale. "Then I hit Tessa, duct taped her, turned the car on and left."

Frankie sat silently for a few moments before asking, "Geoff, you left a big piece out. Help me understand."

Finnegan's gaze fell as he sat quietly.

"Why did you rape her?" Frankie decided to push Finnegan and asked, "And why with a beer bottle and a rose?"

Finnegan didn't answer right away. He ran his fingers through his hair and let out a deep exhale before saying, "We wanted the attack to be more believable. Tessa thought another assault could have looked like a robbery or would be downplayed, but this, this made it more serious. More believable. I think I'll take that lawyer now."

Jim brought him water just as Frankie stood up to leave the room.

CHAPTER
NINETY

FRANKIE LEANED her back against the wall next to the closed door of the interrogation room. She exhaled the breath she didn't realize she had been holding.

Walking back to the squad room she asked Jim, "How could a woman do that to another woman? Much less someone she called friend?"

Jim just shook his head. For once he was at a loss for words. "What do you want to do now?"

"Lock the bitch up and throw away the key," Frankie was angry. It was already so hard for sexual assault victims to get justice. To have a woman go to this extreme for money was unbelievable. She said, "We need to get to her before Finnegan does. I'd put money on her being the first person his attorney calls."

"Why don't you go check on your friend in the hospital? Fitz and I'll go pick her up and let you know when we are on our way back here."

She hesitated before saying, "Okay. But let me call her instead of you picking her up. I'll arrange for her to come give a statement about the phone call. I want her to think I still believe her. Mia, can you call the jail and ask them to wait an hour before letting Finnegan make a phone call?"

"Good call, Frankie," Mia said.

Frankie stood staring at her phone. She took a deep breath, exhaling her frustration and anger. She knew she needed to sound calm and professional.

Tessa answered on the second ring, "Hello."

"Tessa? Detective Thomas. Do you have a few minutes?"

"Sure. What do you need? Hannah's here, too. Should I put the phone on speaker?"

"Um. You can if you want but it isn't necessary."

Frankie waited until Tessa said the phone was on speaker.

"Would you have time to come to my office? I need to get a formal statement regarding the phone call you received. I also have a few voice recordings. I thought we'd try a voice line-up to see if you recognize any of them as the person who called you."

Frankie was good at thinking on her feet, and she knew Tessa would be eager to cooperate.

"Really?" Tessa fumbled with her words, "I, uh, I guess I can."

"I can send someone to pick you up if you'd like. Or you can drive here. I need to run to the hospital, or I'd come out and get you myself."

"Um, no I can drive over. Do you mind if Hannah comes, too? She may want to listen. It'd be great if she recognized a voice, too. Maybe the guy that attacked her the first time?"

"Sure, Tessa. That'll be fine," Truth was Frankie wanted to talk to Hannah, too. She ended the conversation quickly and gathered her things to go see Derek.

Before she could ask, Mia said, "I'm coming with you."

Frankie was quiet on the drive to the hospital. The chatter on the police radio provided a familiar, almost comforting backdrop of sound. She was wondering what to expect. Would Derek be conscious? Would they even let her in to see him? She wasn't family. Was his family there? This would be an awkward way to meet them for the first time. Did they even know about her?

The five-minute drive to the hospital felt like an hour. Mac had texted Frankie Derek's room number. They rode the elevator to the fourth floor in silence. They turned to walk down the hall. Frankie suddenly stopped, took a deep breath, and said a silent prayer.

Mia grabbed her hand, squeezed it tight, and said, "He's going to be okay, Frankie."

Frankie returned Mia's squeeze, nodded, and continued to walk.

The women greeted the officer standing outside the hospital room and after a moment of small talk Frankie looked to Mia and said, "Give me a minute, okay?"

Mia nodded, "Take your time. I'll be here waiting when you're ready to go."

Frankie slowly and quietly pushed open the door of the hospital room. The only light came from behind the bed. Derek looked small and frail lying on the bed with tubes flowing from his body like the tendrils of an octopus. The beeping of the monitors told her how fast his heartbeat and how strong the pressure of blood pumped through his veins. His eyes were closed and his face pale.

Frankie felt tears well in her eyes as she walked to his bedside. She placed her hand gently on top of his, leaned down, and kissed his white lips. She leaned her head close and whispered in his ear, "I'm here, baby."

Frankie lifted her head and gazed at the man whom she had unwillingly fallen in love. She watched as his eyes fluttered.

"Hey," Derek's voice was soft, hoarse, and weak.

"Hey, yourself," Frankie gave him a half smile and held his hand lightly in her grasp.

"I'm glad you're here."

She nodded, "I can't stay long but I'll come back after I finish my shift."

Derek nodded as he closed his eyes. "Good," was the last word he said before he drifted back to sleep.

NINETY-ONE

FRANKIE WAS EXHAUSTED. She couldn't remember when she last slept, and the night was far from over. She looked at Mia and asked, "Ready?"

"Yep. Let's do this." Once outside Mia asked, "Are you okay, Frankie?"

Before she could answer, the emergency room doors burst open. Paramedics rushed through the entrance shouting vitals to the hospital personnel. Frankie and Mia stepped out of the way. An oxygen mask covered the face of the man on the gurney. A paramedic straddled him while administering CPR.

"Mommy," the sound of Dani's voice startled Frankie and caused Mia to turn.

"Dani? Sweety, what happened?"

Dani ran to Frankie and collapsed in her arms. Frankie held her sobbing daughter and stroked her flaxen hair. Confused, she asked, "Where's Tyler? What happened?"

"He's with Keith. Bruce saved me. This man was going to take me. He shot Bruce. Is he going to die? It's all my fault. Bruce wouldn't have gotten shot if he wasn't trying to help me." Dani spoke swiftly, her breath in gasps. A new wave of sobs swept over her.

"It's not your fault. What man, Dani?" Frankie's hands were trembling. Tears welled in her eyes.

"I don't know. He came up behind me while I was working on my computer. He said he'd kill me if I yelled. He tried to get me inside the car but then Bruce came home. He said my name. I shouldn't have yelled. It's my fault. If I wouldn't have…"

Frankie interjected, "It's not your fault, baby. You did everything right." She tried to comfort her daughter as she silently blamed herself.

"Dani, what did the guy look like?" Mia stood beside Frankie with her notebook open and a pen in hand.

"He had on a suit. I think it was black. But I don't think he had a tie on. I don't remember seeing one. He was taller than me but not as tall as Bruce."

"Bruce is 6' Mia. Go on Dani."

"He had black hair, but I don't know what color his eyes were. I didn't really see his face because he was behind me. I kept looking at his gun. It was black. It looked like yours. What if he comes back? What if he tries to take Ty?"

"You get all that, Mia?"

Mia nodded and said, "I'll get it out on the air."

Frankie ushered Dani to the waiting room and closed her eyes as she dialed Keith's number. He answered on the second ring.

"What's up, Frankie?"

She took a deep breath, "Keith, you need to get to the county hospital."

"What happened, Frankie? Are you okay? Want me to grab Dani?"

"She's here with me. Keith, Bruce has been shot. They are taking him into surgery now."

"I'll be there in five."

CHAPTER
NINETY-TWO

KEITH WALKED into the waiting room holding Tyler's hand. Keith's pale blue eyes glistened with fresh tears. When he saw his mother and sister, Tyler let go of Keith's hand and ran. Frankie squatted to meet him and enveloped him in her arms.

His face searched hers, "What happened mom? Keith was crying."

"Bruce was hurt. The doctors are trying to fix him now."

"Dani are you okay?" Tyler looked at his sister with concern.

She gave a half-smile to her brother and nodded.

Mia tapped Frankie on the shoulder and said, "The Assault Squad is going to need to talk to Dani."

Frankie nodded,

"Keith..."

"Go Frankie. Do what you need to do. I'll call you if anything changes."

"We'll get him, Keith." Frankie hugged him and said, "I promise. We'll get him."

He laid his head onto hers. Tears caught in his throat, "I know."

Frankie put her arm around Dani and took Tyler's hand in hers. Mia led them down the hall to the parking garage.

Outside the automatic door Mia asked, "Are you okay, Frankie?"

Frankie took a deep breath. The air in the hospital garage was stale with a hint of car exhaust.

Tears stung her eyes as she nodded and said, "Let's finish this."

CHAPTER
NINETY-THREE

FRANKIE ESCORTED Dani to the second floor of police headquarters. Sergeant Millsap met them at the elevator.

"Hey, Frankie. Is this your daughter?" Millsap nodded his head toward Dani, a miniature version of Frankie.

"Mm hmm." She introduced Millsap to Dani and Tyler. One of Millsap's detectives took Tyler to the waiting room while Frankie and Dani followed him to an interview room.

Millsap got a brief statement from Dani, along with the description of the suspect. Frankie signed a consent to search form so his squad could process her house.

When he finished getting Dani's statement, Frankie grabbed her phone, and dialed her sister's number.

"Sophie?"

A sleep-filled voice replied, "Hey sis. What's going on? Everything okay?"

"Can you come to HQ and get the kids?"

"What happened, Frankie? Are you okay?"

"I'm fine Sophie but Bruce was shot. I need you to get the kids so I can finish what I started."

Her matter-of-fact tone got Sophie's attention, "Okay, Frankie. I'm getting dressed now. I'll be there in ten."

Frankie got to the basement of police headquarters just as Sophie arrived. She pulled Dani and Tyler into her arms and spoke softly, "Go with Aunt Sophie to her apartment. I'll come and get you when I finish here."

"But what if he comes back mom?"

Frankie smoothed Dani's hair before kissing the top of her head, "He won't. I'm going to have a car outside until I get home."

Tears trickled from Dani's eyes, "Okay, mom. I love you."

"I love you too, Angel-girl. Take care of Ty, okay?"

"Yes ma'am."

She mussed Tyler's hair and asked, "Do you know how much I love you, Ty?"

"More than all the sand and water in the sea," Tyler repeated what he had heard from her daily since the day he was born.

"That's right, buddy. Don't forget it."

"Love you too, mom."

Frankie watched Sophie's car drive down the block. Jim came up behind her and asked, "Are you ready?"

Frankie looked up, anger filling her, and said, "Let's do this."

NINETY-FOUR

FRANKIE PUSHED OPEN the door of the interrogation room and walked in with Jim close behind. Tessa and Hannah sat at the table talking quietly.

"Tessa, would you mind waiting outside?"

Frankie kept her voice steady as she motioned toward the door.

"Sure," said Tessa.

Once the door closed, she sent Mia a text, *"Make sure she isn't listening at the door."*

Frankie made small talk with Hannah until she got a message from Mia, *"Taking her to the breakroom for coffee."*

"Hannah, how well do you know Tessa?"

"Pretty well. She's really looked out for me these last few months. Why?"

"Did you know she had financial problems?" Frankie attempted to downplay Tessa's situation.

"Well, we were both out of work for a few months, so I'm not surprised. She never said anything though."

"Do you know anything about her gambling problem?"

"I...what does that have to do with anything?" Hannah started scanning the room. Her eyes darting like a frightened animal.

Frankie sat and looked at Hannah without saying a word. She sensed the words she needed to say were going to break Hannah's heart.

Unable to handle the silence Hannah softly asked, "How bad is it?"

"She was about to lose everything."

Frankie opened her notepad. She was unsure how Hannah was going to take the information that her friend had set her up. Switching gears, she laid a photograph of Finnegan in front of her.

Hannah glanced at the photo and asked, "Did something happen to Geoff?"

"How do you know the man in this photo?"

"He's a friend of Tessa's. I've only met him a couple of times. Always at the casino. Why?"

"We think he had something to do with your attack," Frankie said, and took note of the look of incredulousness on Hannah's face.

"Why would he want to hurt us? He and Tessa are friends."

Frankie sat silently, waiting for the reality to hit Hannah.

"Wait a minute. You don't think? Tessa wouldn't..." Tears slipped from Hannah's eyes as it all became clear. "That's why you asked Tessa to come in, isn't it?"

"Yes."

"You think she's working with Geoffrey. But why would they want to hurt me?" Hannah fumbled with her bag and asked, "It's money, isn't it? I thought she was just pissed off. I can't believe she'd do this."

"What are you talking about, Hannah?"

Hannah looked toward the door. Sweat began to bead on her upper lip as she moved in her chair.

Frankie looked from Jim to the door and asked, "Did you ride with Tessa?"

Hannah nodded her head and asked, "Do you think she can hear what we're talking about?"

Frankie shook her head, "No. Mia took her to get coffee and said she'd text me when they're on their way back."

Hannah sat silently. She appeared to be unsure if she should talk but eventually looked to Frankie and said, "Right after that guy threatened me at my house, we were scheduled to do depositions. We finished the first deposition and took a break and were talking about what happened to me. Marzullo started to laugh and next thing I know they were all laughing and making jokes at my expense. I left the room in tears and hid in the bathroom. Tessa came in and tried to comfort me. We ended up going to the casino afterwards for dinner and drinks. We ran into Geoff there."

Frankie couldn't believe what she was hearing. Was it possible Hannah was part of the planning? With a poker face she asked, "What happened next?"

"I was complaining about those assholes and Geoffrey made some stupid crack about the mob. Before I could say anything Tessa chastised Geoff and told him he shouldn't be making fun of me. Then she made a comment like, 'can you imagine if something worse had happened? What kind of money they'd be willing to pay?' I looked at her like she'd lost her mind. The look on my face must have said it all because she quickly said, 'God forbid.' Then Tessa told me I must know she was kidding. I really thought she was. I mean, she had always been so good to me. I cannot imagine her wanting to hurt me."

"Did the two of you leave the casino together?" Jim's voice seemed loud in the small room compared to Hannah's soft one.

Hannah looked at her hands thoughtfully as though they held the answers. The red of her eyes were a direct contrast to her pale skin. A barely audible, "no" escaped her lips.

Jim looked at Frankie, nodded, and softly asked, "Do you want to help us nail them?"

Hannah raised her head and nodded an almost imperceptible nod.

"HANNAH, DO YOU UNDERSTAND THE PLAN?"

Frankie and Jim had outlined what they expected. Frankie felt confident Hannah could do it, but Jim was not as sure.

"Yes. And you all will be close by the whole time, right?"

Frankie nodded and said, "We will have eyes and ears on you the entire time. Do you think you can get her to talk?"

"Yeah. I'm pretty sure," Hannah pulled her compact and eye drops from her purse. "You can tell I've been crying. Fortunately, that's a common look for me these days. Tessa probably won't even notice. I can't believe that bitch did this to me."

Jim was kind but firm.

"Hannah, you've got to pull it together. She has to believe you two are still allies. If you let your anger show she'll know we're on to her."

"I know," Hannah snapped. "I'll keep it together."

Frankie watched the interchange and said, "Okay. When you leave here make plans for her to come to your house tomorrow night. Tell her you want to try a new recipe or something. We'll come and wire your house in the morning."

"Okay. I'll call you when I have it set up. What are you going to say to Tessa tonight?"

Frankie looked at Jim and said, "I'm going to rush out of here. Jim will tell her I have a family emergency and had to leave. We'll need to reschedule."

Hannah nodded and said, "Okay."

As planned, Frankie rushed through the office door without stopping to speak to Tessa. Mia bolted from the opposite end of the hall and said, "Frankie, I'll drive."

The pair pushed the door open to the stairwell and let it slam behind them.

Jim watched as Frankie rushed down then hall, then said, "Tessa, my apologies. Detective Thomas has had a family emergency. We'll need to reschedule."

Tessa picked up her bag. Tersely she said, "Oh. Okay. I hope every-thing is alright."

Jim gave a non-committal answer and ushered the women to the elevator.

"Thanks for coming in ladies. Detective Thomas will call you in a couple of days."

CHAPTER
NINETY-SIX

"JIM, put a mic in the kitchen over the island. See if you can hide it on the pot rack. Put a second one under the kitchen table. Is there anywhere else you all will be Hannah?"

Hannah chewed on her lower lip and twisted the fingers of her clasped hands. "The bathroom?"

"We won't put one in there. We'll have a boom mic in the car. We'll be parked up the block and will be able to catch her if she is talking outside." Frankie could tell Hannah was nervous and asked, "Do you want one of us to stay inside with you? Is there somewhere Tessa wouldn't go?"

Hannah plopped herself on the barstool. Her elbows hit the table and she rested her chin on her hand. "She never goes upstairs. Detective Thomas, can you stay in the house? I would feel much safer if someone were inside."

Frankie looked from Jim to Mia as Frankie nodded her head.

"Frankie, we have the mics placed. Why don't you and I go to the car and make sure they work. Mia, can you stay with Hannah and help us test it?"

"Sure, Jim."

Frankie shot a questioning look toward Jim and Mia then followed

Jim as he stepped out the backdoor of the house. "So, you think this will work, Jim?"

Jim didn't immediately answer. He walked with purpose, causing her to walk faster. When both car doors were closed, he turned to her and asked, "What the hell are you doing, Frankie?"

Frankie was confused by his questions.

"What do you mean? I thought we were trying to nail this bitch."

"Why did you agree to stay inside the house? You know how dangerous that can be. What if Tessa hears you? What if she decides to wander around the house?"

Frankie was surprised by his response. Jim seemed worried.

"I didn't think…"

His voice was sharp, "No, you didn't fuckin' think. This chick is crazy! Do you have a death wish?!"

"Whoa, Jim. Hold on. I'll have my earpiece in. You can communicate to me without being heard. Hannah's obviously nervous. I was afraid she'd back out if I didn't do something. What the hell was I supposed to say? We can't let Tessa get away with this."

Jim rubbed his head. His voice was softer as he said, "I know. I'm just…I don't want…the mission to fail."

Frankie took a deep breath and reached over to touch his hand, "I know. This is going to work. It has to."

The sound of Mia's voice broke into the conversation, "Frankie. Jim. Are you getting this?"

Frankie sent Mia a text, "*Loud and clear.*"

"Let's go in and run through the plan one more time."

Jim and Frankie exchanged a final look as she opened the door.

"Hannah, I'll be in the closet listening. Make sure Tessa doesn't find a reason to open the door. Get her talking about Geoffrey and the plan. We're recording everything. We want a confession but be careful. We don't want to tip her off."

Hannah's voice cracked as she said, "O – kay."

Frankie got firm, "Hannah, you need to pull it together."

With tears in her eyes Hannah said, "I know. I'll be fine. I can do this."

Jim looked from Mia to Frankie. Frankie nodded her head and looked

Jim in the eyes. She believed in Hannah and wanted him to have faith in her, too.

"Okay ladies. Let's do this. Get in the closet, Frankie."

Jim shot her a wink.

Mia and Jim left through the back door. Frankie sat at the table with Hannah. "You can do this, Hannah. If you feel like you are going to slip up, ask her how her dogs are. Mia will call your phone and say there is an emergency at work. That will be your out. Do you understand?"

Hannah nodded.

"Frankie, she's pulling up now," Mia's voice whispered in Frankie's ear.

"Got it, Mia. Hannah, Tessa is pulling up now. Are you good?"

Hannah nodded. Frankie stepped into the dark closet.

CHAPTER
NINETY-SEVEN

"IS THERE anything I can do to help?" Tessa's voice was upbeat as she chattered mindlessly about her day.

Hannah fought to keep her voice normal as she asked, "Can you wash and tear the lettuce?" Hannah wanted to confront Tessa head on but knew it would ruin everything.

Grabbing the head of lettuce Tessa moved to the sink and said, "So, I told my attorney we weren't willing to settle. They think $250,000 is going to cut it after everything we've gone through? Puhlease. Those assholes need to pay."

Hannah stirred the sauce simmering on the stove, "Mmhm. They have a lot of nerve. I just wish this was over. I'm so tired of being scared all the time. I keep thinking those guys are going to come back. My parents didn't want me to come back here but I needed my space."

Tessa walked over and put her harm around Hannah's shoulders and said, "Oh sweety. I know but trust me when I say you're safe."

"How can you be so sure?"

"I just am." Tessa pushed Hannah's hair from her eyes. Her eyes bore into Hannah's. "Trust me, Hannah."

Hannah stood toe to toe with her and asked, "Is there something you aren't telling me? Did Detective Thomas call you?"

Tessa dropped her hand from Hannah's shoulder and went back to tearing the lettuce and stared out the window as she washed the lettuce in the sink.

"No. I haven't talked to her since she ran out of the office the other day. How fucking rude was that? Calling us in and then running out. I have half a mind to call her sergeant."

"She couldn't help that there was a family emergency. I mean, it wasn't like she planned it."

"I guess you're right, but it still irritates me. She could have called after her little emergency was handled."

"Tessa, how do you know I'll be safe? I mean, I'm afraid to walk outside of my house after dark. I haven't even been to yoga since that guy put a gun to my head. I'm even thinking of selling my house, but you seem so calm."

Tessa stood at the sink, her back to Hannah. She slowly turned the faucet off, grabbed a tea towel, and turned around to face Hannah. "Can I tell you something without you freaking out?"

Hannah's hands began to tremble. She tried to remain calm as she prepared for her friend to confess what she did.

"Tessa? What is it? You're scaring me."

Tessa took two wine glasses and a bottle of wine from the counter. After opening the bottle, she motioned for Hannah to sit at the table, "You should probably sit for this."

Hannah complied with Tessa's request. She placed her clasped hands in her lap to hide their tremble.

"The attack on you was a set up."

Hannah decided to play along, "I know. Maggio orchestrated it."

Tessa looked into Hannah's eyes and said, "That's not entirely true. Geoff and I..."

Hannah jumped from the chair yelling, "What the fuck Tessa? What did you do?"

Tessa's voice remained calm as she said, "Hannah. Sit down. Please. Let me explain."

Hannah locked eyes with Tessa before returning to her seat.

"It all started after that asshole held you up at gunpoint. We were trying to settle the lawsuit and their attorneys were laughing at you and the cops weren't doing anything. It looked like Maggio was going to win. Then the idea came…"

Hannah interrupted, "That day at the casino."

"Yes."

Tessa looked down at the table. Slowly her gaze returned to Hannah.

"We were talking about how they would offer a better settlement if something more serious happened. After you left the casino Geoff and I had a few drinks and continued talking. You weren't really supposed to be hurt. I mean, I told him not to do anything too crazy. It was just supposed to look bad.

"When we left your house the night of the attack, I made sure things were set up for Geoff. I unlocked the garage door so he could get inside and wait. When we left the restaurant, I texted him to tell him we were on the way back. Geoff went inside and waited. I thought he was just going to grab you and knock you out. He hit you with one of the beer bottles we left in the garage. That was all he was supposed to do, I promise. But then he brought out the duct tape. He tied you up and hit you again to make sure you were knocked out. The next thing I knew he was hitting me. He put duct tape on me and then went back to you." Tessa looked down and covered her eyes with her hand. "I didn't know he was going to…I'm so sorry Hannah. I would never have allowed him to…I wish I could have stopped him."

Tessa reached out to Hannah who swiftly pulled her hand away. Hannah spat the words, "Don't. Touch. Me."

HANNAH COULDN'T BELIEVE Tessa had just admitted to having her attacked. Her mind was reeling.

"Why? Do you really hate me that much?"

Tessa's face softened as she looked at Hannah.

"No! Sweetheart, I was trying to help. I thought if something else happened they would offer us a better settlement. I didn't know Geoff was going to…"

"Rape me?! He raped me, Tessa! He raped me with a beer bottle and the thorny stem of a rose. I may never be intimate with anyone ever again. Every time I close my eyes… The nurse said I may have long-term damage. What the hell did you think would happen?"

"Hannah, I'm so sorry. It wasn't supposed to be like that. I need the money. Fast. Or…"

"Or what?"

Tessa took a drink from her glass, finishing the wine it contained. She stood, uncorked the bottle, and poured more into the waiting glass. Tessa took the glass and walked back to the sink. As she sipped from the fresh pour she stared into the dark night. Her mind drifted as she watched the leaves blow around the yard.

Tessa turned back toward Hannah. Taking another sip of wine, she said, "The people I owe money to. I'm afraid they're going to kill me."

Hannah gave Tessa a look indicating she should continue.

"I got in over my head. The money from the lawsuit was going to pay them off. Without it I don't know what they'll do."

"Why didn't you just tell me?"

"I didn't want you to worry. You became so jumpy after you were attacked. I figured if I told you about my debt then you would worry more. I was trying to protect you."

The timer on the stove sounded.

"Looks like dinner is ready," said Tessa.

Hannah busied herself getting the dinner from the oven and plates from the cabinet. Tessa finished preparing the salad and placed it on the table. Hannah was sickened and didn't think she could swallow the food. Tessa made small talk while Hannah pushed the food around her plate, pretending to eat her dinner.

After the dishes where rinsed and loaded in the dishwasher Hannah told Tessa she had a headache and needed to go to bed.

"Are we okay, Hannah? You aren't going to tell Detective Thomas, are you?"

"I just need to process this, Tessa. You understand that, right?"

Tessa gave Hannah a hug and said, "Of course. I'll call you tomorrow."

Hannah nodded. She held the door as Tessa walked out into the dark night.

Frankie found Hannah crying at her kitchen table.

"Mia? Jim? You guys can come inside once you're sure Tessa's gone."

Hannah turned to face Frankie, "I still can't believe it. How could a friend do that? I thought she cared about me."

Frankie sat in the chair next to Hannah and said, "Money makes people do strange things."

Frankie was interrupted by a light tapping on the door. Hannah walked to the door and peeked out. Seeing Mia and Jim she opened the door and let them in.

"Now what?" asked Hannah. She wiped the tears from her face and looked at the trio. Jim busied himself retrieving the bugs from the house.

Frankie didn't know how to answer but said, "I'll call the prosecutor and see what they say. The final decision will be theirs."

"Will he go to jail for what he did? What about Tessa? Will she go to jail?"

Frankie exchanged a knowing look with Mia then said, "Hopefully they'll both go to prison."

Hannah nodded and said, "Thank you."

"Ladies, I've got all the mics. Anything else you need me to do?" Jim's accent was thick as he looked toward Frankie.

She caught his eye, "Thanks Jim. I think we're ready."

The trio stood outside the back door and waited for the door lock to latch.

JIM DROPPED Frankie and Mia at the door of police headquarters.

"I'm going to park and then will come up and help out with the paperwork."Frankie and Mia nodded. As the two walked toward the garage entrance Mia asked, "Penny for your thoughts?"

Frankie switched her bag from one shoulder to the next then said, "Derek. Keith. Bruce is his life. I don't know what Keith will do if he doesn't make it."

Mia put her hand on Frankie's shoulder, "He's going to make it. I can feel it."

Frankie nodded. The two rode the elevator in silence. Frankie, lost in her thoughts, jumped at the sound of her phone. "Thomas."

"He's awake," She could hear the relief in Keith's voice. She nodded at Mia to go into the office without her.

"Thank God! What do you need? Can I bring you anything? Whatever you want. Name it." Frankie's voice cracked with the words.

Reading her mind, he said, "It's not your fault, Frankie. You didn't do this. We're good. I just wanted you to know he's okay. I'm going to stay the night. Are you going to be okay going home? What about the kids?"

Frankie felt the warm tears escape her eyes. She faced the wall, placed her forehead against the plaster, and thanked God for not letting Bruce die.

"Frankie?"

"Yeah? Sorry Keith. The kids are with Sophie, and I have a car parked out front. I'll be fine. I may pull an all-nighter. I'll check in with you later."

"Okay girl. Don't work too hard."

"Mhm. Hey Keith?"

"Yeah?"

Her voice was barely above a whisper. It cracked with each word. "I love you guys."

"I know, Frankie. We love you, too."

Frankie disconnected the call. Before walking back into the office, she dialed Derek. After three rings she disconnected. Looking down she debated on sending a text. Pushing the door to the office open, she returned the phone to her pocket. Frankie thought, *"I'll stop by on my way home."*

FRANKIE PUSHED the office door open and released a deep sigh. Mia tapped on her computer. Jim skimmed over the case file. Both looked up when they heard the door open.

"Frankie?" Mia sent her a questioning stare.

She nodded to Mia. With a crack in her voice she said, "Bruce is going to be okay."

Jim patted her on the shoulder. "Great news, Frankie. Are you ready to write these warrants?"

Frankie nodded and smiled, "Mia, will you work on Midori? Jim and I will work on Finnegan and Tessa."

Mia nodded.

Frankie paged the on-call prosecutor. Within minutes the phone was ringing. "Sex Crimes, Detective Thomas."

"Hey Frankie, it's Tim Rodriguez. What do you have?"

Frankie put the phone on speaker as she updated the prosecutor on the facts.

"We were hoping to get three arrest warrants."

"Sounds like an easy day. What about search warrants? Are you going to need any of those?"

She looked at Jim then said, "Yeah. We're going to need warrants for the phone, bodies, car, and maybe even Midori's house. Can you think of any others? Jim? Mia?"

"Let's write one for Tessa's house, too. Who knows what we'll find," Jim said as he continued scanning the reports.

"How long is it going to take you, Frankie?"

"Two hours?" Her voice raised on the word hours.

"Okay. Call me on my cell when you are done so I can be ready for you."

Frankie assured the prosecutor she would call. Without missing a beat, she made a list of warrants on the white board then pulled out her notes and began typing. Jim scanned over the reports and her notes. He moved between her and Mia, providing them the information they needed.

Hours passed. The only words uttered were the occasional case fact or curse word. One by one she and Mia crossed the items off the list.

Standing up to stretch, Frankie walked to the board and crossed the last one off the list. She looked to Mia whose head was lying on her desk and asked, "How are you doing kid?"

Mia groaned unintelligibly.

Jim stood and twisted his body from left to right and asked, "Are we finished?"

"Mia, will you read over them one more time before I call Tim?"

Mia perked up. She removed the cap from her red pen and placed the tip to her tongue. With a smirk she said, "My pleasure."

"Go easy on me, girlie. It's been a long day!"

Mia and Jim laughed and said in unison, "You can say that again."

Frankie laughed as she grabbed her jacket, "I'll be right back. I need some air."

Jim asked, "Want some company?"

Mia gave her a knowing look, "Jim, would you mind giving my warrant a onceover?"

"Uh, sure Mia."

When Jim turned his back to her Frankie mouthed, "Thanks."

ONE HUNDRED ONE

"HEY BABE. I'm sorry, I know it's late. Hopefully you're sleeping. I just wanted to tell you I'm thinking of you. I'll come by on my way home. And Derek...I need you to be okay."

Frankie disconnected the call when she was certain the voice mail was sent. She stood on the front stairs of the headquarters building. Blowing warm air onto her cold hands she thought to herself, *"I should have said I love you. Why can't I say those words to him?"*

Frankie looked toward the prosecutor's office and took note of the yellow crime scene tape snapping in the wind. She stared at the red and blue glow of the lights as their reflections pierced the night. The vibration of her cell phone pulled her from her reverie.

"Thomas."

"Detective Thomas, it's Tim Rodriguez. Do you have those warrants ready for me?"

"Yeah. I was just getting ready to call you."

"Great. I'm going to come to my office. Can you meet me at the basement entrance in ten?"

"I take it you haven't heard. Two prosecutors were shot last night. Crime scene tape is still up."

"No shit? I hadn't heard. Who was it? Do you know?"

"Derek Kensington and Jessica something."

"Jessica Moon? I heard them talking about going out to celebrate when I left. Damn." Rodriguez exhaled loudly. "I guess it'll be easier if I come to your office. I'll see you in ten."

"Thanks Tim."

Frankie stared at the courthouse. The officers were laughing as they removed the yellow tape.

"I wonder what's so funny?" Frankie thought.

Frankie stared at the scene until flakes of snow began falling. An involuntary shiver ran down her spine. Pulling her coat closed, she turned and went back inside.

ONE HUNDRED TWO

"MIA, you and Fitz head out and pick up Midori. Jim and I are going to go pick up Tessa." Frankie grabbed her keys and said, "I'm driving."

Jim looked from Fitz to Mia to Frankie, "You got it boss."

Frankie navigated the roads to Tessa's house. Jim stared out the window waiting for her to speak.

A block from Tessa's house she extinguished the car lights. Putting the car in park she stared at the house. She hoped the dogs were locked up and Tessa came quietly.

Frankie and Jim approached the door. Frankie stood to the side and listened. She could hear Tessa singing as Jim rapped the door.

From inside they heard a cheery, "Just a second."

Jim was about to rap on the door a second time when it opened.

"Detective Thomas. Agent Craven. What are you doing here? I mean, it's nice to see you but I'm a bit surprised. Would you like to come in?"

"Actually, we'd like you to come downtown with us."

"Oh sure. Do you want me to follow you in my car?"

"No Tessa. We'd like you to come with us. In our car."

"Um. Okay Detective Thomas. Let me get my purse."

Frankie and Jim stepped over the threshold into the dark living room. Tessa walked to a table across the room and reached for her bag. When she turned the light from the kitchen reflected against the black metal of her gun.

In one fluid motion, Frankie's gun was out of her holster, "Drop the gun, Tessa."

Tessa didn't flinch, "I. You. I'm not. How did you know?"

Jim's voice was loud and firm, "Drop the gun, Tessa."

Frankie and Tessa's gaze locked, "Put. The. Gun. Down. Now."

The seconds felt like hours in the dark living room. Every sound was amplified in the silence. Frankie could hear the steady drip of water from a faucet, but her gaze did not waiver.

Jim watched Tessa twist the barrel of her gun toward her body. Frankie lunged forward and grabbed Tessa's wrist, pointing the barrel of the gun upward.

"You don't get to take the easy way out, bitch."

Jim grabbed Tessa's left hand. The three wrestled, landing in a heap. The sound of a gunshot pierced the air as their intertwined bodies rested on the hard, wooden floor. Jim pinned Tessa's hand behind her back. Grabbing for her right hand, he felt a warm, sticky liquid.

"Frankie?" Panic punctuated the word. Louder he said, "Frankie!"

Breathlessly she stood, "I'm okay."

"You fucking, bitch. Why didn't you let me shoot myself? Don't you realize I'm as good as dead anyway?" Venom dripped from Tessa's lips.

She grabbed Tessa's elbow, stood her up and said, "Let's go."

ONE HUNDRED THREE

"MIDORI'S IN CUSTODY. He confessed to everything. He was in on the deal with Tessa and Finnegan. He said he thought if he took Dani I'd walk away from the case, and they'd get the big payout. We found the gun he used to shoot Bruce. He's done," Frankie said.

Keith put his arm across Frankie's shoulders, squeezing her toward him lightly. "Thanks Frankie. That's great news. Are you going to get the kids now?"

She laid her head onto Keith's shoulder and said, "In a few. I'm going to see Derek first."

The pair stood and watched Bruce's chest rise and fall while he slept. Frankie closed her eyes and said a silent "thank you" as a tear slipped down her cheek.

She lifted her head and wiped her face, "Are you sure you're good?"

"Go on, Frankie. Check on Derek then go get some sleep. You look like hammered hell."

Squeezing his waist, she replied, "I love you, too. I'll be by in the morning. Call me if you need anything."

Keith kissed the top of her head, "You got it."

Frankie leaned against the wall and closed her eyes as the elevator climbed to Derek's floor. The ding of the door opening startled her.

"Damn."

Her walk down the hall towards Derek's room was interrupted by medical personnel rushing toward it. Frankie's feet felt like lead weights as she made her way to the room.

"Get me that cart! He's crashing. Push the epi."

Frankie stood in the doorway. Nurses were on either side of Derek's bed; one administering care. The doctor was barking orders as he performed CPR.

"Charging. Clear."

Frankie watched as the paddles were place on Derek's chest. She listened as the doctor barked orders and repeated, "Clear" before reapplying the paddles to his chest.

"Ma'am, you need to wait outside." Frankie could hear the nurse talking but was unable to move. "Ma'am! Come on, let them do their job."

The nurse ushered her to the hallway. The officer who had been sitting next to Derek's room said, "I'll take her to the waiting room."

The nurse nodded and went back into the room.

A preview of book 2 in the City of Fountains Series
No Stone Unturned

Chapter One

THE SOUND of the howling wind was shrouded by the thump, thump of the music coming from the club. Laughter floated from the door as Sarah stepped out onto the sidewalk. Shivering, she suddenly wished she had brought her coat with her. With her arms wrapped around her body and her car keys clutched in her hand she began to walk.

"Where the heck did I park my car?"

As Sarah approached the corner it started to rain.

Behind her a deep, booming voice said, "It sure is cold tonight."

In a chivalrous manner, the man took off his coat and started to place it around Sarah's shoulders.

With a half-hearted laugh she replied, "You're not kidding. I forgot how cold winters could be in Missouri."

The man did not remove his arm from Sarah's shoulders after covering her with the coat.

"Can I give you a ride?"

"Um, no thanks. My car's just ov…"

In one swift movement, before Sarah could say a word, she felt her body pivot toward the car on the street.

"It's cold. I'll take you."

"No, really it's not far—I can walk."

With one hand on her shoulder and the other on the small of her back the man pushed Sarah toward the car. Gruffly he said, "Get in."

Stumbling on the curb, Sarah fell into the open car and felt the door slam behind her. She reached for the handle to open the door, but the handle wasn't there. Panic began to set in as she grabbed for her cell phone to call 9-1-1.

ACKNOWLEDGMENTS

This novel may never have been written if it were not for my dear friend Teresa. She encouraged and pushed me to go for it. For that I will always be grateful.

Thank you to my family for the years of support and sacrifice. We are a small tribe but a strong one. I especially appreciate the support of my son and daughter as I have pursued my dream. Many of the changes in plot direction stem from brainstorming sessions with my son, who will someday be the author of his own story.

A special thank you to my friends and fellow authors Kym Roberts, Roger Canaff, Jennifer Jaynes and Carol Ann Ross. Each of you took the time to read my manuscript, answer my questions, and provide invaluable feedback on my work and the process. Your input and guidance is appreciated more than I can ever express in words.

To all of my friends who did not laugh when I said I was going to write a novel, but instead provided encouragement, insight, laughter, and feedback, thank you. You know who you are – and without you I would not be who I am.

Thank you to my editors Kimberly Hanson and Connie Pletl for the time, effort, skill and patience you had with my manuscript. It is the polished piece it is, in part, because of you.

Thank you to my cover artist, Jaycee at Sweet N' Spicy Designs. Your talent created a cover that exceeded my expectations and imagination.

ABOUT THE AUTHOR

CJ Johnson was born and raised in the mid-west and spent over ten years working for a major metropolitan police department with the last six spent as a detective in the Sex Crimes Section of the Special Victims Unit. Passionate about her work, she fought hard for justice for every victim – especially those others often overlooked.

In 2012, she left the high-stress, fast paced career of law enforcement investigations to spend more time with her family. As a nationally recognized subject matter expert on sexual assault investigations, she focused on developing and executing training curriculum focusing on sex crime investigations to law enforcement agencies and their officers for the state of North Carolina.

She continues to play an active role in her mission to end interpersonal violence through training, volunteerism, and leading a team of investigators for an organization with an aligned mission while working on the *City of Fountains* series.

BOOKS BY C.J. JOHNSON

FEATURING FRANKIE THOMAS

Thorns of Deceit

No Stone Unturned

Across State Lines

Moonglow Road

Visit:

https://www.cjjohnsonbooks.com